# TALL COTTON

CATHERINE TUCKER

Tall Cotton
Red Adept Publishing, LLC
104 Bugenfield Court
Garner, NC 27529
https://RedAdeptPublishing.com/
Copyright © 2025 by Catherine Tucker. All rights reserved.

Cover Art by Streetlight Graphics[1]

No part of this book may be reproduced, scanned, or distributed in any printed or electronic form without permission. Please do not participate in or encourage piracy of copyrighted materials in violation of the author's rights. Thank you for respecting the hard work of this author.

This is a work of fiction. Names, characters, places, and incidents either are the product of the author's imagination or are used fictitiously, and any resemblance to locales, events, business establishments, or actual persons—living or dead—is entirely coincidental.

---

1. http://StreetlightGraphics.com

*To my mother, Mary Lee Owens. Thank you for giving me the gift of prayer.*

# Chapter 1
# Lowell, Mississippi, May 9, 1970

Saturday started like any other beautiful sunny day. My sister Josephine and I were playing kickball in our front yard, filled with excitement. I was particularly elated because of my recent promotion to the fifth grade.

Just as I kicked the ball hard and watched it skitter past Jo, I heard a rumble. I whirled around to witness my mother and father tumbling through our screen door, locked in a fierce struggle. Blood trickled from Momma's nose, and fear registered in her brown eyes. My heart pounded so hard I thought it would explode in my chest. I tried to run to her aid, but my legs trembled like those of a newborn calf, and my feet felt as though they were submerged in a bucket of clay.

"Woman, you *gon'* do what I told ya!" Daddy landed a hard backhand across Momma's face.

She staggered back then crumpled to her knees. Like a panther, he pounced on her. She fell back hard under his weight onto the dusty front porch. His meaty dark fingers were clamped around her neck. Gasping for air, Momma kicked, clawing vigorously at his hands.

"Bailey, do something! He's killing her!" Jo screamed.

When I didn't move, couldn't move, Jo looked around frantically for something to use as a weapon. She went around the side of the house and emerged seconds later, wielding a rusty ironing board almost twice her size. She ran up the steps, and with all the strength she could muster, she pounded Daddy across his head and back.

"Get. Off. My. Momma! Get. Off. Her!"

"Stop, Jo! Get off me, Jo." Daddy whirled around, shocked, his bulging eyes red from rage and alcohol. Usually, no one dared raise a hand at him.

He snatched the ironing board from Jo's hand and slammed it onto the porch. He grabbed for Jo, too, but she dashed down the steps as fast as her twelve-year-old legs could carry her. She raced across the yard and disappeared into the thick cotton field to the right of our home.

Daddy staggered down the four concrete steps. "I'll kill ya, you hear? I'll kill all of ya!"

After a moment, he turned and stumbled back up the steps. He threw open the screen door and thundered into the house. Struggling to her feet, Momma wiped the blood from her nose with the back of her hand. Then she raced into the house after him.

"Otis, what you gonna do? Please don't do nothin' crazy."

I felt as though I was watching a horror movie. Still unable to move or utter a word, I watched in slow motion as my daddy, shotgun in hand, burst through the screen door. It slammed hard against the aluminum siding. He descended the steps unsteadily and stopped four feet in front of me. He raised the shotgun and aimed it toward the field Jo had run into. He cocked it. My entire body trembled. My breath hitched in my throat.

Momma flew down the steps, her feet barely touching them. "Otis, please, please! Don't shoot my child! I'll do it. I'll send her away for good."

Daddy waited a moment then released the hammer on the shotgun and lowered it. He climbed up the steps and staggered into the house.

"Thank you, Lord," Momma whispered, her eyes bright with fresh tears that hadn't yet fallen. As she looked toward the cotton field, relief flashed across her face. Then she looked down at me. "You okay, Bailey?"

When I nodded, she brushed away a single tear that raced down her cheek then walked quickly up the steps and into the house.

The remainder of the day felt sullen and sorrowful. I went to the room I shared with my three sisters. Too embarrassed to come out, I stayed there all evening. I'd failed my mother. I was the only boy, yet I'd stood there like a statue while Daddy practically choked the life out of her. He probably would have killed her if Jo hadn't acted so quickly.

My oldest sister, Priscilla, had remained in our room with the baby and Tamara, shielding them from Daddy's fury. She'd heard the commotion because the argument between Momma and Daddy had started in the house before it escalated to an all-out war that spilled outside. The fight had been about her. I could see the sadness in her eyes. Priscilla kept peeking out of our window and looking out toward the cotton fields where Jo had gone.

Jo stayed away most of the evening. But a little after dark, she knocked on our bedroom window, and I snuck her into the house through the back door. By then, Daddy had passed out on the sofa after downing a fifth of gin. Jo said she'd stayed with our neighbors, the Taylors, until she felt she could safely return home. The Taylors lived about a quarter of a mile from our house on the opposite side of the road.

My daddy wore a look of satisfaction the rest of the day since Momma had agreed to send Priscilla away again. She'd only been back home two months. Momma wanted her there for when Matthew was born, because she planned to help Priscilla take care of him. That was what the fight had been about. Priscilla had become pregnant in June the previous year while she was staying with Big

Momma, at the age of fifteen. She'd been heartbroken when she found out the father, a man in his twenties, was already married. She'd stayed locked in her room all summer and most of the fall, wearing the grooves off Al Green's 45 single "Call Me." I felt sad for her but couldn't cheer her up. Nobody could. From the time Daddy had found out Priscilla was pregnant, during her fifth month, he'd demanded that she leave. He said good girls were married before they had a baby, and if they had a baby before they got married, they were nothing more than tramps. In Daddy's eyes, Priscilla had committed the crime of the century and deserved maximum punishment. But in her state of gloom and doom, it seemed to me she'd been punished enough. Our grandmother—my mother's mom, Big Momma—took her in. Priscilla had just returned home in February, and we'd been hoping she was back for good, but she would have to return to Big Momma's and stay there awhile longer. Daddy had demanded that Priscilla leave the house when he first learned that she was pregnant. Momma had stood her ground and refused to let Priscilla go. But her ground had suddenly become a lot shakier, and she'd given in so no one would have to die.

Priscilla was four years old when Momma and Daddy got married. Momma would often say she looked just like her daddy. She wouldn't talk a lot about Priscilla's dad—only said he was kind and smart. And Momma wouldn't talk about him at all when Daddy was around.

At sixteen, Priscilla was as tall as Momma, with long black hair and big brown eyes. She loved ribbons and bows and pretty things. Jo, on the other hand, was a tomboy. She didn't worry about her hair or her clothes. We would race and turn flips and cartwheels and play kickball with our bare feet. She was the total opposite of Priscilla. I had one other sister, five-year-old Tamera. We called her Tammy. Daddy didn't normally pay much attention to me or Jo, but that day, he had to notice Jo after what she'd done. Because of it, she'd become as much of a pariah as Priscilla.

A LITTLE PAST NOON the next day, as I sat in our big blue-and-brown-floral chair next to the window facing the front yard, I heard a vehicle roll slowly up the gravel driveway. I had just watched Momma's brother Willie Earl drive away with Priscilla and Matthew. He was taking them back to live with Big Momma until heaven knew when. I was surprised that someone else was coming to our house. Momma hadn't said anything about it. The car was a shiny blue 1968 Chevrolet Impala driven by my great-uncle Winston Walker, Big Momma's younger brother. He parked behind Daddy's black Volkswagen Beetle. Uncle Winston's cars always looked new despite being a couple of years old.

Uncle Winston must have been in his late forties or early fifties. He had a slender build and was clean-shaven. The crown of his head, bare as the palm of my hand, shone like a tawny polished marble under the noonday sun. What remained of his wavy black hair was neatly trimmed and peppered with gray. As always, his gray slacks were sharply creased, and his light-blue service station work shirt with the Gresham Oil & Gas logo was neatly pressed. He wore his short sleeves rolled up like Popeye, only without the muscles. I thought Uncle Winston had a lot of money because he always had a nice big car and a nice home. He was divorced and had three grown children. None of them lived with him. They'd all moved to Texas.

Momma must have gone across the road and used Ms. Clara's phone to call him. She parted the curtains and peered out the window as Uncle Winston made his way to the porch. "You children, go pack up some of your things. We're gonna stay with Winston for a while until I can find us a place."

This wasn't the first time Momma had left Daddy. She'd done it once before after taking a pretty good beating from him. To her credit, Momma always fought back. But being a man and stronger, Daddy usually ended up hurting her pretty badly. Most often, he waited until she was drunk so he would be sure to have the upper hand. The last time, we'd stayed with Big Momma about a week, long enough for Daddy to sweet-talk her into coming back home. But she hadn't talked about getting her own place back then. The shotgun play Daddy had made this time must have been the final straw.

Starting a new life without Daddy's wrath sounded appealing, so I hurried into our bedroom and grabbed my two pairs of jeans that didn't have holes in them, some shorts, a few shirts, underwear, and my toothbrush. I stuffed everything into a brown paper bag and headed for the living room. I was wearing my only pair of shoes, low-top Chuck Taylors I'd gotten for Christmas. Daddy must have been pretending to be asleep, because as soon as we headed for the door, he surged from the bed and raced into the living room. A wave of fear seized me.

Daddy rushed out on the porch, his face contorted, his eyes wild, and his mouth twisted like a rabid dog. "Annie, if you leave, don't you come back! You hear me? If you come back, I swear I'll kill ya!"

He lunged for Momma, but Uncle Winston stepped in between them. "That's enough, Otis. We don't need no trouble today. Just go on back in the house. Let thangs settle down for a spell. Everythang gon' be all right in a day or two."

Daddy took a step back and blinked a few times. He seemed to have been assessing the situation. He never displayed too much bravado when another man was around.

"You better get her outa here, then! Annie, don't come crawling back here, you hear me? Stay wherever the hell you goin'!"

"Don't worry—I won't be back. I had enough of your craziness. Twelve years have been twelve years too long. Come on, kids. Y'all get in the car." Momma walked swiftly toward the Chevy.

Jo, Tammy, and I piled into the back seat. My heart was still pumping hard, but it slowed down a beat or two after Momma slid into the front seat next to Uncle Winston and locked the door. As we backed out of the driveway, Daddy went inside, pulled the screen door shut, and slammed the front door. On a hot, muggy day without air-conditioning, I hoped he would roast like a Christmas turkey.

We sped down the two-lane blacktop road toward Belzoni, Mississippi, a small town with half the population of Lowell, fewer than six thousand people. I scanned the endless rows of cotton without really seeing any of them. Hope and despair flooded my mind. Leaving Lowell meant being rid of Daddy, but it also meant changing schools and finding new friends.

My stomach was twisted into a tight knot, so I sank back into the smooth vinyl seat and closed my eyes. Uncle Winston blasted the air-conditioning and pushed in an 8-track tape. The soothing sound of the Isley Brothers' "Voyage to Atlantis" calmly beckoned me to an imaginary place of peace and tranquility.

# Chapter 2
# Washington, DC, May 30, 1970

Jonathan Streeter removed his navy-blue silk tie and threw it on the bench. He loosened the first two buttons of his neatly starched white dress shirt.

"Guys, gather around quickly. We can still win this thing." Jonathan looked up at the scoreboard in the YMCA gymnasium. His basketball team was losing sixty-one to sixty, with five seconds left on the clock. "Here's what we're going to do. Benji, you inbound the ball to Christopher, then you sprint to the corner. Chris, you pass the ball to Benji in the corner. Benji, you look for Tommy cutting across to the low post. Get the ball to Tommy. Tommy, you take the inside shot. Got it?" All heads nodded. "On three. One, two, three. Eagles!"

The buzzer sounded for play to resume at the Washington, DC, citywide summer basketball tournament. Jonathan stood on the sideline. Sweat rolled down his back. He wiped the beads from his temples with a white hand towel. His team sprinted to the floor and took their positions. With his defender's hands flailing in his face, Benjamin James inbounded the ball to Christopher Gaines then sprinted to the corner. One second ticked off the clock. Chris threw an overhead pass to Benjamin in the corner. Benjamin looked for Tommy Robinson, their center, but two lanky players guarded Tommy, with upstretched arms towering over him. Two seconds ticked off the clock.

"Benji, take the shot!" Jonathan yelled.

Eyeing his defender, Benji heaved a towering Hail Mary toward the goal. The buzzer sounded. The ball sailed high in a perfect arc. It came down, hitting the far side of the rim. It sprang to the top of the backboard then bounced out of bounds. The game ended. Jonathan's heart sank. He watched his players drift from the basketball court with slumped shoulders and downcast eyes while the winning team leaped and shouted and celebrated their victory.

Jonathan walked over and congratulated the other coach. He started rehearsing in his mind what he would say to a locker room full of preteen boys whose hearts had been crushed by losing a tournament they'd worked so hard to win. Jonathan had become accustomed to preparing opening arguments and closing arguments to present to juries, but this was different. The hearts of these young boys were still tender, and he needed to say the right thing to bind their wounds.

"Fellas, go on to the locker room and get dressed. I'll be there in five." Jonathan grabbed his tie and clipboard from the bench and walked briskly into his office.

He slid into the rolling chair and pulled out the bottom drawer of his desk. His fingers searched until they found the small metal container. Jonathan pulled out the flask and took two long gulps, allowing the lukewarm alcohol to flow down his esophagus. He took a third swig, replaced the top of the flask, and shoved the container back into the drawer. He wiped his mouth with the hand towel and grabbed the roll of mints from his top drawer. He threw three into his mouth and crunched down on them as he headed to the locker room.

Stepping into the locker room, which smelled of sweat and mint ointment, Jonathan looked around. It was as quiet as a mausoleum. Twelve pairs of eyes bored a hole in the concrete floor. Several boys, including Benjamin, had draped towels over their heads in a vain attempt to hide their tears.

"Listen, fellas. Look at me. Hold your heads up. You've got nothing to be ashamed of. Yes, we lost this game, but you played like champions. And you should be proud of that. You worked hard, and it got us to the finals of our first tournament. What it came down to is the Blue Devils played a better game *tonight*. More balls fell for them *tonight*. Does that make them a better team? No, it does not. On any given night, the outcome could have been very different. I'm proud of you guys. Now, this was our first tournament, but it won't be our last. Go home. Get some rest. Remember to hold your heads up high and be proud of what you've accomplished. Tommy, will you close this game night with a prayer?"

"Sure, Coach." Tommy, the team captain, said a quick prayer for the team.

When it was done, Jonathan looked around the locker room. The boys started talking to one another, congratulating each other, and even smiling. He exhaled. Then he saw Benjamin. The towel still covered his head, and he remained seated on the bench with his back turned to Jonathan and his head bent down.

"Benji, go ahead and get dressed, and let me have a word with you."

"Okay, Coach," he said without turning around.

Jonathan waited for Benjamin on the bench where the team sat during the second half of the game. Minutes later, Benjamin approached, his eyes puffy and bloodshot.

"Have a seat, Benji." After a beat, Jonathan said, "Now, listen. I know how much you wanted to win this game. It was a tough loss. And even though it was a tournament game, it was only one game."

"But, Coach Streeter..." Benjamin's voice cracked. "I missed the last shot. I lost the game."

"No, son, you didn't lose the game. How many other shots were missed by you or your teammates during the game?"

"I don't know. Lots."

"That's right. If any one of those missed shots had fallen, we would have won the game. So it wasn't your final shot that cost us the game. It was every other missed shot as well. Basketball is not an individual sport. It's a team sport. We win as a team, and we lose as a team. The team lost tonight. But listen to me and listen well. If you keep up the same discipline and work ethic you showed tonight, you can be one of the best ball players around. You will go on to score many points to help this team win. You are a player a coach can depend on. That's why I told you to take the final shot. So keep your head up. This was our first tournament. We have two more before the championship. And listen—in a hundred years, who's going to remember this loss anyway?"

"In a hundred years, Coach Streeter?" Benjamin chuckled. "No one."

"That's right. You played a heck of a game tonight. You gave it your all. That's all that matters to me. So, are we good?"

"Yes, Coach, we're good." Benjamin smiled.

"All right. Let's go home."

# Chapter 3

After two weeks of us staying with Uncle Winston, Daddy sweet-talked Momma into coming back to him. And sure enough, bright and early on Saturday morning, Daddy arrived, and Momma, Jo, Tammy, and I all piled into his Volkswagen and headed back to Lowell. I wasn't thrilled to be going back to Daddy and whatever hell would be waiting for us in Lowell. For a while, things were nice. Daddy and Momma talked to one another with kindness and consideration. But I couldn't help but wonder how long the sunshine days would last.

In early June on a Saturday evening, we all sat around our small black-and-white television to watch *Hee Haw*. We laughed, watching Uncle Buck and Roy Clark picking and grinning along with Minnie Pearl and the gang. Then we watched *The Lawrence Welk Show*, which had one Black man, Arthur Duncan, who tap-danced as gracefully as a swan moving across a tranquil lake. I felt such pride seeing him on television, gliding across those polished-marble floors, the only Black man in a sea of white singers and dancers.

When *Lawrence Welk* went off, Momma and Daddy settled back on the sofa to watch the weekend news as they started on their second six-pack of beer. Whenever they weren't out drinking, they enjoyed the weekend news, anchored by Frank Reynolds, a stone-faced white man with a somber voice. I wasn't sure why they liked watching him. I found him to be as exciting as a box full of rocks. So I headed toward our bedroom to find a game to play with Jo and Tammy.

"In other news," Frank Reynolds said in his stoic monotone, "Cleveland's first Black mayor, Carl Stokes, traveled to Washington, DC, on Wednesday. He met with DC Mayor-Commissioner Walter Washington, SNCC Chairman Marion Barry, and local civil rights attorney Jonathan Streeter. The men came together in response to the murder of Chauncy Jackson, a defendant acquitted last year for the murder of a white liquor-store owner in the high-profile case litigated by Mr. Streeter."

Hearing a thump, I stopped and turned around. Momma had dropped her beer. She stared at the TV screen while the frothy amber liquid spilled in all directions.

"What's the matter with you, Annie?" Daddy said. "You act like you seen a ghost."

"It's nothing." Momma sprang from the sofa and rushed past me to get the mop from the kitchen.

"It musta been somethin'. You done wasted a good can of cold beer."

"I heard a name mentioned on the news that surprised me—that's all." Returning to clean up the spill, she swung the mop from side to side with more vigor than necessary.

"Whose name was it?"

"I went to school with a boy named Jonathan Streeter a long time ago. But all those people sound like big shot mayors and lawyers, so it's probably not the same person."

"He musta been somebody you was sweet on for you to be gettin' all shook up."

Momma stopped and held the mop in front of her. "He was just a classmate in the fifth or sixth grade."

"Naw, Annie. I thank this fella was more than what you tryna say. Did you have somethin' goin' on with this negro? From what it look like, maybe you still do."

"Otis, you must be getting drunk. You're making a mountain out of a molehill." Momma walked back into the kitchen with the mop in one hand and the empty beer can in the other.

Daddy surged from the sofa and met her as she walked back into the living room. He grabbed her by the back of her neck. "Annie Lee, if you don't tell me the truth about this fellow, I swear I'll knock yo' teeth down yo' throat."

Momma's body stiffened. Her eyes widened.

A sudden knock at the door stopped Daddy in his tracks. He released her, walked over, and peered out the window. I exhaled the breath caught in my throat.

"It's Eli. I wonder what the hell he want at this hour?" Daddy said.

Elijah Clark worked on the plantation with Daddy. He was also Daddy's fishing buddy. According to Daddy, his boss, Mr. Jim, wasn't too fond of Mr. Eli as a worker because he took his time getting things done, which was probably more out of necessity than negligence because of his age. He was thirty years older than Daddy, which meant he was in his late sixties. So Mr. Eli was more of a liability than an asset to his boss. But since there was no such thing as a retirement plan for sharecroppers, Mr. Eli had to keep working. Despite their age difference, Daddy and Mr. Eli got along very well. Perhaps Daddy saw him as a kind version of a father.

"Come on in, Eli," Daddy said, his voice level and calm as though he hadn't just threatened to do Momma bodily harm because of a man mentioned on TV. "What wind brought you by tonight?"

The scent of stale cigar smoke and sweat floated in on the warm summer breeze that accompanied Mr. Eli when he stepped into the living room. His faded blue jean coveralls fit around his rotund body, giving him the look of a human barrel. He pulled a white handkerchief from his overalls' breast pocket and mopped the beads of sweat from his bald crown.

"Evenin', Otis. Evenin', Annie Lee." Mr. Eli nodded toward Momma, huffing to catch his breath from the short walk from his pickup and up our four concrete steps.

"How are you this evening, Eli?" Momma asked.

"Oh, fair to middlin'. I just stopped by to tell y'all the sad news that Ms. Georgia Chambers done gone on to glory. Passed on last Thursday morning."

"That's too bad," Momma said. "Do you know what happened to her?"

"Well, you know, she'd been sick for some time, and she was well into her seventies. Her funeral gon' be this Monday at Mt. Olive Baptist Church at eleven o'clock in case y'all want to stop by and pay your respects."

"That's mighty nice of you to come by and tell us, Eli. Ms. Georgia was always so nice to me when I ran into her at the grocery store." Momma paused. "I wonder what Mr. Jim's gonna do now. Ms. Georgia's been cooking and cleaning for him since he moved into that house."

"And before that," Mr. Eli said, "she was his parents' maid for more than fifty years."

"I'm sho' he'll find somebody else before long," Daddy said, draining his beer can and handing it to Momma. "We sho' thank you for stoppin' by to let us know about Ms. Georgia."

"Well, y'all folks have yourselves a good evenin'." Mr. Eli turned and waddled toward the door.

I knew Daddy had no intention of paying any respects to Ms. Georgia. Mr. Eli knew it too. The invitation was more for Momma. Daddy's feet had never crossed the threshold of a church, and the death of an old Black woman he barely knew wouldn't be his motivation to start. I could tell he wasn't the least concerned about who Mr. Jim would find to clean his house.

# Chapter 4

Mockingbirds chirped and flitted from one oak tree to the next on a beautiful golden Saturday morning. It had been a week since Momma and Daddy's last altercation, and I hoped this weekend would not be a carbon copy. I sat in the chair by the window facing our front yard. Hearing a car door slam, I looked up from the pages of *Black Beauty* to see a tall white man wearing a cowboy hat, blue jeans, and scuffed-up brown cowboy boots approaching. Even with his cowboy hat and sunshades, I knew it was James Cunningham. Mr. Jim, as my daddy and the other workers called him, was the only white man who lived on the C&S Plantation along with nine Black families including us.

Mr. Jim was the owner of the C&S Plantation, one of the largest and most profitable cotton-producing companies in the Mississippi Delta. Daddy and the rest of the men living on the plantation were sharecroppers, operating tractors, combines, and other massive types of equipment to plant and harvest cotton. Tall and slender with dark-brown hair and warm brown eyes, Mr. Jim lived alone in a stately white house with thick white columns, surrounded by towering magnolia trees and accented with manicured flower beds. His house sat to the right of ours and looked to be three times its size. There could have been at least three houses between our house and Mr. Jim's, but there were none, just rows and rows of cotton.

Mr. Jim had stopped by the house a couple of times before to talk to Daddy. Both times, he'd worn khaki pants, a plaid short-sleeved shirt, and cowboy boots. Jo and Priscilla thought Mr. Jim looked like the movie star Robert Wagner. Momma thought he was rather handsome, too, but she was careful not to say anything like that when Daddy was around.

Daddy said Mr. Jim was popular with women and had more than one girlfriend. It must have been true because we often saw him speed past our house on the weekends in his black convertible Jaguar, with a blonde one day, a brunette the next, and a redhead another. Momma said because Mr. Jim was a rich, good-looking playboy, he lived in tall cotton.

With long, confident strides, Mr. Jim made his way up our makeshift concrete walkway. A woman sat in the passenger seat of the Jaguar. She had brown shoulder-length hair and wore sunglasses with big black lenses. I dog-eared the page and closed my book so I could give my full, undivided attention to what Mr. Jim had come to talk to Daddy about. Apparently, Daddy had heard the car door slam, because he got up and peered out of the window.

He immediately headed to the door and stepped out on the front porch to meet Mr. Jim before his boot could touch the first of our four concrete steps. "Mornin', Mr. Jim. How you doin', suh? Mighty fine day, ain't it?"

"Mornin', Otis. It sure is."

"What brings you by today, suh? Is everything all right?"

"Well," Mr. Jim said, hooking his thumbs in his belt loops and standing wide-legged. "You might've heard that I lost Georgia, my maid. She was sick for about five months before she passed last Thursday."

"Yes, suh, I sho' did hear about Ms. Georgia. I feels real bad about it too."

"Thank you. She was a good, godly woman. Took care of me and my family for more than sixty years total. I miss her terribly."

"I 'spect she's gon' be hard to replace."

"Yes, she will. And that's what I wanted to talk with you about, Otis." Mr. Jim removed his sunglasses and hung them in the collar of his aqua shirt. He crossed his arms, covering the green crocodile emblem, and shifted his weight to one leg.

"Yes, suh?"

"Well, I wanted to talk with you about Annie Lee coming to work for me. Not full-time, because I know she's got you and the kids to take care of. But maybe she can work a couple of days a week for a few hours and some Saturday mornings. What do you think about that?"

Daddy scratched the back of his head. "Yes, suh, I thank that's a mighty fine idea. I'm sho' Annie Lee will be okay with it too."

"That's great, Otis. Can you let me know by Monday morning when she can start? I need the help PDQ because my laundry has piled up a mile high." Mr. Jim chuckled, showing a perfect set of white teeth.

"Yes, suh, I will let you know first thang Monday mornin'."

"All right. I'll see you then. Enjoy the rest of your day, Otis." Mr. Jim gave a casual wave as he strode back to his shiny black convertible.

"You too, Mr. Jim." As the man sped away, Daddy said, "Damn cracker. I'll let you know by Monday all right."

LATER THAT EVENING, I heard Daddy walk into the kitchen while Momma prepared dinner. "Guess who stopped by the house earlier today?"

"I don't know. Who?"

"The big boss man, Jim, came by to tell me that his housekeeper, Ms. Georgia, had passed on."

"Oh, he did? We already knew that. Eli told us about that last Saturday night."

"He said she was his momma's maid and that she took care of his entire family for some sixty years."

"Eli told us that too."

"Well, after that, he mentioned that he wanted you to do some light housework and cook for him a few days a week. Wanted to know if it was okay with me."

Momma was silent for a moment. "Well, you know we could use the money. I wouldn't mind doing it. What do you think?"

"I don't thank so. Won't look right. You and him 'bout the same age and all. Naw, he need to get a much older woman."

Momma laughed. "What do we care about how it looks? We need the money. And he's your boss. How you gonna say no to him and expect him to keep you on as one of his workers? Honestly, I'd rather work inside his cool air-conditioned house than bake in the hot sun, picking or chopping cotton, or work in a hot cotton gin."

Daddy thought for a minute. "Naw, that ain't gon' work. I ain't havin' my wife down there at that house with that cracker all day long. I can hear it now. Tongues gon' start waggin' about some monkey business goin' on down at that house, and I will have to stomp a mudhole in somebody. Nope. Um gon' tell him you was offered another job and you took it."

"Otis, you gonna lie?"

"I done worse."

"But I think..."

"I don't care what you think, Annie. I'm done talkin'. It's settled."

"Fine, Otis. Whatever."

Daddy stalked out of the kitchen and into the bathroom and slammed the door. And just like that, it was decided. Daddy wouldn't let Momma work for Mr. Jim. He was extremely jealous, so he wouldn't want Momma around a rich, handsome man without him being there with her. He was particular about where she went without him, and it must have made him feel good to think he provided for her so that she didn't have to work. Daddy probably also realized he'd gotten lucky with my mother. He was no Sydney Poitier, yet he was married to a beautiful woman.

# Chapter 5

"Bailey, Bailey," someone whispered from a faraway place. "Bailey, Bailey." Then I felt a tug on my shoulder. "Bailey, wake up. Wake up, Bailey."

When I opened my eyes, I saw the sun peeking through the curtains, and Momma stood below my bunk bed, fully dressed. Jo and Tammy still lay snuggled under the threadbare rose-colored bedspread Big Momma had given them the previous year after she bought a new one.

"What is it, Momma? What's wrong?" I didn't know what day it was. Then I remembered.

*But why has Momma awakened me on Sunday?*

We always slept late on Saturday and Sunday. And Momma wasn't dressed for church. She wore a fuchsia-and-green floral-print blouse, fuchsia slacks, and fuchsia slip-on flats. Being shaken out of my sleep when it wasn't a school day made my heart flutter. I feared Daddy must have done something to Momma.

"Shhh. I don't want to wake the girls."

"Okay," I whispered. "But what's wrong?"

"Nothing's wrong, son. Your daddy went fishing with Eli this morning, and I need you to walk to Fratelli's Grocery Store with me. I have to pick up a few things to fix lunch. I'm sure Otis will be hungry as a pack of wolves when he gets home." Momma tapped my shoulder. "Come on, now. Get up before the sun gets too hot."

"Shoot!" I muttered as Momma strode from the room. I rubbed the sleep from my eyes and reluctantly swung my feet out of bed, wanting only to fall back onto my pillow, pull the covers over my head, and sleep for a few more hours. "Okay, Momma."

I climbed down the ladder, lumbered over to the dresser, and grabbed a pair of blue jean shorts and a plain white T-shirt, the first two items I saw. After pushing my feet into my dusty Chuck Taylors, I moseyed into the bathroom to wash my face and brush my teeth.

"You ready, Bailey?" Momma said as I walked into the living room. She dabbed her nose with a tan face powder while looking into a small, round compact mirror.

I thought by the time we reached the store, which was more than a mile away, the powder would have melted off her face faster than a snow cone on the fourth of July. I nodded as Momma dropped the compact into her purse and grabbed the keys from the coffee table by the front door. As we stepped outside, the morning sunshine felt warm and welcoming on my face. I inhaled the clean, fresh air that smelled of dewy grass and newly sprouted cotton bolls, and my resentment for having to get up so early on Sunday morning started to fade. Momma and I headed out on Tribett Road, a two-lane blacktop that ran east to west directly in front of our house. As we passed Mr. Jim's house, I wanted to ask her about Daddy's decision not to let her work for Mr. Jim. But since I didn't want her to know I'd listened in on their conversation, I kept quiet.

"Thank you for walking to the store with me, Bailey. I didn't want to go alone."

"You're welcome, Momma. It feels nice being out here this early in the morning. It's not too hot, and there are hardly any cars passing by." I paused then said, "Momma, will I be like Daddy when I grow up? Will I be... mean like he is?"

"No, Bailey, of course not. You are a kind and loving boy, and you'll grow up to be a kind and loving man."

"But why is Daddy the way he is?"

"Your daddy wasn't always mean and angry."

"So, what happened to him?" I asked.

"Life happened to him, son. When a man is treated like a dog by some people—called names, disrespected, made to feel like he is less than human…"

"You mean by white people?"

"Yes, by white people. Men like your daddy—Black men, I mean—push all of that nastiness down because they can't fight back. Often, they're beaten, put in jail, or worse."

"What could be worse than being beaten or locked up in jail?"

"Killed, son. Beaten to death, shot, or even lynched. So they take the abuse and push it way down deep into their souls. And when their souls fill up, all the bad stuff comes out in the form of rage, and some of them hurt the people closest to them, like their family."

I let that sink in as we neared Marah's Pass, which intersected with Tribett Road. Marah's Pass was a winding gravel road that ran alongside a scary ravine for about half a mile, with no barrier and a steep thirty-foot drop-off. Momma and I walked on the left side of the road near the cotton field, opposite the drop-off.

"Grandpa Willis, Otis's dad, was pretty mean to him too. I remember Otis told me about the last time he played baseball with his friends."

"What happened?"

"Well, he said he must have been around thirteen at the time. One Saturday afternoon, he and the other boys who lived on the same plantation met up to play baseball. He said they had themselves a nice game going. Your dad's team was down by one in the last inning with two outs, and Otis was up to bat. The outfielders started moving back because they knew your daddy could hit the ball far out. Suddenly, everybody froze, he said. Their eyes got big like silver dollars. It looked like they were in shock. Then they started calling Otis's name, trying to warn him. He didn't know what was going on. But when he turned around to see what everybody was gawking at, the strong smell of alcohol hit him in the face. Then he saw the bat coming toward him. He jumped back, but the bat caught him right in the ribcage. He fell to his knees and doubled over in pain. Then his papa started kickin' and stompin' him. He said a big kid called Sluggo and his brother Larry pulled Papa Willis off your daddy.

"He said Papa was shouting, 'You got chores at the house. You ain't got no time to be out here chasin' after no damn ball. I bet' not *ever* catch your Black ass playin' this game again.' Your daddy said he struggled to his feet with the help of his friends. His lip was busted, and he probably had a few bruised ribs. Lucky for him, nothing was broken, because they couldn't afford a doctor. Your daddy had a dream of playing in the big league, but that was the last time he ever played baseball."

"So Daddy is mean and hurtful because Grandpa Willis was mean to him?"

"We don't inherit behavior from our parents, Bailey. I believe we learn things from their actions, either good or bad. But every person's got a choice. When we know right from wrong, we've got the responsibility to choose right instead of wrong. You won't grow up to be like your father or your grandfather."

"Why not?"

"Because people raised on love see the world differently from people raised on survival. And because you see the world differently, you will act differently."

I considered what Momma had said. Even though I didn't like Daddy at certain times, I felt sad for him, learning for the first time that he would never get a chance to live his dream of playing baseball in the major league. He never even came close. My grandpa, who was as mean as a barrel full of rattlesnakes, had snuffed Daddy's dream out like a cheap cigar.

Before I knew it, we'd crossed Highway 82 and were just a few steps away from the store's front door. Two tiny gold bells chimed when we entered. The cool air shooting from the air-conditioner in the window hit my bare arms and face and sent a chill through my body. The shiny hardwood floor squeaked as we walked past the counter holding large jars of dill pickles, pickled eggs, and pickled pig feet.

*Yuck. Disgusting. Who'd want to eat pig feet, let alone ones that have been soaked for weeks in vinegar?*

Jars filled with penny candy and bubble gum also lined the counter. They were more to my liking. The store owner, Antonio Fratelli—Mr. Tony—had crammed shelves five rows high with various food items. Momma and I made our way down the narrow aisles. She picked up a bag of sugar, a package of spaghetti, a bag of rice, and a bag of pinto beans and handed them to me. She then grabbed a pack of ground beef and a whole chicken. She knew I was hungry, so she picked up a small carton of chocolate milk and a honey bun for me and a bottle of orange juice for herself. After that, we headed to the front counter.

Mr. Fratelli stood as tall as he was wide, with a balding crown. "Will this be all, Annie Lee?"

"Yes, sir. This is everything."

His stubby fingers punched the keys on the cash register. "That'll be three dollars and fifty-five cents. Where's Otis this morning?"

"He went fishing with Eli." Momma reached into her purse and gave him the exact amount. "Thank you, Mr. Tony. You have a good day, now."

"You too, Annie."

Momma grabbed one bag off the counter, and I took the other one. As we headed toward the door, the gold bells chimed again. A tall man wearing a cowboy hat and sunglasses entered the store. He removed his shades. When he saw Momma, a look of recognition flickered in his brown eyes, and he smiled.

"Hi there, Annie Lee."

"Hi, Mr. Jim." Momma smiled back.

"I'm surprised to see you. I didn't see Otis's Bug parked outside."

"Otis went fishing with Eli this morning. And the weather was so nice, I decided me and Bailey would walk to the store."

"I see. Well, can I give you a lift back home? I just stopped in to get a pack of cigarettes and some gas." He handed Mr. Fratelli a ten-dollar bill. "Fill 'er up please, and let me get a pack of Marlboros."

"Oh no, I couldn't bother you to do that. We'll just walk back."

Momma couldn't feel the rumble in my gut or see the panic in my eyes. I could only imagine what Daddy would do to her if he saw her riding in the front seat of that fancy new Jaguar, sitting beside Mr. Jim. Deep down, I knew Momma wanted to say yes. I wanted to say yes for her. I wanted her to see what the inside of a fancy new car looked like and smelled like. I wanted her to ride back home instead of walk. But none of that was worth dying over.

"Well, here, let me get the door for you." When we walked outside, Mr. Jim started walking toward his car, then he paused. "Annie, did Otis tell you I came by yesterday?"

"Yes, sir. He did."

"He told you that I'm looking for someone to do some light housekeeping and cooking on a part-time basis?"

"Yes, sir. He told me."

"He said he'd let me know tomorrow morning when you could start."

Momma looked sheepish, and I knew why. Daddy had lied to Mr. Jim about her working for him. But before she could say anything, Mr. Jim continued.

"I don't want to pressure you, but I'm in dire straits and could really use your help sooner rather than later."

"I'm sorry, Mr. Jim. I can't work for you. You see, I just accepted another job last week... uh... Otis didn't know about it."

"How about I pay you twice what they're offering to pay you?"

I could practically see the wheels turning in Momma's head and the dollar signs flashing in her eyes. Last night, she'd told Daddy we really needed the money, and now Mr. Jim had offered to pay her twice as much as her imaginary job. But she'd have to convince Daddy to let her work for Mr. Jim. Would it matter to him that Mr. Jim would pay her double?

Momma paused. "You know, we really could use the extra money. When would I need to start?"

Momma was good with numbers. It was a natural ability for her. It would have been an easy calculation for her to double the amount of her imaginary job. She had a good grasp of the English language, too, and had helped me with both subjects since first grade. Momma often downplayed her ability to speak proper English, especially around Daddy. I suspected she didn't want him to feel insecure about the way he spoke.

"As soon as you want. My laundry and dirty dishes have stacked up a mile high."

"I will take the job, Mr. Jim, under one condition."

"Sure, what is it?"

"I don't want Otis to know."

My stomach lurched. I wondered if she had any idea what Daddy would do to her if he found out.

"Why not, Annie?" Mr. Jim removed his sunglasses.

"It's so silly. Otis doesn't think we should have the same boss. So he told me I couldn't." Momma waved a dismissive hand. "But we really need the money."

"Okay. Then it's settled." Mr. Jim put his sunglasses back on. "You can come work for me, but as far as keeping it a secret from Otis, that's on you. I don't want to be in the middle of your business." Mr. Jim started walking toward his car. When he reached it, he opened the gas cap and pushed in the pump nozzle. "Can you start next week?"

# Chapter 6

We started our trek back home after Momma told Mr. Jim she would start working for him the following Saturday. I didn't say anything for a long time while I tried to figure out what to say. Kids weren't supposed to question their parents, so I wanted to make sure I didn't come across as disrespectful. So I nibbled on my honey bun, drank my chocolate milk, and otherwise kept my mouth closed.

"Listen, Bailey," Momma said as we made our way along Marah's Pass. "Don't you say anything to your daddy about the conversation I just had with Mr. Jim. He can't know that I plan to work for him. Do you understand?"

"Yes, Momma, but how are you going to keep this from Daddy? When you walk down to Mr. Jim's house, won't he see you?"

"No, because I will be working part-time. I'll go to Mr. Jim's house after Otis goes to work and be back home before he gets off work. And I'll go on Saturdays when he's gone fishing."

"But what if Daddy finds out somehow? He will be so mad."

"He won't find out if I'm careful and if you keep your mouth shut. Also, we can't say anything about me working for Mr. Jim around Tammy because she's too young to keep a secret. She'll just blurt it out."

"I won't say anything, Momma. I know how Daddy is when he gets mad, especially after he's been drinking. The last time he got real mad at you, he tried to choke you to death. And he didn't even have a good reason to be that angry."

"You let me worry about your daddy. You just do what I asked you to do."

"I will, Momma." After we'd walked almost half the length of Marah's Pass, I said, "Momma, can I ask you a question?"

"Sure, Bailey."

"Is it right for you to keep a secret from Daddy? I mean, isn't keeping a secret like fibbing in a way? And didn't you tell us we weren't supposed to fib?"

"Listen, Bailey, life is complicated. It's not always black and white. It's not always simple. Our life with your daddy is hard. I want us to have a better life. And working for Mr. Jim can help us get that life."

"Without Daddy?"

"Yes, without your daddy," she said.

"But you said we should always be truthful."

"Bailey, do you remember the story in the Bible that I told you about where the woman helped the two spies get away?"

"Do you mean Rahab?"

"Yes. She told a lie to protect those men. Do you remember that?" Momma asked.

"I remember."

"God didn't punish her for lying, because she did it for the right reason. In fact, God blessed Rahab."

"So sometimes it's okay to fib?" I asked.

"Sometimes, son, doing the wrong thing for the right reason makes it okay. You understand?"

"I think so."

According to Momma, God blessed Rahab for fibbing to protect the two spies. I sure hoped God would bless us even though we were keeping a secret from Daddy. Otherwise, the situation could turn deadly before either of us could say "Jesus wept." A queasy feeling rumbled in the pit of my stomach.

# Chapter 7

Jonathan Streeter stood at the large picture window of his Florida Avenue home in Washington, DC. From this vantage point, he could see a handful of people milling about on U Street. He glanced at the buildings, a depressing vestige of what they'd once been. Some were burned-out hulls, while others had chain-locked doors and windows boarded up with plywood. Since the riots two years prior, after an assassin's bullet had killed Dr. Martin Luther King, the once vibrant hub for people dining and going to bars had become a ghost town. In his split-level condo, with his law office on the first floor and his living quarters on the second, Jonathan had been fortunate that his building sustained little damage.

Developers had finally purchased many of the buildings, and construction would begin soon. He'd even gotten a hefty offer to sell his property. He'd declined. The neighborhood would look significantly different because the developers were white and the previous owners had been Black.

*Urban renewal is a double-edged sword—a blessing and a curse.* He sighed.

When his desk phone rang, Jonathan was jarred out of his revelry. "Yes, Beverly?"

"Mr. Streeter, I have a long-distance call for you. He said he's your cousin, a Titus Jones from Greenville, Mississippi."

A smile spread across Jonathan's face. "I haven't heard from Titus in a month of Sundays. Put him through." He heard the click of the call being transferred. "Titus, what's going on, man?"

"Everything is everything, my brother. What's shaking?"

"I can't complain." Jonathan sat on the corner of his polished-maple desk with the receiver to his ear. "How long has it been since the last time we talked—three or four years?"

"Something like that."

"Man, we've got to do better."

"No jive," Titus said. "I've been watching the news, and I see the residents of DC are making their feelings known. They are literally taking it to the streets."

"I guess you mean the demonstrators protesting the Vietnam war?" Jonathan walked to his black leather executive chair and sat in it. He swiveled around to face the window.

"Yeah, man. It looked like a thousand people marched to the Capitol last month."

"That's true. At least it was peaceful, and nobody got hurt. It's bad enough with the killing going on in the war. Crime is up in America. And here in DC, man, crime has skyrocketed. It's not even safe to walk downtown anymore."

"Since that fool killed Dr. King, it seems the entire country is a powder keg waiting to explode," Titus said. "Speaking out against the war just might have gotten Dr. King killed."

"I think you're right. J. Edgar Hoover labeled him a communist and said he was the most dangerous man alive. Can you believe that?"

"Yeah, I can believe he said it. Now, if that doesn't cause some redneck to come out of the woodwork to do something crazy, I don't know what would."

"Sho' you're right." Jonathan leaned forward in his chair. "Say, man, I know you didn't call me to talk politics. Are you sure everything is okay at home?"

"Well, I guess you're right about that. The reason I called is to let you know that a good friend of yours, Lorenzo Cain, got shot two nights ago. Attempted robbery, they say."

"Aw, man. How is he?" Jonathan asked, a knot in his stomach.

"The bullet barely missed his brain. It's touch-and-go. The doctors aren't sure he's going to make it. I know you were close, so I wanted to let you know in the event you decided to fly down and see him." There was silence on the phone line. "Hello, Jon? You still there?"

"Yeah, I'm here. You're right. Lorenzo means a great deal to me. He was a good friend to me and a mentor when I was an undergrad. He took me under his wing and shielded me from some things that could have cost my scholarship."

"So, are you coming down to see him?"

"I don't know, Titus." Jonathan squeezed a small rubber basketball. "When I left Mississippi after Mom died, I vowed I would never return."

"The past has got a lot of ghosts that you don't want to revisit. But will you be able to live with yourself if Lorenzo doesn't make it?"

Jonathan released the small basketball, aiming it at the miniature goal affixed to his door. "I... I don't know."

"If you decide to come, he's at the Delta Medical Center in Greenville. I'd be glad to pick you up from the airport."

"How's your family?" Jonathan asked, switching subjects to avoid committing one way or the other. "Your mom and everybody... are they good?"

"Everybody's good. You probably don't know that Monica and I divorced about three years ago."

"Sorry to hear that."

"Apparently, the life of a cop's wife had become too stressful for her, worrying about whether I would come home every night. What about you? Did you get married?" Titus asked.

"Right now, I'm married to the law. Maybe one day."

"Well, I know you're busy lawyering, so I'm gonna let you slide. Let me know if you decide to come home."

"Is your number still the same?" Jonathan asked.

"No, it changed when I moved into my own pad."

"Can I get it? I'll give you a call later."

Titus gave him the phone number, and Jonathan scribbled it onto his desk calendar.

"Okay, stay loose, my man," Titus said.

"Right on, brother." Jonathan hung up and rocked back in his high-back leather chair while the ghosts of Mississippi past did the hustle in his brain. He swallowed hard to resist the itch he felt in the back of his throat.

# Chapter 8

Momma's first day of work at Mr. Jim's home happened the following Saturday. Daddy left at the crack of dawn to meet at Mr. Eli's house because Mr. Eli owned the boat they used for their weekend fishing expeditions. They never returned home until two or three in the afternoon.

Around eight o'clock that morning, I tapped on the half-open bathroom door. Momma was looking in the mirror, applying rose lipstick. When she gestured for me to come in, I entered the bathroom and stammered over every other word while asking her if I could go to work with her.

She snapped the top on the lipstick tube then turned to face me. "Bailey, I don't have time for your foolishness this morning. I'm trying to get ready to go to work."

"I know, and I want to go with you."

"Why, Bailey? Why do you want to go to work with me? You don't want to do the chores you have around here. Why do you want to go down to Mr. Jim's house to help me do housework?"

"I just want to help you, Momma, like a good son would."

"Boy, do I look like I just fell off a turnip truck? Now, spill it."

"Oh, all right," I said, letting out a theatrical sigh, my shoulders slumping in resignation. "I want to go down to Mr. Jim's house so that I can watch *Bugs Bunny* and *Road Runner* on his color TV."

"Oh, absolutely not!"

"Momma, please."

"Bailey, I can't take you down to that man's house while I'm working. He'll think you're gonna get in my way and keep me from getting my work done. Maids don't bring their children to work with them. Do you want me to get fired on the first day?"

"No, Momma, I don't want you to get fired, and I won't get in the way. I'll be real, real quiet—as quiet as a teeny, tiny mouse. Mr. Jim won't even know I'm there."

"I said no."

"Please, Momma. Just let me come for a little while just to see a few minutes of *Bugs Bunny* and *Road Runner*. I'll even pick up leaves outside if Mr. Jim wants me to. I can be your helper."

Momma exhaled loudly. "Okay, but if he says you can't stay, you're gonna have to leave right then. You understand?"

"Yes, I understand."

"Okay, go wake Jo up, and tell her that you're coming with me. She and Tammy will be okay here alone for the few hours we'll be gone."

"Yes!" I leaped into the air, thinking I would have the best bragging rights among my friends.

Momma and I began our trek down Tribett Road to Mr. Jim's house around eight in the morning. She'd planned to work until noon. Mr. Jim's house was built on the same side of Tribett Road as ours. Rows of cotton separated the two houses, though there was enough land to build two additional houses between the two. At night, when it was quiet, we could hear talking and laughter coming from his house.

There was no sidewalk, so we walked alongside the blacktop road because it had rained the day before, and the grass was still damp. The rain added freshness to the air. It was as though God had sent the showers to cleanse everything just for us. Chased by a gentle breeze, the thick white clouds began to part, allowing the sun's bright radiance to burst through.

As we approached Mr. Jim's home, my breath hitched. We'd walked past his residence many times before and observed its grandeur, but realizing I was about to go inside, I suddenly felt overwhelmed. The brick two-story with thick white columns and large windows framed with black shutters and a wraparound porch appeared larger the closer we got. Oak and magnolia trees towered in Mr. Jim's yard. Sculptured hedges and mounds of pink, purple, and white flowers accented curved flowerbeds that decorated the front yard.

We veered off the blacktop road to the right and walked along the gravel driveway, which led to the back door. Black folk didn't enter white people's houses through the front door. Actually, no one entered Mr. Jim's home through the front door because a carport had been built at the back of his house, so even he entered through the back door. Mr. Jim's brown Chevy pickup was parked in the driveway, but his convertible Jaguar wasn't there. Instead, someone had parked a shiny candy-apple-red Mercedes Benz behind his truck. Momma thought perhaps Mr. Jim's fiancée had bought a new car.

But when Momma climbed the steps and knocked on the door, a woman in her early thirties with ginger hair that cascaded down to her shoulders opened the back door. She greeted us with a big Ellie May Clampett smile, revealing perfect pearl-white teeth that undoubtedly had been straightened. She wore a sleeveless pink-and-orange-paisley minidress and pink sandals. Her nail polish matched the pink in her dress. Her rosy cheeks and hot-pink lipstick added much-needed color to her pale face, which looked as smooth as a Barbie doll's.

"Hi," she said with a decided Southern drawl. "You must be Annie Lee. Jim told me you'd start working here today. I'm Caroline, Jim's cousin. Come on in."

Daddy said Caroline Cunningham kept Mr. Jim's books for the plantation. He also said the two of them were more like brother and sister than cousins.

Ms. Caroline gestured for us to come in, and she opened the door wide for us to enter the kitchen.

The aroma of freshly brewed coffee mixed with cedarwood greeted us when we walked in. Coffee had never smelled so rich and inviting before. Daddy heated water in a small boiler for his instant coffee, which I could hardly smell. Mr. Jim brewed his coffee in a white coffee maker. Apparently, that made all the difference.

"Good morning, Ms. Caroline." Momma extended her hand to the woman. "I'm pleased to make your acquaintance. This is my son, Bailey. I told him he could be my helper today. I hope that's okay."

"Of course. Hello, Bailey." She smiled politely at me, but the warmth of her smile never reached her green eyes. "That won't be a problem at all. Jim had to run into town to take care of some business. He should be back in an hour or two. In the meantime, he wanted me to get you started on your chores. Follow me. I want to show you the house so you'll know where everything is."

Ms. Caroline led us past the kitchen. On the right, through an arched doorway, was a dining room with a shiny wooden table that looked to be half the length of our football field, along with ten or twelve high-backed cushioned chairs. Tangerine floral curtains hung at a huge window draped at the top like a woman's skirt in western movies. Two massive gold chandeliers dripping with hundreds of crystals hung over the table. A large cabinet filled with crystal glasses and china in various styles adorned the back wall.

Momma and I followed Ms. Caroline as she led us from the kitchen to the hallway and into a huge living room. A step down led into a spacious room with dark paneled walls and hardwood floors covered with a red-and-blue rug. The brown leather sofa and chairs of powder blue had also been crafted in dark wood. The living room opened to an expansive space with white marble tiles and a white spiral staircase. In the center of the foyer hung an enormous gold chandelier with dozens of candle lights and row upon row of sparkling crystals.

"Those stairs lead to the guest bedrooms. Nothing needs to be done in those rooms today. Everything you need to do today is on this level," Caroline said.

We followed her down the hallway as the soles of her sandals tapped softly on the polished floor. The scent of her rose-petal-and-vanilla perfume drifted behind her. We passed two bedrooms. The first, on the right, had a bed with posts made of thick dark wood and covered with a gold bedspread and matching drapes. The bed in the second bedroom, on the left, was made of a lighter-colored wood Momma said was oak. It had a lime-green-and-gold bedspread and curtains. Midway down the hall was a bathroom on the right. Across the hall from that was the laundry room. We continued down to the end of the hall, where there were two more rooms.

"This is Jim's bedroom. His bathroom is through that door once you enter his room." Ms. Caroline pointed. "And across the hall is his office. You can start wherever you want. However, Jim wants the kitchen, the two bathrooms, and his bedroom cleaned. His laundry also needs to be washed, dried, and folded. Any questions?" She smiled.

"No, I don't have any questions. Thank you for showing us around."

"I need to run to the bank downtown and make Jim's deposit. I'll be back in about forty minutes or so." Ms. Caroline walked back into the living room, grabbed her orange patent-leather handbag from the sofa, and strutted toward the back door. "If you get thirsty, help yourself to any of the cold drinks in the fridge."

"Yes, ma'am," Momma said.

I thought about whispering to Momma to ask her if I could watch TV, but I changed my mind after seeing the strange look in Ms. Caroline's eyes earlier. I felt a sense of relief watching her skip down the steps, slide into the seat of her Mercedes, and back out of Mr. Jim's driveway.

"She was nice, wasn't she?" Momma said.

I shrugged. "I don't know."

"You didn't think she was nice?" Momma walked over to the sink, removed the dirty dishes, and filled it with hot, soapy water.

"She sounded nice, and she smelled nice. But when she looked at me with those green eyes, I felt a chill go through me."

"You're just not used to seeing a person with green eyes—that's all."

"I see kids at school all the time with blue eyes and green eyes. But I never felt weird when they looked at me."

"Maybe it's because she's a grown woman and not a kid." Momma handed me a plate, and I dried it with a white dishtowel. I decided perhaps she was right.

Before I knew it, we had finished washing and drying the dishes. We headed down the hall to Mr. Jim's laundry room, and I watched as Momma stuffed a load of clothes into the washing machine. It took her a while to figure out how to use Mr. Jim's new model, which had several knobs and multiple settings. It looked like a gold gift box with a lid instead of a bow. Our washing machine was big, white, and round and looked like Will Robinson's robot.

Momma had finished more than half of her chores, but Ms. Caroline still hadn't returned. After Momma dried and folded Mr. Jim's laundry, she put fresh linens on his bed. Then we went across to his office, where she began dusting his large maple desk and organizing the files and folders on his desktop. I stared out of the back window, captivated by a red-headed woodpecker hammering away at one of the magnolia trees. When I heard a strange voice echo through the room, I jerked around.

"Why are you looking through Jim's ledger?" Ms. Caroline stood in Mr. Jim's office doorway with her arms folded. Her green eyes blazed kryptonite daggers at Momma, who quickly closed the book and placed it back on Mr. Jim's desk.

"I didn't mean any harm. I was just curious about it because the cover was so nice. I haven't seen anything like it before."

"Weren't there enough bathrooms to keep you busy? If you haven't cleaned them, you can do it now and then leave."

"I've already cleaned them," Momma said. "I'll just get my purse. Come on, Bailey."

Caroline turned and stalked ahead of us into the living room. She pulled out a pack of Benson & Hedges cigarettes from her purse and tapped one out. After lighting it, she took a long draw and expelled a white funnel of smoke toward the ceiling. Without looking in our direction, she said, "Goodbye."

Momma grabbed her purse from the kitchen counter, and we headed toward the back door. I scampered down the steps and walked briskly down the driveway until I reached the blacktop road. Momma was two or three steps behind me. I stopped and waited for her.

"Momma, Ms. Caroline was kind of scary just now."

"I guess she was just upset because I had been looking in Mr. Jim's book. When people get upset, they look and act different."

"She sure looked different than before she left." I thought about it for a while. "Momma, I don't want to come to Mr. Jim's house again if Ms. Caroline is going to be there."

"Don't worry, son. I wouldn't let her touch a hair on your head." Momma hugged me around my shoulders, and we continued walking down Tribett Road.

"She didn't scare you?"

"Bailey, I've come up against a lot worse than that green-eyed she-devil back there. I live with your daddy, remember?" Momma chuckled. "If she gets cut, she'll bleed just like anybody else."

"Yeah, but I bet she'd bleed green Vulcan blood like Mr. Spock."

Momma chuckled again. "It's okay, son. You don't have to go back when she's there."

"What was in that book, anyway? Anything good?"

"Rows and rows of numbers."

"That's it? She was upset about some numbers?"

"Those numbers meant something, Bailey."

"What did they mean?"

"I'm not sure. Mr. Jim is making a whole lot of money, and I bet some of it ain't coming from these cotton fields."

"So, what's wrong with that?" I asked.

"Not all money is good money."

"I thought it was."

"Not if you got it by doing something dishonest or illegal. That's why I think Ms. Caroline was so upset. I might have seen something I shouldn't have."

# Chapter 9

Jonathan looked at his watch. His summer-league basketball team had five minutes remaining to finish running the suicide drill. They all hated the drill and groaned when he sent them to the baseline to run it. When he heard the gym door open and saw his old friend Robert Donnelly walk in, Jonathan stood to greet him. At six feet, nine inches tall, Robert towered over Jonathan.

"When *the* Jonathan Streeter, attorney extraordinaire, calls, you show up." Robert smiled, showing a perfect set of white teeth.

Robert Donnelly had played college basketball with Jonathan, and he'd gone on to be drafted in the second round by the Los Angeles Lakers. He'd since retired and had become a sports announcer for a local DC television station.

"Listen, Bob, I appreciate you bailing me out. As I said, I need to travel to Mississippi for a couple of weeks, and I couldn't think of anybody better to coach my team while I'm away."

Jonathan remembered Bob's strong work ethic even as a college player and his drive and determination to win as an NBA player. He also had integrity. What Bob would teach the boys would be in line with what Jonathan had taught them.

"I'm glad I could do it," Bob said. "It'll give me a chance to give back to the community in a small way."

"The guys are going to be thrilled to be coached by a former NBA superstar."

"I'm way before their time. I'm not sure they'll even recognize me." Bob chuckled. "Besides, they are junior high school boys. Nothing much impresses boys that age."

"I think they'll be impressed. I'm going to call them in to meet you. I'd like you to stay and coach one of the teams in a scrimmage game if you have the time."

"Sure, that'll be fun. I'll try to take it easy on your team too." After a beat, Bob said, "It surprised me when you said you were going to Mississippi. You said it would have to be a life-or-death situation for you to ever go back."

"It is. A close friend was shot in a robbery attempt. The doctors don't know if he'll make it or not. You may remember Lorenzo Cain. He was a junior when we were freshmen. He helped bail me out of a few tough situations. So despite my reservations, I feel compelled to go."

"Understood. Yeah, I do remember him. I'm sorry he got shot. I hope he pulls through."

"Yeah, me too." Jonathan looked at his watch again then blew his whistle. "Time's up! Go get a drink of water then hustle to center court."

The boys trotted to the water fountain and gulped the water as though it were a gushing spring in a desert oasis. Then they jogged to center court, where Jonathan and Robert stood. A few bent down, grabbing their knees while sucking in air. Others leaned on the shoulders of teammates.

"Good job, everybody. I know the suicide drill is tough, but you'll thank me for it the next time you go up against the Blue Devils and you run their butts into the ground."

The boys grumbled.

"Listen, I want to introduce you to a good friend of mine. Some of you may know him. His name is Robert Donnelly. Robert played several seasons in the NBA with the Los Angeles Lakers, helping them to win three championships."

Some of the boys stood up straight. The eyes of a few brightened with interest.

"Bob—or as you will refer to him, Coach Bob or Coach Donnelly—will be standing in for me for the next two weeks, coaching you guys, while I travel to Mississippi on personal business."

"Coach Streeter, we just started to get real good," said Tommy Robinson.

"Aww shucks. Two weeks is a long time, Coach Streeter," said Christopher Gaines.

"Listen up. I'm leaving you in great hands. After two weeks, you guys probably won't even want me back as coach." Jonathan chuckled.

"Naw, Coach, we're glad you brought in your good friend who is a former NBA superstar, but nobody can replace you," said Benjamin.

"Okay, time will tell. But listen, all jokes aside, I want you to give Coach Donnelly the same respect and cooperation you give to me. Is that understood?"

"Yes, Coach Streeter," the boys said in unison.

"Okay, fellas, I'm going to divide you into two teams. The remainder of today's practice will be a scrimmage game. Coach Donnelly will coach one team, and I will coach the other."

The boys smiled and high-fived each other. Jonathan rattled off the starting five for both teams then blew his whistle. The boys sprinted to the center of the court.

# Chapter 10

It had been a month since Momma began working for Mr. Jim, and Daddy still didn't have a clue. Jo and I had been careful not to mention Mr. Jim when Daddy was around. We also tried not to say his name when Tammy was around, but we slipped a few times in our exuberance over Momma bringing home half a cake or cookies from Mr. Jim's house. Jo and I were convinced rich white people's desserts tasted much more delectable than ours. We were also convinced they cost a lot more than ours.

One Saturday morning in late June, Momma asked me to go to work with her. She wanted to keep an eye on me because my stomach felt achy and queasy from eating cold spaghetti the previous night. I'd taken some Arm & Hammer baking soda and water, as she'd instructed, to settle my stomach. Momma assured me that Ms. Caroline would not be there. She even promised to give me two dollars for helping her.

Daddy had gone fishing with Mr. Eli again, so Momma and I left home at eight thirty to start our trek down to Mr. Jim's house. Momma knocked, and Mr. Jim opened the back door. A rich coffee aroma drifted over us.

"Good morning, Annie. Y'all come on in." He smiled, revealing perfectly straight white teeth. "I see you brought a helper today."

"Good morning, Mr. Jim. You remember my son, Bailey. He had a stomachache. And I wanted to keep an eye on him. I hope it's okay."

"It's fine." He motioned for us to come in. "Hi, Bailey. So, you gonna help your momma today?"

"Yes, sir," I said, looking around the immaculate kitchen with all its new-looking appliances in a harvest-gold color. It stood in stark contrast to our old worn refrigerator and stove.

"Well, I'm not going to keep you from it. Annie, if Bailey starts feeling better, I've got some weeds out in the flower beds that need to be pulled and a few leaves that need to be raked up." As Mr. Jim headed toward the living room, he stopped. "Also, Annie, can you fix me a light breakfast? You know how I like it." He winked.

"I sure do." Momma smiled sheepishly.

Mr. Jim smiled and made his way down the hall, his cowboy boots thumping on the hardwood floor. He disappeared into one of his back rooms.

Momma walked into the living room, turned on the television, then came into the kitchen and began fixing Mr. Jim's breakfast. I sat on one of the chairs at the round table in the kitchen area and took my book, *Sounder,* from my jeans back pocket. Before long, the aroma of bacon started to waft in the air. Usually, bacon would have my taste buds jumping for joy, but that day, it caused my stomach to somersault as a wave of nausea passed over me.

"Momma, can I go outside? That bacon is making my stomach feel queasy."

"Okay, son. Go on outside. If you start feeling better, you can pull the grass out of the flower beds for Mr. Jim and rake up the leaves. No need to be in a rush to get finished. I have at least about two hours of work here anyway."

"All right, Momma."

"Wait a minute, Bailey." Momma handed me two white trash bags she'd taken from under the sink. "Here. Take these to put the grass and leaves in. The rake's in the shed out back."

"Okay." Carrying the bags, I headed out the back door and down the steps.

Chirping mockingbirds greeted me, darting from branch to branch and tree to tree as they flew high up in the magnolia tree. The flower beds in front of the house were a bouquet of pink, purple, and white. I didn't know what kinds of flowers they were, just that they smelled as sweet as some of the perfumes Momma wore.

When I kneeled and started pulling the weeds, I found it easy because the ground was soft. Soon, I'd forgotten about my upset stomach. It didn't take me long to finish pulling the weeds. I walked around to the back of the house and found the rake in the shed, just as Momma said. Thirty minutes or so later, I had finished. I carried the trash bags to the back of the house and placed them in Mr. Jim's big black trash can. Then I jogged up the steps, pushed open the back door, and entered the kitchen.

"I'm done, Momma." I looked around the kitchen and in the living room, but Momma wasn't there. "Momma, where are you?"

"I'll be right there, Bailey."

I sat at the table in the kitchen, pulled out *Sounder*, and started reading again. Several minutes later, I heard soft footsteps coming from the back.

"I'm almost done, son." Momma walked past me and went into the kitchen. She carried Mr. Jim's empty breakfast tray. "I just need to wash these few dishes. Why don't you go into the living room and watch TV until I'm ready to go? Sit on the rug since you've been working in the yard."

"Okay, but can I have a glass of water, please? I'm so thirsty."

I gulped down the cool water Momma gave me. Then I walked into the living room, admiring the dark paneled walls and polished hardwood floors. As I stepped down to the sunken floor, I was captivated by the colorful images on the television. A commercial for the *Beverly Hillbillies* came on, and I was amazed by the brilliant-golden shade of Ellie May's hair and the dazzling blue of her eyes. I sat on the soft rug, pretending that I was home and the floor-model color TV, comfortable sofa and chairs, and thick dark-wood furnishings were ours.

After a while, Mr. Jim brought his empty coffee mug back to the kitchen. He thanked Momma for another delicious meal. Then he said something to her in a tone too low for me to understand. If the television volume had been a little lower, I probably could have heard, but I was more interested in seeing the hilarious antics between the Road Runner and Bugs Bunny. Even so, I could hear Momma's playful laugh, and I wondered why she didn't laugh that way with Daddy.

"Well, I'm almost done here. Do you need me to do anything else before I go?" she asked.

"Can't think of anything. Thank you for your help today, Annie. You'll be back on Tuesday?"

I glanced around and saw Momma smiling. She wiped her hands on her white apron, then her gaze met Mr. Jim's. "Yes, sir. I'll see you then. Same time?"

"Perfect." He smiled.

Momma took off her apron and grabbed her purse. "Let's go, Bailey."

"Bye, Jim... Mr. Jim. See you Tuesday."

"See you Tuesday, Annie. Bye, Bailey. Oh, and take those chocolate chip cookies with you. I'm sure Bailey and the girls will enjoy them." Mr. Jim strode down the hall, whistling a jovial tune.

As we neared our home, I looked up, and my heart started to pound erratically. I almost dropped the box of cookies I was carrying. Momma stopped in her tracks. She gripped the straps of her shoulder bag. Panic flashed in her eyes. Daddy's Volkswagen was parked in the driveway.

# Chapter 11

The glass double doors slid open when Jonathan approached the entry to the Delta Medical Center in Greenville. A blast of cool, sterile air greeted him as he crossed the threshold. A woman with frizzy strawberry-blond hair looked up when Jonathan approached the nurses' station.

She smiled perfunctorily. "May I help you?"

"Yes. I need the room number for Lorenzo Cain, please."

"Just a minute." With a pen in hand, she scrolled down a list of names on a printed page attached to a clipboard. "Mr. Cain is in ICU. Only family members can visit him. Are you family?"

"Yes, he's my brother." Under the circumstances, Jonathan didn't think a little white lie would do any harm. Besides, once upon a time, they'd been as close as brothers.

"The ICU is located on the third floor."

"Thank you."

Jonathan took the elevator to the third floor and looked for the ICU. When he located the room, he eased the door open so as not to disturb the comatose man with his head wrapped in white gauze. Jonathan realized the irony of his attempts to be quiet as the heels of his Italian leather shoes tapped softly against the tile floor. The room was as silent as a graveyard except for the clicks and beeps of the machines. A nurse with chestnut-brown shoulder-length hair stood beside Lorenzo's bed, taking his vitals. She glanced up at Jonathan and smiled politely.

"How is he?" Jonathan said.

"As well as could be expected under the circumstances."

"Will he pull through?"

"We don't know. At this point, it could go either way. But it's believed that comatose patients can hear when you're talking to them. So do what you can to encourage Mr. Cain to fight." After annotating Lorenzo's chart, the nurse left the room.

Jonathan sat in a club chair next to Lorenzo's bed. "What people won't do to get a little attention." He chuckled. "How you been, man? It's been a long time. We said we'd stay in touch, but I guess we both got caught up in life. Me chasing hot cases and you chasing hot chicks." He laughed. It sounded hollow and empty in a room where no one could share in the conversation.

"Man, it looks like things got rough down here for you. I wish I'd been here for you the way you were always there for me. The way you were there after Pops was killed. I was so angry."

Jonathan adjusted the soft tan blanket across Lorenzo's chest then cradled his friend's hand in his own, like a handshake. The silence in the room weighed in on him. The machines beeped.

"When my dad died, I couldn't understand why God would choose him instead of all the other bad dads running around, cheating on their wives, robbing, stealing, some killing."

Jonathan let the words settle, let the sounds of the machines fill the air as his mind drifted back to the boy he'd been. He wondered how he'd even graduated from high school, let alone summa cum laude.

"I thought I finally had it all together. Everything was fine for a while until it wasn't. I realized I hadn't dealt with Pops's death the way I should've. Once I got to college, everything came rushing back, and I started to spiral out of control. I couldn't sleep. I hardly ate. The anger crept right back, and I blamed everybody for everything I did wrong. I felt like the world was against me. I would have lost my academic scholarship, for sure, with my crazy antics—skipping classes, fighting, drinking, and bringing girls to the dorm. But, man, you were there for me all the way, even when I didn't want you to be. I never really thanked you properly for it. Pride. Foolish pride—that's all it was. But that's all going to change. When you get out of here, we're going to paint the town red and a few other colors."

Jonathan paused and looked at his watch. "I've been rambling for a while now. I think that's enough for one day. I'll be back tomorrow. You've got to pull through. I love you, man."

He waited as though he expected Lorenzo to respond. There was only silence. Jonathan stood, feeling a deep sadness for his friend, and left the room.

# Chapter 12

I'd known the day of reckoning would come. I just hadn't known it would be *that* day. The panic-stricken look on Momma's face told me I should be worried. I knew that already. The drumbeat thrumming in my chest had alerted me.

Momma grabbed me by my shoulders and spun my mannequin-like body toward her. "Listen to me, Bailey. This is very important. Our lives, and especially my life, depend on what happens when we walk into that house. We knew this could happen. We planned for it. And if we stick to the plan, everything will be fine. I will talk to your daddy. Don't you say anything, you hear me?"

I nodded, incapable of formulating words. But I felt a tiny sense of relief, knowing I didn't have to look Daddy in the eye and lie to him.

"Won't... won't Daddy ask Jo where we are?"

"I'm sure he already asked her. I went over this several times with Jo. She knows what to tell him. There's no reason your daddy shouldn't believe our story—unless one of us slips and tells him."

"I won't tell, Momma."

"Bailey, I know you're scared, but today, we've got to look fear in the eye and say, 'Get the hell out of the way!' Now, that's the only way we'll get through this situation without things turning bad. You hear me?"

"Yes, Momma," I said, but I found it hard to stand firm in my conviction to be brave when my legs felt like noodles. I drew in a deep breath and exhaled, praying that God would give me courage.

"All right, let's go."

We continued toward home on the blacktop road. When we turned up our pathway, we cautiously approached the house as though we expected Cerberus to greet us. And he just might, depending upon how much alcohol my daddy had consumed.

When we walked into the living room, a pungent fish odor assaulted my nostrils. Music from *American Bandstand* blared from the television. Jo sat in the big chair by the window, with her nose in a book. She didn't seem to notice we'd entered the house. I saw no sign of Daddy, and I didn't know what his state of mind would be. A knot twisted in my stomach. My feet became glued to the planks in our floor.

"Jo," Momma said, "where's your daddy?"

Jo was a voracious reader, just as I was, constantly engrossed in a Nancy Drew mystery or some other novel. We generally had to call her three or four times before she'd even hear us. When Jo didn't answer, Momma called her name again, this time with more urgency.

Jo looked up in her usual nonchalant manner. "Momma, did you say something?"

"Where's your daddy?"

"He's in the kitchen."

"Where's Tammy?"

"She's in our room, playing with her dolls," Jo said.

"Bailey, hand me those cookies," Momma said, "Didn't you say you needed to use the bathroom *real* bad?" She nodded toward the restroom. Then Momma put on an improvised smile and strolled casually into the kitchen. "Hey, you're back early. How'd you do at the lake?"

The smell of fish guts permeated the air, and I couldn't determine whether the stench of alcohol was mixed in with the disgusting odor. And I needed to see whether Daddy was drunk or not before I left Momma alone with him, so I crept from the living room to our bedroom, which also had an entrance into the kitchen. Daddy looked up from the table, where he sat gutting a fish with a sharp-looking pocketknife with a silver handle.

His bloodshot eyes locked onto Momma. "Where you been?"

"Didn't Jo tell you?"

"Um asking you. Where you been?"

"Down to Ms. Barbara's house. Ms. Clara told me she wasn't feeling well, so I made some soup and took it to her."

Daddy sucked his teeth. "What you got there in that box?"

"Cookies," Momma said, lifting the lid. "Ms. Barbara gave them to me for the kids. She was so thankful that I came to visit her and brought the soup. Do you want one?"

"Naw. You know I ain't particular about no damn cookies." Daddy reeled from side to side. "I thought it might be cake." He paused. "I seen a box like that b'fore."

Momma looked down at the box. With an unsteady hand, she closed the lid. "Well, they sell them in all the grocery stores."

That was a lie. I never saw those cookies in any of the grocery stores where we shopped.

"Naw, I seen it someplace else."

"I don't know, Otis, but do you need help with the fish?"

"Um almost done. Only caught these five perches right here. They wasn't bitin' too good today." Daddy's words slurred a bit. "The bait house was almost out of worms, so we had to buy some of them fake baits. Fishes didn't like 'em too much."

"They are a nice size, though," Momma said, "I'll just fry the fish for you and me and fry some chicken for the kids."

Daddy nodded, placed the knife on the table, and wiped his bloodstained hands on one of his old T-shirts. As he wrapped the fish guts in the newspaper, I turned to go to the bathroom because it appeared the drama was over. Tammy walked into the kitchen from the living room, holding Barbie by her straw-colored hair. She stopped right beside Momma, whose body became as rigid as an ironing board.

"Hey, Daddy," she said, "why them fishes stink so much?"

Daddy chuckled. "It's them fish guts that stank so bad, not the fishes. I gotta take the guts out so we can eat the fishes."

"Well, I don't want to eat none of that stinky fish with his ole stinky guts!"

"You don't have to, baby girl. You can eat the chicken yo' momma's gon' cook. How's that?" Daddy swayed from side to side.

"Okay, Daddy." Tammy gave a big grin. Then she looked up at Momma holding the box of cookies. "Hi, Momma. Can I have some of that sweet Mr. Jimmy cake?"

# Chapter 13

Daddy's brows knotted, and his face twisted into a scowl. "Sweet Jimmy cake? What that child talkin' 'bout? I thought you said them was cookies."

Momma fumbled with the lid on the box and eventually took out a chocolate chip cookie and gave it to Tammy. "Here you go, sweetheart. Now, go on back in your room and play with your dolls. Bailey, you and Jo can have a cookie too. And take Tammy to your room so I can start cooking."

Tammy jumped up and down. "Thank you, Mommy! Thank you, Mommy!"

I took the box of cookies in one hand and Tammy by the other and led her into our room. I was too nervous to eat a cookie. I placed the box on the top of our dresser. I feared for Momma because I wasn't sure how she would explain to Daddy what sweet Mr. Jimmy cake was. Jo didn't move from the chair, where she sat with her eyes glued to the pages of her mystery novel, unaware of the danger unfolding in her own home. I stood frozen in the living room doorframe, waiting to see how Momma would explain what Tammy had said.

"What she talkin' 'bout, Annie? Sweet Jimmy cake. I know I done seen that box before."

"Like I said, these are just chocolate chip cookies Ms. Barbara gave to the kids. Tammy is probably repeating something she heard on TV. You know how kids are. There's no cake, but you can have a cookie or two."

"Naw, you know I ain't particular 'bout no damn cookies. These children sho' can come up with somethin'. Sweet Jimmy cake." Daddy shook his head. "We got any beer in the icebox? Me and Eli drunk the twelve-pack I brung and a half a pint of gin."

Daddy really didn't need anything else to drink, but I knew Momma wouldn't challenge him because he was like a keg of dynamite with a short fuse.

"I think we have a couple of cans left," Momma said.

"I'll take one after I clean up." Daddy stood and walked unsteadily to toward the living room. "Throw out this mess, will ya?"

Momma grabbed the fish guts wrapped in newspaper and threw them into the trash can outside. Afterward, she fried the fish for the two of them and fried chicken for us kids. She cut up potatoes to make french fries and sliced juicy red tomatoes then seasoned them with salt and black pepper.

While Momma cooked, Daddy bathed and dressed in fresh clothing. He sat in his recliner watching *Gunsmoke,* sipping on a beer, and nodding. When Momma finished cooking, she brought Daddy a plate with fish fried to a golden brown, piping-hot french fries, and cool seasoned tomatoes. His catch was cooked to perfection and adorning his plate. He grinned with satisfaction. Momma fixed her plate and Tammy's. After that, Jo and I raced into the kitchen to fix our plates while the chicken and french fries were still hot.

For the next hour before he fell asleep in the recliner, Daddy prattled on about Mr. Eli and their dismal day of fishing on Lake Ferguson. Momma listened and laughed at the appropriate times and reminded Daddy what a good fisherman he had been despite having a bad day at the lake. Her high-pitched laughter was a sure sign of relief, knowing we'd narrowly escaped what could have been a tragic day.

# Chapter 14

Uncle Earl climbed down the ladder and looked up, admiring his handiwork. He'd hung the basketball goal Mr. Fratelli had given me after buying a new one for his son Mark.

"Now you and Jo can play basketball instead of playin' kickball all the time and learn some real skills. How does it look to you?"

"It looks great!" I bounced the basketball in the dusty area where no grass grew then released a long shot—an airball. "Aw, shucks!"

"Keep shootin', young blood." Uncle Earl chased down the ball and passed it back to me. "You gotta warm up some."

I continued to dribble and shoot. "I think I'll ask Ray and some of my other friends to play sometime."

"I'm sure that'll be okay with your mom and dad."

"Uncle Earl, you want to play horse?"

"Sure, why not. I wanna see what you can do since I spent the last hour hanging this thing."

"Okay. But I won't take it easy on you because you're my uncle and you're old." I grinned.

"And I won't take it easy on you because you're ten and a midget." Uncle Earl chuckled as he swatted the ball from my hand and started dribbling. "Let's play."

Uncle Earl and I played three rounds of horse, the best two out of three. I won, but he let me. At six foot two, he towered over me with long spider arms. He could have dunked every shot if he'd tried.

Hearing Uncle Earl laugh and have fun reminded me of how it used to be when Daddy would play catch with me. It had been years since he'd tossed me a glove and taken me out into the backyard, but one of my best days with him had been in the spring several years back.

His voice sounded in my head, and I was lost in the memory.

"Come on, Bailey, let yo' glove touch with the ground and grab the ball up," Daddy had said. "Here it come again."

He rolled the ball over the green grass. It sped toward me. I had it for sure. But for the third time, the ball rolled under my glove and between my legs. It stopped at the edge of our vegetable garden.

"Go get it, son—hurry up." Daddy chuckled. "Toss it back to me."

I raced over, scooped up the ball, and with all the strength I had, I thew it back to Daddy.

"This time, I want you to make a alligator mouth. That'll help you be able to pick the ball up better."

"A what?" I asked.

"A alligator mouth." Daddy tossed the ball back to me. "I'll show you. Now, you roll the ball back to me."

"Okay, Daddy." I rolled the ball to him, and as he touched the ground with his glove, he clapped his other hand over the top of the ball to mimic what the top of an alligator's mouth would look like. I thought that was pretty clever.

"Now, um gon' roll the ball back to you, and I want you to make a alligator mouth and pick it up just like I did. You thank you got it?"

Nodding enthusiastically, I said, "Yep, I got it, Daddy." As the ball rolled toward me, I moved into its path. I touched the ground with my glove, and when the ball rolled into it, I clamped it like an alligator with my other hand.

"That's good, son." Daddy beamed with pride. "Okay, we gon' do it a few more times to make sho' you got it, then we gon' work on fly balls."

# Chapter 15

I asked two of my friends, Leo Ware and Ray Martin, who didn't live far from us, to come and play with Jo and me the next day. The boys had a slight height advantage over me because they were both eleven. However, Ray was in the same grade as I was because he had been held back in the second grade. We played horse, pony, and two on two from noon until almost sundown, stopping only to get water or use the bathroom.

We were starting to get tired, so we decided our final game would be two on two. Jo and Leo were teammates, and so were Ray and I. After playing awhile, Leo attempted a long shot to tie the game, but I blocked it.

"Foul!" Leo said.

"That was all ball!" I shouted.

"No, you hit me on my wrist, so I get to shoot two free throws."

"No, you don't. I blocked you fair and square."

"No, you didn't, Bailey," Leo said. "You're trying to cheat us out of this game."

"I'm not! You're just a crybaby trying to cheat us out of the game!"

Before long, all four of us were shouting at each other without any words being heard. Then Leo pushed me in the chest. "You cheat, Bailey Connor, just like your momma. She's cheating with Mr. Jim."

"You're a lying piece of dog shit!" As heat rose up my spine, my fingers curled into tight fists.

"And your momma's a tramp."

I swung, striking Leo hard across his left cheek. Stunned, he grabbed the side of his face, then Leo charged me. When he tackled me, I landed on my back, underneath him.

"What the hell is goin' on out here?" Daddy said, racing out of the back door.

"Stop them, Daddy!" Jo screamed.

"Naw, let 'em fight." Daddy took a drag from his cigarette and blew out a funnel of smoke. "This how you learn to defend yo' self. Now, Bailey, if you don't kick Leo's li'l ass, I'm gon' kick yours."

I flipped Leo over. He landed on his back. I straddled him, but he flipped me over his head. We squared off like opposing linemen and charged at each other. I extended my leg, flipping Leo onto his back again. When he scrambled onto his stomach, I grabbed his arm and twisted it behind his back.

"You're breaking my arm! Get off me! Get off me!" he yelled.

"Okay, that's 'nough, Bailey. Get off the boy," Daddy said.

We both stood and dusted the dirt and grass off our clothes.

"Y'all supposed to be friends. What y'all fightin' about?" Daddy looked from one of us to the other.

No one responded.

"I said, what you boys fightin' about?"

"No reason," I said.

"Yeah, no reason," Leo said. "Just a silly foul."

"Well, you boys is friends. You need to apologize and shake hands."

"I'm sorry, Bailey, for what I said about..."

"It's okay, Leo. I'm sorry that I hit you in the face," I said through clenched teeth, my fists still half-cocked. I wanted Leo to know that if he said anything else about my momma, I would sock him in his jaw again.

"All right. Now, y'all boys gone on home," Daddy said to Leo and Ray. "Bailey, you gone on in the house. It's almost suppertime anyway."

"Okay, Daddy." I watched him disappear inside.

Leo and Ray had almost reached Tribett Road.

As Jo and I began walking toward the house, I grabbed her by the arm. "Jo, what did Leo mean when he said Momma was cheating with Mr. Jim?"

"How should I know? Probably some worthless gossip. Maybe you should have asked Leo before you punched him in the face. But what does it matter? He was just mad because you're shorter than he is but you blocked his shot. Forget about it."

# Chapter 16

Friday came, and Jo and I played basketball for hours. The afternoon turned into evening, and the sun, dressed in shades of lavish orange and spectacular reds, descended into a lavender sky. The cicadas sang, and fireflies blinked on and off as they darted in a zigzag pattern. We decided it was time to go inside since we could hardly see the basketball anymore. We'd neared the back door as a dark automobile pulled into the driveway and parked behind Daddy's Volkswagen. Jo continued inside, but I walked around to the front of the house to see who the visitors were. The car's headlights turned off, and the driver's side and passenger doors swung open almost simultaneously.

A young woman wearing bell-bottom blue jeans and a sleeveless canary-yellow silk blouse stepped from the passenger side and pranced unsteadily over the gravel in yellow platform sandals. It was Momma's younger sister Bernadette. Her fiancé, Walter—a tall, slender man with a neatly trimmed Afro and a full beard—lumbered behind her, carrying a brown paper bag in one hand and a twelve-pack of Budweiser in the other. Bernadette was three years younger than Momma, which made her thirty-one and on her way to her third marriage. I heard Momma say Aunt Bernie's marriages lasted about as long as a common cold. She always dressed as though she were on her way to someplace fancy, even when she came out to our house in the middle of nowhere. She and Momma were the closest out of the six sisters, despite their age difference.

"Hey, Dr. Bailey," Aunt Bernadette said with a smile as I met her at the bottom of the steps. "How you doing, little man? Still making straight *A*s?"

"Yep." I felt my face flush with embarrassment and pride.

"Good." She patted me on the back. "You keep that up. We need a rich doctor in the family. You dig where I'm coming from?" Bernadette threw her head back with laughter.

"Yes, Aunt Bernie." I followed the grownups into the house.

I'd never thought about being a doctor before, let alone a rich one. I couldn't even stand watching myself get vaccinated, so I'd probably faint if I had to administer a shot, extract a bullet, or stitch up a wound. The thought of it made me feel queasy, though I had to admit it sure did make me feel good that Aunt Bernie thought I could be someone that important someday. I didn't have the heart to tell her I'd never become a doctor.

"Y'all come on in and take a load off," Momma said, greeting Aunt Bernie and Walter at the door. "I just finished dinner. If you're hungry, I can fix you a plate."

"Chile, Walter and me just left Benny's Burger Joint down on Nelson Street. I had the biggest burger you ever saw. Ate the whole thing too." Aunt Bernie chuckled, taking the beer from Walter. "Here, Annie, put this beer in the fridge, but take us out a few before you do. It's been a long ride out here from Greenville."

I didn't think Greenville was that far from Lowell. Actually, it was in the same county. But listening to Aunt Bernadette, you would have thought she'd ridden a covered wagon across the western plains.

"Thanks, Bernie. I sure could use a beer myself. It's been a long day."

"Where's Otis?" Walter said.

"He's in the back. He'll be out in a minute."

Just as Momma finished the sentence, Daddy strolled into the living room with a big grin on his face. He knew how to turn on the charm when other people were around.

"Hey, Bernie. What's goin' on, Walter?" Daddy said.

The adults exchanged greetings then sat in the living room, talking about grownup stuff. Music from the turntable played in the background. After playing basketball all afternoon, I was famished, so I moseyed into the kitchen and fixed myself a sizable helping of Momma's collard greens, macaroni and cheese, cornbread, and the best fried chicken in the entire state of Mississippi. Jo fixed her plate and Tammy's, and we sat at the kitchen table and devoured our meal. Afterward, we retreated to our bedroom. Jo flung herself across her bed and began reading a novel, while Tammy sat next to her and began scribbling in a coloring book. I grabbed one of the Hardy Boys mysteries, climbed up on my bed, and started reading.

After about an hour, Jo must have grown tired of reading. She asked me if I wanted to play Old Maid, which I agreed to do because I'd become drowsy reading my book, and it wasn't yet nine o'clock. Music from the living room floated melodiously through our thin walls. I could hear "Midnight Train to Georgia" and Aunt Bernadette straining her vocal cords, trying to out-sing Gladys Knight. She must have been pretty tipsy.

I went into the kitchen to get a glass of iced tea and saw Aunt Bernie and Walter two-stepping in the center of the living room. Red plastic cups lined the coffee table. Whatever Walter had brought in that brown paper bag probably filled those cups.

Daddy sat in his recliner, smoking a cigarette and nodding to the beat. Momma sat on the sofa across from him, sipping from her cup, with a lighted cigarette between her fingers. It appeared the grownups were having a good time in their cigarette-hazed, booze-infused Friday-night escapade.

I went back into our room and continued playing cards with Jo. A short time later, I heard the adults deciding to play cards too. They estimated their books and placed their bids, so I surmised they were playing spades. Jo and I finished our card game, and I dozed off fully dressed, lying across my bed.

A loud crash sometime later yanked me out of a deep sleep. Disoriented, I couldn't determine what had made the noise, but it became clear when I heard the loud, angry voice that followed. So I slid down the bunkbed's ladder and tiptoed up the hall to the living room. Daddy had flipped over the coffee table. Red plastic cups, ashtrays, cigarette butts, and ashes littered the floor. Aunt Bernie stood frozen next to the stereo. Walter's red eyes looked like he'd just been jarred out of sleep. Daddy held the Queen of Hearts in his hand, jabbing it in the air toward Momma. She stood about three feet from him.

"I know I seen them gotdamn hearts on that box before. Now I know where I seen them," Daddy said, huffing like a demented bull intent on goring its victim to death.

"Man, what are you talking about?" Momma placed a defiant hand on her hip.

"Jim brought that same box with them damn hearts on it to the shop with leftover cake."

"Anybody can buy a damn cake."

"I ain't crazy, Annie. Ain't no niggas buying no cakes or cookies like them. Hell, we wouldn't even know where to get 'em."

"So, what you saying, Otis?"

"You know what I'm sayin'. Same thang people sayin'. You been sneakin' down to Jim's house, laying up with that cracker behind my back."

"Don't be crazy, Otis," Momma said. "That white man don't want me. He's got three or four white women that he's playing around with."

"Otis, that's enough!" Aunt Bernie said. "Do you know what you sayin'?"

"You stay out of this, Bernie," Walter said. "This ain't none of your business."

"It is my business. This man just accused my sister of screwing a white man."

"I think it's time for us to go, Bernie." Walter placed his red cup on the side table.

"Yeah, y'all need to go—this between Annie Lee and me. But I ain't crazy. Folks been talkin', Annie. But I said not my wife. Not behind my back."

"Don't be a damn fool. That's just gossip—"

"A fool... shut the hell up, you slut!" Daddy lunged for Momma.

My heart thundered in my chest.

"Whoa, whoa, Otis." Walter sprang from the sofa and dashed between Momma and Daddy. "Maybe you should calm down a little." He attempted to place a hand on Daddy's shoulder, but Daddy swatted it away and glared at Momma with hate-filled eyes. "Come on, Otis, man—"

"Get the hell outa my house, Walter." Daddy stalked into the bedroom and slammed the door so hard the frame rattled.

Bernadette grabbed her purse, and she and Walter headed for the front door. "You gonna be okay, Annie?"

"Yeah, yeah, I'll be fine. Otis is just blowing off steam right now. He'll calm down and go on to sleep."

"I hope so because he was madder than a one-eyed billy goat. I've never seen him like that before."

"Consider yourself lucky." Momma gave a weak chuckle. "I'll be fine. Y'all be safe on the road back to Greenville."

"We will." Bernadette hugged Momma.

As she and Walter stepped out onto the porch, I wanted to scream, "Stop! Y'all come back!" My confidence wasn't as great as

Momma's, thinking that Daddy would calm down and go to sleep. And I didn't know what I would do—or could do—if Daddy burst back through that bedroom door.

# Chapter 17

I watched through the living room window as Momma walked out onto the porch and waved goodbye to Aunt Bernie and Walter. The bright headlights pierced the darkness as the car backed out of the driveway and headed back toward Greenville. Momma sat on the porch, with her feet resting on one of the steps. She lit a cigarette and blew a plume of smoke into the air. I decided to join Momma, so I eased the front door open, hoping not to disturb Daddy and raise his ire again. I tiptoed over and sat down beside her.

"Bailey, what are you still doing up? It's past midnight."

"I was asleep, but a noise woke me up, and I got up to see what it was."

"Your daddy, up to his old tricks again."

"I'm just glad Walter and Aunt Bernie were here."

"Yeah, so am I." Momma took another long drag from her cigarette and blew streams of smoke through her nostrils. She was quiet for a while, and I didn't know what to say, so we just sat in silence as the crickets and cicadas sang a joyful tune.

"Momma, are you going back down to Mr. Jim's house to work?" I finally asked.

"Hush, boy!" Momma jerked her head around and looked toward the window. "As far as I'm concerned," she whispered, "I was never at Mr. Jim's house. You understand me?"

"Yes, Momma."

Momma drew another drag from her cigarette, tossed it onto the step, and stubbed it out with the bottom of her shoe. "It's time for you to go to bed, Bailey."

"But what about you? I don't want to go to bed. I want to stay with you in case Daddy comes out here and starts fussing again."

"No, you go on to bed, now. I can take care of myself. Go on, you hear?"

"Yes, ma'am." I rose slowly and skulked to the door. "Good night, Momma."

"Good night, son."

FORTUNATELY, MOMMA had been right about Daddy. He fell asleep and snored loudly throughout the night. The next morning, it was as though the North Pole had sent a frosty chill through our house. Daddy didn't talk to Momma at all. He wouldn't even look at her. She'd fixed his breakfast, but he ignored that as well. Instead, he boiled water on top of the stove and made himself a cup of coffee. He went outside, sat on the porch, and drank it. Afterward, he brought the cup back inside, set it on the kitchen table, and left, slamming the front door on his way out.

It remained the same all week long. Momma would try holding a conversation with Daddy, and he'd completely ignore her. Finally, by midweek, she'd stopped trying, and they passed each other both day and night like total strangers, one not recognizing the other. It was quiet in the house, except for the chatter we kids made. And we even found ourselves lowering our voices. It had become a strange and eerie kind of quiet, like being in the eye of a hurricane.

# Chapter 18

We spent the Fourth of July holiday at Big Momma's house as we did every special occasion. This was our great escape from the humdrum existence of living two miles from downtown Lowell and out in the country. Big Daddy, my grandfather, had died of a heart attack three years earlier at the age of fifty-five. His bigger-than-life presence was still missed, especially by Momma, who cried whenever she thought about him.

Momma was the oldest of four brothers and five sisters, a total of nine siblings. All of Momma's brothers and sisters liked Daddy. Even Big Momma liked him, and she didn't like anybody except her own kids. They were all convinced Daddy was such a nice man because he had the uncanny ability to turn on the charm when it suited him. They never saw the mean, drunken, cursing side that we were privy to regularly. They only saw the good, caring side, the Dr. Jekyll side. But we frequently witnessed the appearance of Mr. Hyde.

The rain started as a drizzle early in the evening, and by nightfall, it had become a raging downpour. But the rain didn't dampen the spirits of my family. There must have been at least fifteen grownups and kids crammed into Big Momma's living room, including Momma, Daddy, Big Momma, three of Momma's sisters—Bernadette, Olivia, and Violet—her brother Willie Earl, and Bernadette's fiancé, Walter. Three of Momma's older brothers had moved north to find better work opportunities.

With the front door open, a cool breeze from the rain blew through the screen. Uncle Earl brought a tall stack of 45s and kept the music going as loud, soulful sounds swirled from the turntable. The grownups snapped their fingers and danced to Stevie Wonder's "Signed, Sealed, Delivered," James Brown's "Super Bad," and a half dozen other tunes.

Uncle Earl slowed the beat down when the grownups grew tired of dancing, playing ballads like Candi Staton's "Stand by Your Man" and the Delfonics' "Didn't I Blow Your Mind This Time." The women sang along. Aunt Bernie sang the loudest because she knew all the words, and she wanted everybody else to know she knew them. Uncle Earl also played records that my young cousins, my sisters, and I liked to dance to, like the Jackson 5's "ABC" and "The Love You Save." Before Uncle Earl cranked the music up again for the adults, he played one of Big Momma's favorite blues songs, "The Thrill Is Gone" by B.B. King. As my aunts and uncles sang and danced, they consumed far too much alcohol, and so did Momma and Daddy.

We left Big Momma's house shortly after midnight amid the occasional *POP! POP! POP!* of firecrackers and the bright explosion of red, white, and blue fireworks against the purple sky. The rain had interrupted the usual nonstop whizzing and booming of fireworks and the heart-stopping sound of firecrackers. I didn't mind the fireworks, but firecrackers reminded me of gunfire, so the fewer I heard of them, the better.

Halfway through the dark seven-mile stretch of the highway to Lowell, Daddy's conversation abruptly shifted from normal chitchat, revisiting the day's events, to loud, venom-laced accusations. My heart pounded hard in my chest as Daddy's vicious rant escalated.

"Don't think I don't know what's going on between you and that white man."

"I don't know what you talkin' about, Otis."

"You know! I ain't no fool, Annie! I know what's goin' on!" He pounded the dashboard to accentuate each word. "I know you been sneakin' behind my back, goin' down to his house every chance you get."

"People just talkin'. It's just idle gossip," Momma said casually, her words slurring a bit. "You just gonna believe what other people tell you?"

"If *everybody* talkin' 'bout it, Annie, it got to be some truth to it. It's over. You ain't makin' no damn fool out of me no mo'!"

"You're already a damn fool for believing it."

"What did you say?" Daddy grabbed Momma by the back of her head and slammed her face into the dashboard.

Alcohol and adrenaline must have dulled the impact. Momma reared back and began throwing wild punches, striking Daddy across his face. He tried to block them with his right hand and control the car with the left. Then Daddy did the unthinkable. He reached across Momma.

"Get the hell out!" Opening her door, he began pushing and shoving Momma. With one hand, he wrestled with the steering wheel. With the other, he forcefully pushed and shoved her. Momma held on, fighting him wildly—fighting for her life.

Jo screamed, "Y'all stop fighting! Please stop fighting!"

"Daddy, stop! Please stop!" I screamed. I began to hyperventilate. Tammy started wailing and crying loudly.

The car skidded to the left and cut across the median, heading into oncoming traffic. Bright headlights cut across our path. Cars swerved and spun out. Horns blared. Drivers fought with their vehicles on the slick pavement, trying to avoid hitting us.

Momma clung to the open door. Half of her body hung outside of the car. I watched in horror as we slid sideways off the wet pavement and down a steep embankment. Hitting the opposite side of the ditch, our vehicle came to an abrupt stop just to the right of a light pole. My heartbeat pulsated in my ears. Hot tears raced down my face. Jo and Tammy cried loudly. Their screams and sobs filled the car's interior.

Momma struggled, finally flinging herself back into the car. She and Daddy sat in stunned silence, knowing we had narrowly escaped death. After a moment, Momma turned in her seat to face us. A purple knot marred her forehead, visible by the car's dome interior light.

"Y'all kids okay?"

Through sniffles and sobs, we all managed to utter some form of yes.

"Annie Lee," Daddy yelled, "look what you made me do!" He swung the car door open. "I'm gon' try to push us out. You come around and press on the gas when I tell you to."

"Otis, you know I can't drive no stick shift."

"You ain't got to drive. Just do what I tell you to get us out of this ditch."

Momma got out, hurried to the driver's side, and slid under the steering wheel. She rolled down the window so she could hear Daddy's instructions. He told her what to do then yelled, "Give it gas, now!"

Daddy pushed. The car rocked back and forth, but it went nowhere. The engine shut off.

"Ease off the clutch, Annie. Don't jump off it. Try one more time."

Momma did as Daddy instructed. He pushed with every ounce of strength he had until his feet slipped in the mud. He fell to his knees.

Daddy pulled himself up and slammed a fist onto the hood. "Sommabitch!" After a brief pause, he walked around to the driver's side and poked his head in the window. Blood trickled from a gash over his left eye. "Guess we stuck. I'm gon' try to flag somebody down to call a tow truck."

One car after another zoomed past Daddy for what seemed like hours. Though the rain had stopped, it brought a damp chill to the early-morning air despite it being the middle of summer. I pulled the collar of my shirt up around my ears and wrapped my arms around my body, trying to keep warm. Tammy and Jo had fallen asleep, and I found myself nodding in and out, fighting to stay awake.

Finally, a white pickup truck eased to a stop in front of Daddy, and a young Black man rolled down his window. "Mr. Otis, is that you? What happened?" It was Ms. Clara Bea's nephew Montrell Jones, whom everyone called Mojo.

"I hit a slick spot back yonder—lost control of the car. My family is in the car down in the ditch. You wouldn't have a chain, would you?" Daddy fished into his pockets and pulled out a fistful of crumpled bills. "I sho' would appreciate it if you could pull me out. Got a few dollars for your troubles."

"No need, Mr. Otis. Keep your money. I always carry a chain in this old truck. Never know when it might come to use."

"Thank you, Mojo. I sho' appreciate you."

"Let me grab this chain." Mojo stepped out of the truck. "I'll have that Bug out of the ditch in no time."

Mojo worked fast and efficiently to hook the Volkswagen to his truck. The cool breeze that nipped at his exposed body parts was at least part of the motivation for him to finish quickly. Before long, the car jerked then began to roll back onto the pavement.

Daddy pushed the gear into park and raced over to Mojo to thank him again as he unhooked the chain. Mojo smiled and mumbled something in return then climbed into the cab of his truck and sped away. Daddy returned to the car and drove the remainder of the way home without uttering a single word. As the full blast from the heater enveloped me like a warm cocoon, the smooth crooning of Clarence Carter on the radio urging his lover to "slip away" lulled me into a nice comfortable slumber.

# Chapter 19

"Y'all wake up. We're home," Momma said. "Bailey, Jo, Tammy, y'all wake up."

After a long stretch, I willed myself back into a state of consciousness. Through sleepy eyes, I squinted to see the neon-green hands on the clock in the dash, which indicated it was 2:35 in the morning. I nudged Tammy, who sat between Jo and me, then reached over and shook Jo by her shoulder.

When I stepped out of the warmth of the car, the cool, damp air chilled me to the bone. As I hurried toward the house, voices at a distance, rising and falling, caused me to stop. Everyone stopped, except Tammy, who didn't seem to notice or care about the voices. She continued her drowsy unsteady trek toward the porch.

"That's coming from Jim's house." Daddy pointed. "What the heck is going on down yonder this time of the mornin'?"

A third car was parked in Mr. Jim's driveway, in addition to his sports car and work truck. The car's headlights shot a straight beam of light over the field beyond Mr. Jim's house. Next to the car, the silhouettes of two people were etched in the darkness.

"If you don't get rid of that Black slut, we're done! It's over!" said the female voice.

Only mumbles were heard from the man I assumed was Mr. Jim.

"Fine! Keep that nigga! But don't be surprised if both of you wake up with a bullet in your skulls!" The female got into the car and slammed the door.

The car shot backward. The headlights swung in our direction as the car spun around and raced out of Mr. Jim's driveway. It turned onto the blacktop road and, within seconds, blazed past our house. With the commotion over, we all went inside the house.

"Ain't nobody no fool, Annie Lee, nobody! That white woman got your number, and I do too! You go down to Jim's house one more time, and somebody's gon' be buyin' a pine box!" Daddy stalked into the bedroom and slammed the door with a loud thud.

"Kids, y'all go to bed. I'm going too. We all had a long night. Good night."

"Good night, Momma," I said.

I went to bed, but I had a restless night of tossing and turning. Terrifying dreams of Momma being shot in the head and placed in a pine box taunted me until daybreak.

# Chapter 20

The week after the altercation in the car, Momma and Daddy barely spoke to one another. And when Daddy did speak to Momma, every other word was a curse word. Daddy generally didn't drink during the week, but that week was an exception. He drank every day after he got off work. My sisters and I hid out in our room, playing checkers or cards and blasting the transistor radio, trying to drown out the loud arguing and cussing. Daddy was in an uproar because "everyone," according to him, knew his wife had been sneaking down to Mr. Jim's house, being alone with him, and doing heavens knew what. That week, Daddy carried his pistol in his pants pocket to frighten Momma. Little did he know, or care, that it frightened us too.

On Friday night, the situation intensified, and Daddy's rage escalated to a fever pitch. Playing games failed as a distraction, and so did blasting the radio. Their voices were louder than the music, so I snuck around through the kitchen and watched Momma and Daddy through the cracked bedroom door, thinking if he tried to harm her, I would run to her defense and save her—this time.

"Um gon' kill you and that cracker!" Daddy stood over Momma, who sat on the bed. He wagged a dark finger in her face to drive home his point.

She brushed his hand aside as though swatting a fly away. "You talking crazy, Otis. Ain't nothing going on between me and Mr. Jim. I don't want that white man, and he certainly don't want me."

"That ain't what everybody's sayin', Annie. And I know the truth. I know you been sleepin' with him. I can smell him on you."

"Otis, you need to calm down." Momma stood up to face Daddy. "You letting your imagination get the best of you. You know for yourself that Mr. Jim's got four or five women."

"I guess that make you number six!"

"Come on, Otis," Momma said, trying to cajole him, wrapping her arms around his neck. "Let's go out and have a good time like we always do on Friday night and put this Mr. Jim stuff behind us."

"Get the hell away from me!" Daddy pushed Momma away from him, sending her flying into the window, glass panes cracking as she fell back. Curtains that hung precariously fell down around her.

My heart thudded in my chest. I was about to race into the room, but Momma's response stopped me. She tossed the curtains onto the floor and pushed herself off the windowsill.

"Take your drunk crazy ass on, and do whatever it is you want to do. It won't be the first time for you to go sniffing around those damn juke-joint sluts. Go on, you dirty Black dog! Go!"

When Momma started to walk past Daddy, he grabbed her by the throat and started choking her. Momma tried to free herself from Daddy's grip, clawing and scratching at his hands. I rushed into the room. "Stop, Daddy! Stop! Please stop! Jo, come quick! Help! They're fighting again!"

My breathing became labored as I stood there, frozen. I wanted to help Momma, but fear coiled around me like a python, restricting my ability to move. Momma scratched Daddy in the eyes. He cried out in pain then backhanded her, sending her stumbling and crashing against the dresser. Losing her balance, she fell to the floor. As she struggled to stand, Daddy kicked Momma in her side, causing her to fall back onto the floor.

"Daddy, stop!" Jo rushed into the room and jumped on Daddy's back, wrapping her arms around his neck in a stranglehold.

"Get off me, Jo! Get off me!" Daddy garbled, swinging to the left and right, trying to throw Jo off him.

But Jo held on like a bronco rider. Compelled by Jo's bravery, I rushed over and grabbed Daddy around his waist and held on for dear life, trying to pull him away. When Daddy raised his foot to kick Momma again, she grabbed it, causing him to lose his balance and sending Daddy, Jo, and me tumbling to the floor. Daddy crawled over to Momma on his hands and knees and grabbed her foot, pulling her toward him, as she kicked and grasped for something to hold on to.

A sudden knock on the door caused Daddy to freeze.

I bolted for the door and swung it open. "Help us! He's killing her!"

Shock registered on Mr. Eli's face as he shuffled into my parents' bedroom. "What's goin' on, Otis? What the hell is you doin'?"

Daddy lifted himself from the floor. "Mind yo' business, Eli." He brushed past Mr. Eli and thundered through the living room and out the front door, slamming it so hard the frame shook. Seconds later, his car door banged shut, and gravel spewed in every direction as Daddy sped out of the driveway.

"You okay, Annie?" Mr. Eli said with concern-filled eyes as he helped Momma stand.

"I think I'm okay. I just need to sit down for a minute."

"Momma, you might need to go to the doctor."

"I'll be okay, Bailey," Momma said as Mr. Eli guided her over to the bed. "I'm glad you stopped by when you did, Eli. I really think Otis has lost his mind over these rumors about me and Mr. Jim. But I tell you what, and I mean this from the bottom of my heart—if he puts his hands on me again, I swear I will kill him."

# Chapter 21

The following morning, I headed into the kitchen to see what Momma had started preparing for breakfast. Much to my dismay, she wasn't in the kitchen, and nothing had been prepared for breakfast. Hearing the front door creak open, I turned as Momma entered the living room, wearing the same tangerine blouse and plaid bell-bottoms she'd worn the previous day.

Reeking of stale cigarette smoke and day-old liquor, Momma dropped her handbag onto the sofa and ambled into the kitchen. She took out a small pot from underneath the sink and filled it with water to set to boil. I followed her into the kitchen.

"Good morning, Momma. Where are you just coming from?"

"Morning, Bailey. Where's your daddy?"

"Daddy didn't come home last night either."

"Oh, really?" Momma scooped instant coffee and sugar into her mug.

Daddy generally stayed out late when he went to the juke joints without Momma, but he'd always come home even if it was just before the sun rose. And Momma had never stayed out all night. A sinking feeling settled in my stomach that told me things were worse than they'd ever been before.

"Where do you think Daddy is?" I asked. "Do you think something happened to him?"

"I don't know and don't care," Momma said, but I could tell she was worried and annoyed by my questions.

She took a few sips of her coffee then started fixing breakfast. When it was ready, I sat at the small wooden table in the kitchen and devoured the cheese grits and bacon. Then I grabbed a copy of *Readers Digest* and retreated to the big chair by the window to tackle the crossword puzzle. I had never finished one without peeking at the answers, but I loved a good challenge all the same. Each time I worked on a puzzle, I got a few words closer to finishing it.

After Josephine finished eating, she bounded into the living room and sat on the sofa. She settled in with her nose in a book. Tammy sat on the floor next to the sofa, playing with jacks. Momma stayed at the kitchen table, smoking a cigarette and sipping her second cup of coffee.

Just as I'd flipped over to my second favorite section in the magazine, *Life in These United States,* I heard a sound that was strangely out of place—one that made my heart race a hundred beats per second. I threw back the curtains in time to see three police cars race past the house, with their sirens blaring and lights flashing. I jumped off the sofa, swung open the door, and dashed down the steps. I stood there in my pajamas, bare feet and all, and watched the three Washington County sheriff's cars pull up in front of Mr. Jim's house and line up one behind the other. I was intrigued about what would warrant not one but three police cars coming this far out in the country.

The officers, five white men in all, rushed to the front door and eventually went inside. I wanted to sneak down through the cotton field to get a closer look and listen in on their conversations, but Momma would have skinned me alive if she found out I left the house without her permission. As I stood there with my eyes and ears tuned for the slightest movement or sound, a white ambulance with big red letters sped past quietly, without a siren. There were no flashing lights. It slowed, turned into Mr. Jim's driveway, maneuvered around his two vehicles, and backed up to the back door.

The two people wearing white got out of the ambulance, walked briskly toward the back door, and disappeared. Then there was no movement. I stood there for several minutes, waiting for some new activity. When there was none, I decided it was time to go back inside the house.

Jo glanced up from her book. "What's all the commotion going on outside?"

I ignored her and ran straight to the kitchen. "Momma, something's going on at Mr. Jim's house."

"What do you mean?"

"I just saw three sheriff's cars and an ambulance speed past our house and park in his driveway. They're still there."

"You sure?" she asked.

"Yeah. I stood outside and watched."

A look of concern swept across Momma's face. She followed me from the kitchen to her bedroom. Jo joined us.

Momma pulled the curtain back and peered out of the window facing Mr. Jim's house. "Hmmm... I wonder what's going on. Maybe Mr. Jim is sick. Or maybe one of his girlfriends or his fiancée got sick."

"Would they need all those policemen if somebody was sick?" I asked.

"I don't know, Bailey. I'm just guessing."

"Maybe they got into a fight, and somebody got hurt," Jo said.

"He's not that kind of man. He wouldn't hit a woman. I'm sure of that." Momma craned her neck, straining on her tiptoes, trying to see more.

The ambulance back doors swung open and remained that way for a while. From our vantage point, we couldn't see what was happening because the ambulance blocked our view. After several minutes, the doors closed. The driver and passenger climbed back into the ambulance and pulled away from Mr. Jim's home. There were no flashing lights as the ambulance headed in our direction. One by one, the police cars turned around and cruised toward our house. I could hear the hum of their engines as they sped past.

Momma let the curtain drop into place and strolled back into the kitchen. She didn't utter a word. I was afraid to ask her what she thought, because of what I saw in her eyes—utter fear.

# Chapter 22

An hour after the ambulance and police cars left Mr. Jim's house, I heard a car door slam. Peering out the window, I saw Daddy's gray Volkswagen parked in the driveway. As he made his way toward the porch, I raced into Momma's bedroom, tiptoed over to the bed, where she napped, and tapped her gently on the shoulder.

"Momma... Momma..."

"What? What's wrong?" she asked.

"Nothing. Daddy's home."

Momma sat up slowly, wiping the sleep from her eyes. She stretched and yawned. Suddenly her eyes widened, then they went dark. "Thanks, Bailey. Go find something to do, you hear?"

I heard the front door open then close as I retreated into my bedroom.

Jo rose up on her elbow and wiped the sleep from her eyes. "What's going on? Is Daddy home yet?"

"Yeah. Just got here."

"Better get ready for World War III." A look of resignation clouded Jo's face as she fell back onto her pillow. "How come they have to fuss and fight so much?"

"Guess that's what married people do."

"I ain't never getting married," Jo said.

"I'm never getting married," I corrected.

"Be quiet, Mr. Perfect. You're so annoying sometimes."

"You be quiet."

We both fell silent when we heard the bedroom door open then close. Daddy's deep voice penetrated the walls, as did the sound of his footsteps as he made his way across the room. "Before you say anything, Annie, let me explain. Not that I should be explainin' nothin' to you."

"Explain what? Why didn't you bring your sorry ass home last night? I already know the answer to that. Is this supposed to be payback, Otis?"

"Naw, ain't nothin' like that."

"What is it like, then, you cheatin', low-down dirty dog?"

"Now, I ain't no low-down cheatin' dog, so you best calm down and let me explain."

"I heard it all before, Otis. But go ahead. Explain!"

"When I left here, I went down to Big Earl's to gamble. Well, guess who walked in the place after I been there about an hour or two," he said. Momma didn't answer, so Daddy continued. "One-Leg Mooch. I ain't seen him in a month of Sundays. He said he'd been back down in them Louisiana swamps, catchin' gators. Guess Mooch wanna lose that other leg." Daddy chuckled. "Anyhow, he pulled out a roll of cash and told me to drank whatever I wanted to."

"And I'm sure you did."

"Free liquor? You know I did. Next thang I knowed, I'm wakin' up on the side of Frazier Road, near the Mennonite church, not too far from Holly Ridge. It was dark as all get out. So I thought I best get from out there before the Klan or somebody like that rolled up on me. But when I cranked up the car and tried to pull off, the car started drivin' funny, draggin' and bouncin'. Even before I got out, I already knowed I had a flat tire and no spare."

"That's a good one. How long did it take you to come up with that lie? All the way home?"

"If you don't believe me, you can come out to the car. I had to flag down this guy early this mornin'. He was nice 'nough to take me to buy a used tire from ole man Jenkins's shop. I swear b'fore God."

"Fine. Whatever, Otis. I really don't have time for your foolishness today. Right now, I'm more concerned about what's going on down at your boss's house."

"What you mean, what's going on at Jim's house?"

"This morning, there were three police cars and an ambulance down there."

"Is that right? You don't reckon him and one of his women got into it, do you? The one down there on the fourth day of July was hotter than fish grease."

Much to my relief, I could tell from my parents' tone the fight was all but over, so I slid off the bed and went through the kitchen and into the living room. I grabbed *Charlotte's Web* and plopped into my favorite chair to get lost in a make-believe world with imaginary problems.

Jo came into the living room and sat on the sofa after turning on the TV. I hadn't read the second page of my story when the words from the news reporter spilled from our twenty-one-inch black-and-white television, sending shock waves to my brain, temporarily suspending my ability to comprehend.

"Mr. James Tanner Cunningham," the reporter said, "a longtime resident of Lowell and one of its most prominent citizens, was found dead early this morning by police. An unknown assailant entered his home and stabbed Mr. Cunningham more than forty times in his face, chest, and neck area. Ms. Sarah Jane Bingham, the fiancée of Jim Cunningham, discovered his body after entering his home around eight o'clock this morning."

I sat upright. My book fell to the floor. "Momma, Momma, come quick!"

I immediately heard the patter of footsteps racing from the direction of my parents' bedroom. "Boy, what's wrong? Why are you yelling?" Momma said.

"Mr. Jim's dead!"

"What? What you talkin' about?"

"They're talking about it on the news."

Momma rushed to the TV and turned the volume up as the reporter continued.

"Jim Cunningham, as he was known by family members and friends, graduated from Mississippi State University in 1960 with a BA in Business Management and became the sole proprietor of C&S Plantation after his father, James Edgar Cunningham III, died in 1967. There have been no arrests made in Mr. Cunningham's murder, but the Washington County Sheriff's Department has started an active investigation. We will continue to update you as details in this shocking story unfold. On the national front, the Charles Manson trial continues for the murder of seven people, including actress Sharon Tate."

Momma punched the off knob on the TV, and the screen went black. Her eyes had become glassy as tears began to form. Daddy, who'd come into the room, too, stood motionless beside her without saying a word.

"Who would want to kill him?" Momma asked, her eyes drifting toward Daddy.

Daddy pushed his hands deep into his pants pockets, his gaze fixed on the dark screen. After a moment, his bloodshot eyes locked with Momma's. "I don't know, but it look like he got what was comin' to him."

# Chapter 23

A week passed before we heard any additional news about Mr. Jim's murder. Daddy started to work half days on another plantation and had been generally in a foul mood because he wasn't sure whether the C&S Plantation would shut down completely or be sold to someone else. If it shut down, he didn't know where he would find full-time work.

Momma had become quiet and sullen most of the time. Jo and I tried to talk to her, to ask her questions about the murder, but Momma, preoccupied with her own worries, wouldn't engage in a meaningful conversation with either of us. I suppose she worried about where Daddy would work and also where she would work. Not having Mr. Jim to work for anymore meant she might have to work in the fields again, especially if Daddy only worked half days. All of this made us sad. But we were also unhappy that a very nice man had been killed and no one knew why.

That Sunday afternoon, a news report about Mr. Jim was shown on television. The reporter said that the sheriff's department had identified a suspect and was close to making an arrest. The reporter dredged up the unpleasantness of how Mr. Jim was killed and the fact that someone had stabbed him forty-six times in the chest-and-throat area.

With the heaviness of Mr. Jim's murder and the crazy eyes of that mass-murderer Charles Manson whirling in my mind, I escaped to our room. I climbed onto the bed to lose myself in *Charlotte's Webb* and see if Charlotte had figured out a way to save poor Wilbur from becoming glazed ham at some family's Christmas dinner. That would take my mind off my family's troubles, at least for a while.

Tammy followed me into the room, carrying a box of checkers. "You wanna play?"

"No, I don't feel like it right now."

"How come?"

"Just don't."

"You think I'm gonna beat you, don't you?"

"Yeah, I do," I said, humoring my little sister, hoping she'd go away.

"Chicken! Bak-a-bak-a-bak-a!" Tammy walked around in a circle, flapping arms she'd folded like chicken wings. "Bak-a-bak-a-bak-a!"

"Stop it. Be quiet."

"Chicken!" Tammy tossed the checkers box onto the floor with a crash. Red and black chips spilled out, rolling in all directions. She poked out her tongue and ran out of the room.

I closed the door behind her. With Tammy out of the room, I fell onto my back, staring at the ceiling. Thoughts of the newscast filled my mind. It made no sense that someone would stab Mr. Jim forty-six times when they probably could have killed him by stabbing him once or twice. Whoever had killed Mr. Jim must have really hated him and really wanted him dead. As my eyelids became heavy, I felt my body drift uneasily into another world.

An hour or so later, around six o'clock in the evening, a shrill cry snatched me from my dream. Dazed and confused, I sat up. My heart pounded fiercely. For several seconds, I didn't know where I was or what was going on. Glancing around the room, I soon recognized the familiar faded wallpaper. It became clear where I was—but not what the sound was.

Then that became clear too. *Sirens.* I leaped off the bed and raced into the living room in time to see Daddy throw back the curtains and stare out the window facing Tribett Road, the blacktop road in front of our house.

"Annie," he said, "a police car done pulled up in front of the house."

Momma rushed out of the bedroom. She stood beside Daddy, looking out of the window. Jo and I slid between them and looked out too. Tammy came running out of our bedroom and pushed her way between Jo and me. We watched as the sheriff and his deputy walked up the pathway to our house.

Within seconds, the pounding on the door almost matched the thudding in my chest. Daddy wiped his hands on his pants legs, swung the door open, and stepped cautiously out onto the front porch. Both officers stood on the porch in front of Daddy. Momma moved closer to the threshold of the door but remained inside the screen door. We continued to gaze through the window.

"Evening, Sheriff."

"You Otis Connor?" The tall, lanky officer had red hair peppered with gray. His top lip was nearly covered by his red push-broom mustache. A lump of tobacco was tucked behind his bottom lip. The officer standing next to him with a surly expression was shorter and thicker, with dark hair and ruddy cheeks.

"Yes, suh. I'm him. What's this 'bout, Sheriff?"

"Now, you just hold your horses, boy, I'm askin' the questions this evenin'. I'm Sheriff Kurt McGowan from the Washington County Sheriff's Department, and this here is Chief Deputy Cody Pugh. Does Annie Lee Connor also live here?"

"Sheriff, what this about?" Daddy repeated.

"This is my last time askin' you, boy. Does Annie Lee Connor live at this residence?"

"Yes, suh, but…"

The sheriff looked past Daddy to where Momma stood. "Are you Annie Lee Connor?"

"Yes, Officer, I'm Annie Lee Connor." Momma remained standing behind the screen door.

"Gal, you mind steppin' out here on the porch?"

Momma stepped out and stood beside Daddy.

"Annie Lee Connor," said Sheriff McGowan, "I've got a warrant for your arrest for the murder of one Mr. James T. Cunningham. Turn around, and put your hands behind your back."

Shocked and confused, Momma stood as still and as straight as a light pole. "Arrest? There's got to be a mistake. I didn't kill Mr. Jim. I swear, I didn't."

"Did you hear me?" the sheriff repeated. "I said turn around and put your hands behind your back."

Momma slowly turned her back to the sheriff. He placed her hands behind her back. When the realization hit us that the sheriff had placed Momma under arrest, loud wailing erupted in the house. My sisters and I clung to each other, weeping. I wrenched away from them and rushed out onto the porch. My sisters followed.

"Don't let them take her, Daddy," I said through my sobs. "Please don't let them take Momma."

"She didn't do anything, Sheriff," Jo cried, tears flowing down her cheeks. "She didn't. Please let her go."

"Mommy! Mommy! Mommy!" Tammy screamed. "You ole mean man, let my momma go!"

"Sheriff," Daddy pleaded, "don't take her away. There gotta be a mistake. She ain't kilt nobody. She ain't kilt nobody!"

"You niggers think you so high-and-mighty. You ain't colored no more. You're Black. You think you can kill a white man and get away with it. Not in Washington County, you won't." Sheriff McGowan locked the cuffs on Momma's wrists. "Gal, you still in Mississippi!" He turned and spat dark tobacco juice onto the porch.

"Please, Sheriff—"

Lieutenant McGowan stared at Daddy with cold steel-blue eyes. One hand grasped Momma's cuffs, and the other rested on his weapon. "Step back in the house now, boy, unless you want to be arrested too."

Daddy took a step back, but he remained on the porch, and so did we. He continued to plead with the sheriff, but his pleas fell on deaf ears. The sheriff read Momma her rights and marched her down the steps. She continued to repeat over and over that there had been a mistake, that she didn't kill anybody.

Glancing over her shoulder, Momma told Daddy, "Call my brother. Call Willie Earl. Let him know."

The sheriff opened the door and shoved Momma into the back seat. As the car sped away, she glanced helplessly through the window in our direction.

# Chapter 24

After the sheriff's car sped away with Momma, Daddy ushered us inside and tried to console us—to no avail. Fear and sadness overwhelmed us. He begged us to stop crying and attempted to reassure us that everything would be okay. Then he hurried over to Ms. Clara's house to use her phone, leaving us alone in our misery. My sisters and I clung to each other and wept bitterly.

When Daddy returned ten minutes later, he gathered us around him. Jo and Tammy were on either side of Daddy on the sofa, and I sat on the floor. Daddy's words were reassuring, but his sad, weak eyes weren't very convincing.

"Y'all listen," Daddy said. "I know thangs look scary, but everythang gon' be all right." He looked down at his folded hands, which trembled. "Y'all Uncle Lance and Uncle Earl, they gon' help us figure thangs out."

"Daddy," Tammy asked, between sniffles, "how come the po-lice took Momma away?"

"They thank she done somethin' bad, baby girl."

Tammy tilted her head to one side. "What did she do bad, Daddy?"

"They thank she hurt Mr. Jim."

"How come she did that?" she asked.

"Yo' momma didn't do nothin'."

"Daddy, what will we do if they send Momma to prison?" Jo asked, wiping her tears with the back of her hand.

Daddy was silent for a beat. "That ain't gon' happen. Um gon' see to it. Now, I want y'all to leave the worryin' to the grown folks. Okay?"

The three of us said, "Okay," almost in unison. But I still worried about Momma's safety. She looked terrified in the back of that police car, and I could imagine how frightened she was at having to be locked up in a cold jail cell.

A sudden knock on the door gave us all a start.

"Who knockin'?" Daddy called out.

"It's Clara Bea from across the way."

Tammy ran over to the door and swung it open. "Come in, Ms. Clara. The po-lice took Momma away."

"I know, baby."

"Come on in, Ms. Clara," Daddy said.

"Hi, kids." Ms. Clara nodded dutifully at us.

The scent of lilacs floated across the threshold when Ms. Clara Bea Walker stepped into the house. Her ebony skin was almost flawless, except for the fine lines that creased the corners of her dark eyes. Her gray hair was pulled into a perfect ball on top of her head. Her petite body seemed strong despite her being almost eighty years old. She'd been our neighbor since we moved into our house seven years prior. Momma said Ms. Clara's husband had died a long time ago, but now she had a boyfriend, Mr. Odell, who often came by to spend time with her. Mr. Odell was in his eighties also. I wondered why they called Mr. Odell her boyfriend. At that age, he was a long way from being a boy.

"Otis," Ms. Clara said, "I just come over to fetch you. Annie Lee's on the telephone. She say she need to talk to you, so I come right over."

"Thank you, Ms. Clara. I been waitin' on her call." Daddy rose and hurried toward the door. "I'll be right back. Bailey, come close the door and lock it."

Daddy was gone for about fifteen minutes, but it seemed like an eternity. I watched from the window, waiting for him to return. I'd cried so much my eyes had almost swollen shut. They ached as though they'd been pricked with a thousand needles, and my nose felt as though it had swollen to the size of my fist. I imagined I looked like a Gila monster. As Daddy crossed the road from Ms. Clara's house, I raced down the steps to meet him.

My stomach fluttered with nervous anticipation. "What did Momma say?"

"She gon' have to stay in jail all night. Court is at nine thirty in the mornin'."

"Her trial starts tomorrow?"

"Naw, somethin' called a arrangement."

"Daddy, are you going to court to see Momma tomorrow?" I asked.

"Yeah, I'm goin'."

"Can I go?"

"No, you can't. Yo' momma said the arrangement supposed to be over real quick."

"You think Momma will be able to come home?" I asked.

"Don't know, son. Depend how much the bail money is."

"Will it be a lot?"

"They thank she kilt a white man, so I 'spect so."

"Would it be less if they thought she killed a Black man?" I asked.

"Boy, you sho' ask a lot of questions." Daddy scratched the back of his head. "She probably wouldna been arrested at all."

"Why not?"

Daddy stopped at the base of the steps and exhaled. "'Cause white folk don't thank a colored person life worth as much as a white person life."

"But that's not true, Daddy. Momma said God created all of us—red, yellow, black, white, and brown. She said underneath our skin, we're all the same."

Daddy started up the steps, and I hurried after him. He turned and looked down at me. "Son, at this point, Um not even sho' there is a God."

He opened the screen door and went inside. I tried to follow him, but I couldn't. I plopped down on the top step. Utter helplessness and sadness draped me like a soggy blanket.

*If there is no God, we have no hope.*

# Chapter 25

Over the course of two weeks, Jonathan visited his friend at the Delta Medical Center almost every day. After his last visit, he'd expected to find him as he'd been previously—still in a coma, no change. But when he eased Lorenzo's door open on this particular Sunday morning, to his surprise, the man was resting against a stack of pillows, reading a newspaper. He turned his head, still wrapped in white gauze, toward the squeaky door.

"Well... well... well. Look... look what the c-cat dragged in." A broad grin spread across his face.

"And look who's in the land of the living. How are you feeling, man?" Jonathan walked over, shook Lorenzo's hand, and hugged him.

"Not b-bad. Being I was on the brink of d-death a few weeks ago. But much better now."

"How long have you been out of the coma?"

"Yesterday morning around ten. Nurse told me my *b-brother* stopped by almost every d-day to talk or read to me. Thanks for coming to see me, Jon. I... I really appreciate it."

"You would have done the same for me. Besides, I was able to get a few words in uninterrupted." Jonathan chuckled.

Lorenzo Cain was a highly respected attorney in Greenville. He'd practiced criminal law for fifteen years. During that time, he'd only lost two cases, and those had happened early in his career.

"Have a s-seat. It's great seeing you after all these y-years. Saw you on the news a month ago. You're doing b-big things in the community."

"Just doing what I can."

"So, how's life tr-treating you? You married? Have kids?"

"I'm married to Lady Law right now," Jonathan said. "My practice is going well, and in my free time, I coach a boy's summer-league basketball team. Everything's solid. How about you? Did you marry that cute cheerleader you dated during undergrad?"

"No, Olivia moved back to New... New Jersey after we graduated. Over t-time we drifted apart. I met my wife right here in Gr-Greenville seventeen years ago. Had you gotten here fifteen minutes e-earlier, you would have met Nora. We have two boys, fifteen and twelve, Lorenzo Jr. and Ca-Caleb."

"That's great, Lorenzo. I know you're a wonderful husband and father."

"I a-appreciate you coming all this way to see about me, J-Jonathan. I realize how hard it was for you to return to Mississippi."

"You know, while you were in a coma, I thanked you for all you did to help me get through my college years when I was about to torpedo my life. I don't know whether you heard me or not, but I want to say it again—thank you, man, for all you did for me back then."

Lorenzo waved a dismissive hand. "You were y-young. Hell, we both were. I'm glad I had s-sense enough to help you." He laughed.

"Man, I wish I'd been here for you when you were attacked. So, what happened, Lorenzo? Do they know who shot you?"

"No, the police don't know who... who shot me. I worked late one n-night and was leaving the office around eleven. Two h-hoodlums approached me in the parking lot as I was about to get into my... my car. They asked for my wallet, m-my watch, my wedding ring, and my pinky d-diamond ring. I complied, but the clowns shot... shot me anyway. Guess they thought I'd be able to ID them. They weren't w-wearing masks."

"Can you ID them?"

"No. I didn't get a g-good look at them. The parking lot is not w-well lit. I'm also dealing with some sh-short-term memory loss." After a pause, Lorenzo said, "Listen, Jon, I was r-reading this story in the newspaper this morning about the Annie Lee Connor m-murder trial. Have you heard about it?"

"I heard a little bit about it on the radio."

Lorenzo rubbed the stubble on his chin and cleared his throat. "Well, as I'm s-sitting here with you, something occurred to me, and I w-want to talk with you about it."

Jonathan raised his hand to protest. "I already know what you're going to say. You are going to ask me to take the case. Am I right?"

"You're right. You'd be the p-perfect lawyer to represent her, and you can work under my banner."

"I already thought about it, and my answer is no. I have too much going on back in DC. I have a law practice to run. I have cases I need to get back to. I have my boys' basketball team that I also need to get back to. There's just too much going on right now for me to drop everything to take this case."

"Listen, Jon, if I w-were in any condition, I would take the case myself. But it will be another two or three m-months, according to the neurologist, before I'm operating at maximum mental ca-capacity again. So just hear me out."

Jonathan laced his fingers together, resting them in his lap, preparing to listen. He was certain he already knew what Lorenzo had to say, but out of respect and admiration for the man who'd helped during a difficult period in his life, Jonathan felt compelled to listen.

"Don't you see, Jonathan? This c-case is bigger than Annie Lee Connor. By winning this case, you could achieve a major t-turning point in our history that says a Black woman or m-man *can* receive a fair trial, not only in America but in the d-deep South, in Mississippi. Do you see the relevance? Do you understand the s-significance of that?"

The room fell silent. The air-conditioner provided the only audible sound, humming like a chorus of mocking cicadas.

"Look, Lorenzo, I do understand. I see the big picture and what's at stake here. I understand the social and political implications. But there has to be another attorney here in Greenville who can take this case."

"I'm not sure th-this lady can afford a top-notch cr-criminal attorney. The only way Annie Lee Connor will get a f-fair trial is to be represented by someone who ca-cares about justice, not some overworked, underpaid, state-appointed p-public defender."

"My answer is still no. I have a life to get back to in DC. The only reason I came to Mississippi was to see you and support you in any way I can. Now that I see you're okay and on the road to a full recovery, I will probably be heading back to DC tomorrow or the day after."

"All right, then. I s-see your mind is made up. I won't try to pressure you. B-But I hope you will give it some more thought." After a beat, Lorenzo said, "Speaking of thought, what do you th-think about this Charles Manson trial? How would you like to r-represent him?" He shook his head.

"You couldn't pay me enough money to represent that psychopath. Though the law says everyone deserves a fair trial, I couldn't be the one representing him. The man is as guilty as homemade sin for orchestrating the murder of those five people."

"It makes me sick to my s-stomach that they killed Sharon T-Tate, who was eight months pr-pregnant. No, Charles M-Manson needs to go straight to hell wearing g-gasoline underwear."

"Kaboom!" Jonathan mimicked an exploding bomb.

Lorenzo nodded and took a sip of water. "On a lighter n-note, have you found anything interesting to get into since you've been in G-Greenville?"

"Not really. I've been busy working on a brief that I'm preparing for an upcoming trial."

"I wish you'd s-stick around a little while longer so I can show you around t-town. I think the chicks would dig you. You turned out to be a nice-looking b-brotha since you grew into that large head of yours," Lorenzo said, and both men laughed.

"I'm going to let you slide with that one since you just came out of a coma and don't have use of all your faculties, but once you're released from here, it's fair game. You dig it?"

"Yeah, I dig." Lorenzo chuckled.

"Well, I think I'm going to go grab some lunch. I will holla back at you later this afternoon. Can I get you anything?"

"Sure. Can you bring me a good b-book to read, something by Chester Himes or Rob-Robert B. Parker?"

"You got it."

"I'll s-see you later, then. Thanks again, Jonathan." Lorenzo extended his hand.

As Jonathan stood to shake Lorenzo's hand, he noticed the *Delta Democrat-Times* on the side table and the headline *Black Woman Charged with Capital Murder Accused of Killing White Landowner.* Jonathan lifted the newspaper and scanned the black-and-white photo of the woman arrested for murder. Something like lead dropped in Jonathan's stomach.

"This can't be... Annie Price," he whispered.

# Chapter 26

Before Momma went to jail, Daddy wouldn't allow anyone in the house to cook but her. I wasn't sure if he was afraid to eat our cooking because he knew it would be terrible or if he thought one of us would poison him. But with Momma being gone, the task of cooking fell to Jo and me so we wouldn't starve to death. Our first attempt at culinary greatness was breakfast the morning after Momma's arrest. The results were disastrous—lumpy, undercooked grits, bland, soggy eggs, and burned bacon. Thank goodness Daddy had gone to attend Momma's arraignment before we finished.

After Daddy left, we waited, with a healthy measure of anxiety, to hear the outcome. When Daddy returned, Uncle Earl followed him home in his 1966 emerald green Ford LTD. Daddy and Uncle Earl walked into the house together. Daddy continued into the kitchen and fixed them both a cup of coffee, even though it was almost noon. Uncle Earl drank more coffee than any person I'd ever seen. He sat on the sofa, his hands cupped around one of our brown coffee mugs with a totem pole image molded into it. Daddy sat in his brown leatherlike recliner. Jo and I greeted Uncle Earl then returned to the kitchen and finished washing the dishes. The furrow in Uncle Earl's brow sent an uneasy twinge through my nervous system.

"I can't believe they charged Annie Lee with capital murder and set her bail at two hundred thousand dollars," Uncle Earl said to Daddy.

"Ain't no way we can come up with that kinda money," Daddy said. "Not anytime soon."

"Two hundred thousand dollars!" I said, walking into the living room and standing next to Uncle Earl. "That's a lot!"

"Yeah, Bailey, it is."

"Two hundred thousand dollars for what?" Jo asked, drying her hands on her blue jean shorts as she followed me into the living room.

"That's how much Momma's bail is," I said, glancing over my shoulder at her.

"For supposedly killing Mr. Jim. I guess Mr. Jim was *real* important," Jo said, plopping down in the big chair by the window.

"The prosecutor, Frank Sutton, say they got enough evidence to convict Annie Lee," Uncle Earl said. "And I heard he got ties to the KKK." Tammy came into the room and climbed up on the sofa beside Uncle Earl. "But the only evidence they got is circumstantial."

"What does circa-stancha mean, Uncle Earl?" Tammy asked.

Uncle Earl explained that circumstantial evidence meant that the prosecutor didn't have anything real, like a knife, to connect Momma to the crime. There was no murder weapon and no eyewitness. I wasn't sure Tammy understood the explanation, but I did.

"But that doggone Sutton also said Annie Lee had motive, means, and opportunity," Uncle Earl said.

"What, what, and what?" Jo asked.

Uncle Earl took a big gulp of his coffee and placed the mug on the coffee table. "A motive is a reason to commit a crime."

"What did they say Momma's motive was?" Jo asked, biting her fingernails.

"They said she was angry at your daddy's boss for something." Uncle Earl shot Daddy a glance that seemed to question how much information he really should share.

"Why was Momma mad?" Tammy asked.

"She wasn't mad at that man, Tammy, and she didn't kill him," Uncle Earl said, continuing before Tammy could ask another question. "But Sutton said Annie didn't have an alibi for where she was early Saturday morning, so she had the opportunity to kill Jim Cunningham. But I know better."

"What's a al-la-by? Is that like a lullaby?" Tammy asked, her face scrunched up as she peered up at Uncle Earl.

Uncle Earl chuckled then explained what an alibi was. He didn't have a high school education—Momma said he'd dropped out of school in the sixth grade to start working in the cotton fields. But Uncle Earl had street smarts and a lot of common sense. He was smart in ways that made up for his lack of formal education.

"Sounds like Momma is in a whole lot of trouble," I said.

Uncle Earl wasn't telling us everything, especially about what the prosecutor said Momma's motive was. But I didn't say anything else. I figured if he'd wanted to tell us more, he would have. Besides, I wasn't feeling brave enough to challenge a grown man. And I was grateful that Daddy actually let us sit and listen to him and Uncle Earl and ask questions. Typically, he would have made us leave the room because "grown folks" were talking.

After Uncle Earl left, I went into our room, flung myself across the bed, and pulled out one of the Hardy Boys mysteries, but I couldn't concentrate well enough to read a single line. Disturbing thoughts and images of Momma crept into my mind, shrouding me with an overwhelming feeling of sadness. I wondered what she had to eat while she was in jail or whether they fed her at all. And I worried most of all about whether I would ever see my momma again.

Daddy left shortly after Uncle Earl. He didn't say where he was going, but I had a sneaking suspicion he'd headed to some juke joint to get drunk. That seemed to be the grown-up reaction to problems they couldn't solve. And with Momma locked up and her bail set at two hundred thousand dollars, Daddy was facing an impossible grown-up problem.

Jo and I waited for Daddy to return most of the afternoon because we needed him to take us to Fratelli's to get food for breakfast and lunch the following day. But by late in the day, he hadn't come back.

"Bailey, we need to go to the store before it gets dark."

"Ten minutes. I'm almost done with this chapter," I said. I had finally settled into my story.

"No, now, Bailey."

"Oh, all right." I rolled over, stretched like a lazy house cat, then sat up and pushed my feet into my sneakers. I gazed past the frayed, partially open curtains nailed to the top of the window frame, my stomach twisting.

"Jo, it's almost dark already. Where's Daddy? He was supposed to take us to the store."

"I know. But as you can see, Sherlock, he's not back. That's why you need to hurry up."

"I am," I said in a huff as I finished tying my shoelaces. "Do you know what we need to get?"

"Yeah—got the list right here." Jo patted the pocket of her hand-me-down black-and-white domino-plaid blouse that was a size too big. Her sturdy bare legs sprouted from her knee-length blue jean shorts as she pranced out of our room and toward the front door.

"Wait!" I raced into the living room to catch up with her. "What about Tammy?"

"We'll take her over to Ms. Clara's. Come on!"

I followed Jo out of the house. When I stepped onto the porch, the muggy summer heat enveloped me like a warm cocoon. We didn't have air-conditioning, but the box fans did a pretty good job of providing some relief. Inhaling the stifling air, I noticed the lilac sky with bright-orange etchings where the sun quietly slipped from view. Ordinarily, I would have been in awe of such beauty, but that evening, awe was replaced by a healthy dose of dread. Darkness would soon follow, and not only did I have to be concerned about my welfare, but I also had my sister to think about. I hurried down the steps, ignoring the ripple of anxiety stirring in my gut. I inhaled deeply then exhaled slowly to strengthen my resolve.

Jo locked the door with Momma's key and pushed it into the pocket of her shorts. We walked Tammy across the road to stay with Ms. Clara until we returned from the grocery store.

Ms. Clara, standing in her yard, took Tammy's hand then waved goodbye. "Y'all kids, be careful, and hurry back. Remember to walk on the same side of the road as oncomin' traffic. Otherwise, you won't know what's comin' up behind you. Walk off to the side of the road near the cotton fields. And don't take no ride from nobody unless you know who it is."

"Yes, ma'am," Jo said.

"Bring me some bubblegum!" Tammy yelled.

"Okay!" I yelled back.

Soon Jo and I had fallen into long easy strides on Tribett Road as we headed east toward Fratelli's Grocery Store. It was about a mile and a half away. As we approached Mr. Jim's house, the hairs on the back of my neck stood on end. Until recently, his house had looked warm and inviting with elegant white pillars and forest-green shutters, but now, with no sign of life, it stood bleak and foreboding.

Suddenly, I wanted to get past it as fast as I could. "Hey, Jo, I'll race ya!" I knew Jo was always up to a good challenge.

"To Ms. Maxine's school bus?"

"Yep. Ready. Set. Go!"

After an all-out seventy-five-yard sprint, Jo stretched out her arms in victory. "I win!" She pranced ahead like a prize-winning filly, hands on her hips, breathing hard and sucking in air.

"Rematch on the way back," I said, my chest heaving and my heart pounding vigorously as I drew in warm air through my mouth.

I didn't care that Jo had beaten me. Sure, she was a girl, but she was also two years older than I was. I was relieved that Mr. Jim's house had faded behind us.

"Do you think Momma killed Mr. Jim?" I asked Jo after I caught my breath.

"Of course not! Why would you ask me a stupid question like that?"

"The police think she did it."

"The police are stupid."

We both forced a brave laugh as we continued up Tribett Road. Pretty soon, we turned onto Marah's Pass. There were cotton fields on the left of the winding road, and on the right was a ravine with a twenty-five- or thirty-foot drop. Tall, leaning trees, thick grass, cattails, and various other plants surrounded it. There was no railing to prevent a car from driving into the ravine or a person from falling off the edge if he wasn't careful. We walked to the left side of the road, far from the ravine side. When we rounded the first bend on Marah's Pass, the chirp of crickets, the loud singing of locusts, and the *rumm-rumm-rumm* call of bullfrogs made my legs feel wobbly. I tried not to look toward the ravine or focus on how scary the evening had suddenly become.

"Since Momma didn't kill Mr. Jim, who do you think did?" I asked.

"I don't know. It could have been anybody. One of his many girlfriends could have done it."

"What... what about Daddy?"

"What about him?"

"You think he could have done it? He was really angry with Momma and Mr. Jim," I said.

"Shoot! Bailey, I don't know. Daddy goes berserk when he's drinking, and he's done some horrible things to a few men out of jealousy, not to mention how he beats up Momma. But kill somebody? I don't know."

"Just like Momma, Daddy didn't come home the night before someone killed Mr. Jim."

"Where did he say he was?" Jo asked.

"He said he was drunk and passed out on the side of the road."

"So he couldn't have done it if he was drunk and passed out. Hey, look!" Jo pointed. "The store is just across the highway. We need to run like crazy when we get a chance, okay?" We watched several cars, trucks, and eighteen-wheelers speed by. "You ready?"

"Yeah."

The way was clear. We dashed across Highway 82 to Fratelli's Grocery Store. Two tiny gold bells chimed when we entered. The air inside was cool and smelled of strong coffee and bleach. I tried to ignore the big jars of pickled pig feet and pickled eggs on the counter.

Jo pulled the list from her pocket. "You go get a dozen eggs, a half gallon of milk, and a box of Corn Flakes. I'll get the two-pound bag of flour, a pound of sugar, and a can of Crisco."

"Can we get a soda too? I'm so thirsty. And don't forget Tammy's bubblegum."

"I'm thirsty too. We'll have to see how much money is left."

After Jo paid for the groceries, she had just enough money left to buy a Coca-Cola for herself, an Orange Crush for me, and bubble gum for Tammy. We grabbed the big brown paper bags and headed for the door, gulping down our cold drinks on the way. After waiting for five or six cars and trucks to whiz past, we darted across the highway.

We hurried along Marah's Pass. The sun had gone down, and it was completely dark. The only thing I could see was a pale crescent moon and a million stars that danced like miniature white flames—ones that offered no warmth. To distract ourselves from the eerie sounds of the night and to make time go by faster, we played a game we called category. One of us would choose a category—such as a type of fruit, yellow objects, or girls' names that started with an *E*—and then each of us had to name an item in the category. The one who couldn't think of an answer was the loser. Concentrating on the game kept our fear at bay.

Finally, we turned onto Tribett Road, and I breathed a sigh of relief. But we still had a mile to go. We'd been lucky going to the store because only two cars passed us, and the drivers had appeared to be in a hurry, so neither seemed to notice us.

From a distance, a pair of headlights appeared out of the darkness, drawing closer to us. My breath hitched in my throat. I swallowed hard. "Jo, do you see those lights?"

"Yeah. I see 'em."

"What do we do?"

"Keep walking. Don't stop. Move closer to the field."

"Okay." I could feel my heart pounding hard against my rib cage. I prayed silently that the car would keep going.

Suddenly, the high beams flashed. I squinted and shielded my eyes. The car drew nearer. It slowed. From the dull-green light in the dashboard, I could see the face of the sheriff who had arrested Momma. He leered at us. My legs became noodles. My heart rate accelerated. The car drove past us. I exhaled. Then the brake lights flashed bloodred. A fresh wave of fear washed over me. The car made a wild U-turn and headed toward us. The engine purred softly as the car rolled alongside us. The window slid down. The stench of alcohol mixed with exhaust fumes made me nauseous.

"Where you kids goin' this time of night?" slurred the pale-faced man looking past his deputy, who sat in the passenger seat.

"We're on our way back home. We went to the store," Jo said, looking straight ahead.

"Won't y'all climb on in the car? We'll give you a ride home. It's hotter than a four-peckered billy goat out there." Both men crowed with laughter.

"No, thank you. We're almost there," said Jo.

"How much farther you got to go?"

"Not far," I said, trying to keep my voice from trembling. "We live right up there in the light-green house, not too far from the one Mr. Jim used to live in." Immediately, I knew I'd said too much.

The expression on the man's face registered realization. "Oh, I see." The sheriff glanced at his deputy, who chewed slowly on a toothpick. He nodded and grinned back at the sheriff in a way that sent a chill up my spine. "Y'all Otis and Annie Lee Connor's kids. Well, guess what? Now, I'm not askin'. I'm tellin' you to get in the damn car!" The sheriff slammed on the brakes, threw the car in park, and swung open the car door.

"Run, Jo! Run!"

Jo bolted for the cotton field to the right, with the big grocery bag clutched to her chest. I dashed behind her. The brown paper sack jabbed at my chin. The white blotches in Jo's blouse bounced up and down. I wasn't far behind her. Then something grabbed my feet. A scream escaped my lips. I fell hard to the ground, crushing the eggs against my chest. I kicked wildly, and the bag Jo had dropped untangled from my feet. Leaping up, I raced to catch up with Jo. My groceries were on the ground where I left them. I watched the two flashlight beams sway ominously overhead.

"You little nigglets, you ain't getting away," the man growled. "Your mammy's gonna be sorry her black ass ever laid eyes on a white man, let alone killed one."

When I caught up with Jo, we kneeled for a second, breathing hard as we watched the lights.

"Keep low so they can't see us," she whispered, her voice quivering, her breathing ragged.

"Okay. We're almost at Mr. Jim's house. Let's cut across the road once we get there. Then we can find a hiding place." My heart pounded in my ears. I realized my fear of the two men was much greater than my fear of Mr. Jim's house.

"Olly olly oxen free!" one of the men called out in a high-pitched tone. They laughed menacingly. "You kids, come on out. We ain't gonna hurt you. We're just playin' with you."

"Let's go," Jo said.

We ran through the tall cotton, keeping low. Jo tugged on my shirt when we were directly across the road from Mr. Jim's house. We crouched and waited until the beams swung in the opposite direction.

"Now!" I whispered.

We dashed across the road. Reaching the other side, Jo tripped and tumbled into the ditch face down. I almost fell on top of her. Grappling for her hand, I practically dragged her to her feet. We raced toward the big butane gas tank on the side of Mr. Jim's house. We crouched, our backs pressed against the tank, gasping for air. The beam from the flashlights swayed back and forth like a watchtower light.

"H-e-e-ere kitty, kitty, kitty. Come out, come out, wherever you are." The men cackled. "H-e-e-ere, kitty, kitty, kitty." The voices slowly moved away.

"Jo, I think we can make it home." I felt my heart beating a hundred beats per second.

"Okay, let's go," Jo said, breathing in gulps.

I dashed toward the cotton field ahead of me. Jo was on my heels, breathing hard. When we reached our yard, we raced around to the back of the house. Still crouching, Jo unlocked the back door, and we tumbled inside.

# Chapter 27

"Hurry, lock it, Jo! Lock it! Hurry!" I swallowed hard, trying to catch my breath, feeling as though I would hyperventilate at any moment. Our house was completely dark. We hadn't thought to turn the lights on before we left because there was still daylight.

"Bailey, follow me. We've got to protect ourselves," Jo whispered.

I followed her silhouette as we crept through the kitchen. We stumbled together through the darkness, making our way to our parents' bedroom. She guided me to their closet. My knees felt rubbery as I realized what Jo was up to. She climbed onto the step stool and fumbled in the dark until she found Daddy's shotgun on the shelf.

"Hold this, Bailey, while I find the box of shells."

I felt the cool steel of the gun's barrel, and a ripple of panic shot through my body.

"Got 'em!" Jo whispered. "We can watch through Momma and Daddy's window to see if those men are still out there." She sat at the foot of their bed and loaded the shotgun. Then she tiptoed to the window and slowly pulled back the curtain.

I stood next to her and peered out. "Jo, are you scared?"

"Yes. But not as scared as I was before. We have to be ready in case those men decide to stop here. They know where we live."

We watched as the pair of headlights crawled toward our house. Bright beams jetted from the car, swaying back and forth, searching the cotton fields. When the car finally reached our house, I could barely hear the quiet hum of the motor over the drumbeat of my heart. I closed my eyes and whispered a prayer that the men wouldn't stop. The engine roared, and the car sped past our house. I exhaled.

"Thank God." I spoke in a whisper. Then I said, "Jo, let's go look out the living room window to see if they're gone for good."

With cautious steps, holding on to each other, Jo and I made our way to the living room and peered out the side window. The red taillights continued up Tribett Road, and the searching beams were gone. Relief swept over me, but we kept watching until the taillights had disappeared. Even then, we watched to see if the car would make a U-turn and come back.

We waited in the darkness for what seemed like hours, occasionally peering out the window. The car didn't return. Jo finally turned on the television to give us a little light.

"I lost our food," Jo said. "I dropped it when I started running. The bag was too heavy." "I dropped mine, too, when I fell down." The tears I'd held back during the night's terror started to burn my eyes, and I swallowed the lump in my throat. I refused to cry. I refused to feel sorry for myself.

"It's okay. Food can be replaced. We did the right thing. We ran, and we made it home safely. And in the morning, we can ask Daddy to go back down there with us to see if anything can be saved."

A sudden knock at the door gave Jo and me a start. We locked eyes. Jo raised the shotgun.

"Hello, is anybody home? It's Ms. Clara."

Relieved, I ran to the door and opened it.

"I thought you kids shoulda been back from the store by now. I was startin' to worry because it's dark outside, and you don't have no lights on in here. Is everything all right?"

"No, ma'am," I said. "Jo and I were chased by the sheriff and the deputy who arrested Momma."

"Oh my, Lord! You kids all right?"

"Yes, ma'am," Jo said, having placed the shotgun on the floor. "We ran through the cotton fields to get away from them, but we lost all of our groceries."

"Well, thank God y'all is safe. Your daddy can buy more groceries." Ms. Clara looked at her watch. "I see he's not home yet. Well, you children go ahead and lock up tight. And be careful with that shotgun. I'm goin' on back across the street. Just wanted to bring Tammy home. She been askin' for you two."

"Thank you for watching her, Ms. Clara," I said.

"Not a problem at all. Good night, kids."

I followed Ms. Clara to the door and locked it behind her. I watched her through the front window as she darted across the road.

Tammy started jumping up and down. "Bailey, where's my bubblegum? Where's my gum?"

I reached into the pocket of my jeans, pulled out a pink-and-blue-wrapped piece of bubblegum, and gave it to Tammy. She grabbed it and threw her arms around my neck.

# Chapter 28

That night, I dreamed of being chased through the woods by men with large baying greyhounds with fiery red eyes that were close to sniffing out my hiding place. I awoke with a start, breathing hard, a drumbeat pounding in my chest. Calming myself, I realized it was only a dream. Then overwhelming sadness enveloped me. I remembered Momma wouldn't be in the kitchen, cooking breakfast. I also remembered Uncle Earl saying the prosecutor wanted to lock her away for good. I swallowed hard. Then my thoughts turned to Daddy. He hadn't come home before we went to bed, which was after midnight. Listening for the rumble of his snoring, all I heard was silence.

I swung out of bed, pulled on a pair of shorts and a T-shirt, and went searching for my dad. When I passed Momma and Daddy's room, it was empty, but the bed had been slept in. I found Daddy sitting on the front porch with his feet propped on the steps, smoking a cigarette and drinking a cup of coffee. He looked up at me with bloodshot eyes. I couldn't tell if it was from drinking the night before or from crying. Maybe it was a combination of the two.

"Mornin', Bailey. Why you up so early?"

"I didn't sleep very well last night. I had a terrible dream. I was glad when morning came."

"Dreamin' 'bout your momma?"

"No, I was dreaming about those two white men who chased me and Jo when we were coming back from the store last night."

"What two white men?" Daddy's brow creased.

"The sheriff and deputy who arrested Momma."

"Why was they chasin' y'all?"

"They asked us if we wanted a ride. And we said no because Momma told us to never get into a car with a stranger. When they realized you and Momma were our parents, they tried to make us get in the car."

"They put their hands on you?" Daddy's red eyes blazed.

"No. The sheriff got angry and started yelling at us. He stopped the car and got out."

"What y'all do?"

"We ran. But we lost all the groceries in the fields between Mr. Mason and Ms. Odell's house."

"But y'all got away from 'em?"

"Yeah."

"Mm-hm." Daddy's jaw clenched. He took a long draw from his cigarette, stubbed it under his boot, and blew out a funnel of smoke.

Then he rose, threw the screen door wide open, and stalked into the house. The door slammed hard against the aluminum siding. We followed him into his and Momma's bedroom.

He entered the bedroom closet and ran his hand across the shelf. "Where's my shotgun?"

"It's under Jo and Tammy's bed," I said.

"What's it doin' there?"

"Jo said we needed to protect ourselves just in case those men came to the house looking for us after they couldn't find us in the cotton fields."

Daddy marched into our bedroom and grabbed the shotgun from under the bed. He checked to see if it was loaded. He headed toward the front door, with me on his heels, my legs barely holding me up.

"What are you about to do, Daddy?"

"Um gon' make somebody thank twice about messin' with my kids."

"Wait, Daddy! Don't go! They'll shoot you!"

Daddy tossed the gun into the back seat and climbed into his car. The Bug shot backward, spewing gravel in every direction.

THREE HOURS LATER, Daddy finally returned home. When I saw his Volkswagen pulling into the driveway, I raced out onto the porch. I'd waited on pins and needles, expecting that at any moment, flashing red and blue lights would park in front of our house, and some stone-faced white man would tell us that our daddy had been shot dead and my sisters and I were orphans. Daddy stepped out of the car.

"Daddy, what happened?" Relief washed over me, seeing that his white T-shirt was not riddled with bullet holes and dripping with blood.

"I went over to yo' uncle Lance's for him to go with me. He wouldn't. Said I was bein' foolish. Said that was one sho' way of gettin' myself kilt. He'll be over later. He's makin' some phone calls, trying to find a lawyer for your momma."

Daddy opened the Volkswagen's trunk and grabbed a bag of groceries. He'd bought corn flakes, milk, bologna, white bread, pork and beans, rice, and smoked sausage. Breakfast, lunch, and dinner. Jo and I decided we wouldn't go back to the fields to recover any of the items we'd lost. We were fearful the men would show up again.

"Are you going to see Momma today?" I asked Daddy.

"I plan on it."

"Can I go?"

"Bailey, jail ain't no place for no kid."

"But I want to visit Momma. See how she's doing."

"I know, son. We workin' on a way to get her out for good, so just hold yo' horses. Like I said, Lance is makin' some phone calls right now to find a lawyer for yo' momma."

"Oh, all right."

Daddy walked into the house, cradling the shotgun in one arm and the bag of groceries in the other. Not more than an hour later, Daddy's brother Lance pulled into the driveway in his shiny sunburst-orange Chevrolet Camaro. We were hoping he would bring some good news about an attorney for Momma.

Uncle Lance was five years younger than Daddy, so that made him thirty-five. And he seemed younger too. He didn't carry the weight of the world on his shoulders the way Daddy did. I supposed his weight wasn't as heavy. He'd finished high school and gone into the army. After an honorable discharge, Uncle Lance had taken a job with the post office.

He and Daddy had different fathers, and Uncle Lance lived with his dad most of the time. He was kind and generous, with an infectious laugh. Daddy and Uncle Lance were as different as a gentle breeze and a hailstorm. When he walked into the house, wearing off-white linen shorts and an orange-and-blue tropical-print button-down shirt, the mood seemed to lighten.

My sisters and I greeted Uncle Lance with a hug. Then Daddy told us to go find something to do while he and Uncle Lance talked. I grabbed a copy of *Readers Digest* and retreated to the kitchen table. My plan was to work the crossword puzzle—and listen.

"I took the liberty of getting us a six-pack," Uncle Lance said. "I figured you wouldn't mind."

"Naw, I don't mind at all." Daddy picked up one of the beers, popped the cap, and took a long guzzle. "Well, did you have any luck findin' a lawyer to help Annie Lee?"

Uncle Lance took a swig of his beer. "Here's the problem—there aren't many Black criminal attorneys in Greenville. And the white ones won't touch her case with a ten-foot pole. I did some calling around, and Greenville's best Black attorney is a cat named Lorenzo Cain. That's the good news. The bad news is Cain is laid up in the hospital with a bullet wound to his skull."

"Somebody shot him?"

"Apparent robbery attempt." Uncle Lance took another gulp of his beer. "So from where I'm sitting, it's not looking too good, Otis. We're gonna need a miracle."

# Chapter 29

Jonathan left the hospital immediately and drove his rental seven miles east to the county jail in the neighboring town of Lowell. He sat at a square wooden table in a small room with dingy white tile and dull gray walls. Various scenarios raced through his mind as to what could have caused Annie Lee Price, as he knew her, to end up in such a dire situation. It seemed inconceivable that the brown-eyed girl with the pretty smile and outgoing personality could commit such a heinous crime. But then he considered that she could be innocent. He knew all too well that Black men and women were often arrested and convicted of crimes they hadn't committed. Countless cases had been documented of such atrocities that began to happen during Reconstruction.

*Is this such a case?*

The inner door opened, and a slim woman with caramel-brown skin and sad eyes stepped into the room. Her black hair had been pulled back into a disheveled twist. She wore a gray jumpsuit. The shackles around her ankles connected with the silver handcuffs around her wrists. They jangled as she shuffled into the room. Jonathan scanned her face to determine whether she was Annie Lee Price, the girl he'd gone to school with from fourth to seventh grade.

He stood at the table and waited. When Annie reached the table, Jonathan extended his hand. Confusion creased her brow as she shook hands with him.

"Hi, Annie," he said. "It's been a long time. It's good to see you again."

She stared at him with a vacant expression. Then a spark of recognition flickered in Annie's eyes. "Jon Streeter? From Indianola, Mississippi? Yes, I remember you." A weak smile spread across her lips. "What are you doing here?"

"Would you care to sit for a moment?" Jonathan gestured toward the chair. "I would ask how you're doing, but that's pretty obvious."

"I'm holding up," Annie said, sitting and folding her hands on the wooden tabletop, making the chains clank loudly against it. "I'm sure you're wondering how I ended up here. Well, it's a long story."

"I have a few minutes."

"It's been a long time since I saw you last. It was the summer of '54 at the Greenville Carnival. Do you remember that?"

"Of course. I'd just graduated from high school, and I was spending the summer with my grandmother in Greenville. You and I bumped into each other at the carnival and ended up spending the entire day and most of the evening together. That was—what, fifteen years ago?"

"Seventeen. And apparently, you left Lowell sometime later that year," Annie said.

"That's right. In the fall, I moved to Atlanta to attend Morehouse College. Then I moved to Cambridge, Massachusetts, and got my law degree from Harvard."

"That's great, Jonathan. You always were smart. I knew you would make it out of these sticks."

"You were the smart one. I always tried to keep up with you, the straight-A student."

"So were you."

"I made an occasional B." Jonathan chuckled. "So, Annie, you asked me what I'm doing here. I read the story about you in the *Delta Democrat-Times*, and I'm concerned about you and your safety. I'm concerned about your case. Do you have an attorney to represent you?"

"My husband, Otis, is trying to find one for me. But as of today, no, I don't have an attorney."

"Listen, I'm planning to stay in town for a few more days to make sure Lorenzo's condition remains stable. Would you mind if I come back to check on you and see how things are going with you?"

"I'd like that a lot. There aren't too many friendly faces in this place." Annie forced a smile.

"It's been seventeen years, Annie, and you haven't changed a bit. You're still that pretty girl with the long pigtails and beautiful brown eyes that I met in the fourth grade."

"As you can see, a lot has changed since then." Annie held up her wrists, and the chains clanked loudly. She rose from the table and shuffled toward the door without looking back. "Goodbye, Jonathan. Thanks for coming."

# Chapter 30

Coping with Momma's absence and the fact that she might never be coming home had started to take a toll on all of us. My sisters and I moped around the house most of the time, and Daddy drowned his sorrows, even during weekdays, in a bottle of Kentucky Tavern Bourbon. It didn't help matters that Big Momma had called Daddy on Ms. Clara's phone and told him Priscilla needed to come back home to help us younger kids since Momma was in jail. Big Momma obviously didn't know how much Daddy hated Priscilla. Otherwise, she wouldn't have made such a horrible decision. I was terrified about what he'd do to her and us in a drunken rage after Priscilla returned. This time, Momma wouldn't be here to protect us.

The second day after Momma's arrest, I sat on the porch for three hours, listening to music on my transistor radio. Tammy had spent most of the day collecting tiny bouquets of wildflowers. We'd left Jo inside. She'd cried herself to sleep. Daddy was watching a baseball game as he drank his bourbon. He was staring out the window more than looking at the TV screen.

The afternoon drifted into evening, and the mandarin-orange sun began her graceful descent in an amethyst sky. The crickets chirped mirthfully, and fireflies flickered as they danced around Tammy and me. We were headed indoors when Aunt Bernadette and Walter pulled into our driveway and parked their dark-blue automobile behind Daddy's Volkswagen. Tammy continued inside, but I waited on the porch for them. The headlights blinked off, and the driver's side and passenger doors swung open almost simultaneously.

Aunt Bernadette and Walter made their way up our gravel walkway. I greeted the two of them and followed them to the house.

Daddy met them at the door. "Hey, Bernie. Hey, Walter. Y'all come on in and take a load off. I was just sittin' here, watchin' a ball game and tryin' to figure out what we gon' do about Annie Lee's situation."

"Well, I knew you wouldn't be up to cookin', so I made you and the kids some spaghetti and meatballs and one of my delicious peach cobblers."

"Thanks, Bernie. I really 'preciate it. The kids ain't had a decent meal since the law picked up Annie Lee."

"Here, Otis," Bernadette said, taking the beer from Walter. "Put this beer in the fridge, but take us out a few before you do."

Walter followed Otis into the kitchen and placed the bag with the spaghetti and the cobbler on the table. Then they returned to the living room, and Daddy went back to his recliner. Walter sat on the sofa, and Aunt Bernadette sat next to him.

"Bailey, go tell yo' sisters to come get somethin' to eat."

"Okay, Daddy." I went to tell Jo and Tammy to come and fix their plates.

Then I went back to the kitchen to fix myself some of Aunt Bernadette's spaghetti and meatballs while it was still warm. She was an excellent cook and an even better baker. I couldn't wait to dig into that peach cobbler. After I fixed my plate, I sat at the kitchen table, which provided the perfect vantage point to watch and listen while not appearing to be doing so. Jo fixed her plate and Tammy's, and they went back into our room to eat.

"Otis," Aunt Bernie said, "what's the lowdown with my sister's situation? I went to see her yesterday. She didn't know what was going on with her bail or getting a lawyer."

Daddy took a minute to answer. "I don't know, Bernie. I just don't know."

"We all know Annie Lee didn't kill that man. She didn't have no reason to."

"We know she didn't kill him. But knowin' is one thang, and provin' is another," Daddy said.

"You suppose they gonna let Annie Lee out on bail?" Aunt Bernie asked.

"They set Annie Lee's bail at two hunda thousand dollars," Daddy said.

Walter let out a low whistle.

"We tryin' to raise the money now, but we got a ways to go. I called my other brothers—all five of 'em—to see how much they can give."

"You need to start looking for a good lawyer too." Walter took a swig of beer. "A Black woman accused of killing a white man is just as bad as if a Black man had been accused. Ain't no difference."

"That's what me and my brother Lance been tryin' to do. A good lawyer gon' cost good money. But we tryin' to find one."

"I wonder who really killed that man," Aunt Bernadette said. "I heard he was cut up worse than a pig that's been to slaughter. Somebody was real angry with him. And even though Annie Lee didn't do it, she's a Black woman accused of killing a white man. They've pinned it on her, and they'll do their damnedest to make it stick."

"Jealousy has killed more people than cancer," Walter said. "And it's the oldest reason for committing murder. I think his fiancée probably did it."

"Well, like I said, I know they are trying to pin this murder on Annie Lee because she's Black. But they can't do it because she's got a rock-solid alibi." Aunt Bernie released a sigh after sipping her beer.

"I know she got a alibi," Daddy said. "She was here with the kids."

"No, Annie wasn't here with the kids," Aunt Bernie said. "She was with Earl from around eight o'clock that night until around seven the next morning. She told me they listened to records, drank almost a fifth of Seagram's gin, and then both passed out on the sofa." Aunt Bernie laughed. "So I know for a fact that she didn't kill that man."

# Chapter 31

Being a criminal attorney, Jonathan Streeter knew how critical and urgent Annie Lee Connor's case was, so he returned the next day to visit her in jail. But Jonathan knew the prosecutor would move quickly for a speedy trial. And if Annie Lee could not afford an attorney, a state-appointed public defender would be assigned to her.

When she walked into the small dingy room, surprise registered on her face. "I didn't expect to see you back so soon," she said, taking a seat across from Jonathan.

"I didn't expect to be back so soon. But your case weighed heavily on my mind. I couldn't rest, thinking about it. How are you holding up?"

"About as well as can be expected."

"Any threats? Anybody tried to harm you?" he asked.

"No, just the usual hateful looks and mean, barking commands. Nothing I can't deal with."

"Okay. Good. Yesterday, you told me your husband had been trying to find an attorney for you. How's that going? Any success?"

"No. All of the Black attorneys my brother-in-law Lance called would charge an arm and a leg. And of course, none of the white attorneys will come near this case."

"Listen, Annie, I had only planned to be in Lowell for another week or so to see if Lorenzo's condition would change, but after talking with you yesterday, I realized I have to do whatever I can to help you. A Black person accused of killing a white person in the deep South will never get a fair trial. Especially if they don't have good representation. The odds are totally stacked against him or her from the start.

"I don't know if you remember what happened to my dad. Pops owned a barbershop when we lived in Indianola. One evening, he was working in the shop, and the police charged in and arrested him for the rape of a white woman, somebody he'd never heard of. They said the woman reported she had been knocked out with a strap. And since he had several barber straps in his shop, they arrested him. He had six witnesses who were prepared to testify that he was at the barbershop at the time of the rape. But he never got to go to trial. A mob overran the jail, dragged him out, and lynched him. They drug his body behind a truck through town until practically nothing was left. That happened in August 1948. I was twelve years old. It broke my mother's heart. I couldn't help my father, but I vowed to help as many other innocent Black people as I can."

"That's why your family moved to Lowell."

"Yes. We moved shortly after Pops's murder. Now, in your case, Annie, if you don't have an attorney representing you, a state-appointed public defender will be assigned to you. This person would most likely be white. He'll have thirty or forty other cases assigned to him. Being severely underpaid, he'd hardly put forth the effort to mount a strong defense for you, a Black woman."

"Jonathan, I know I'm in a bad situation, so why are you telling me this?"

"I said all of that to ask you if you'd like me to represent you."

Annie Lee laughed. "I saw you on television last month. You were meeting with the DC mayor, Thurgood Marshall, and a couple of other bigwigs. Look at your clothes. I'm sure your tie alone costs more than I earned in a month working for Jim Cunningham. And your watch probably costs more than Otis's Volkswagen. We can't afford you."

"I know life can be tough. I'm no stranger to hardship myself. When we moved to Lowell, we lived in the projects across the tracks just south of downtown. Fortunately, I was blessed with an academic scholarship to Morehouse then went on to get my law degree from Harvard. I've done pro bono work before, Annie, and I'll represent you pro bono as well. So don't give the cost another thought."

"All right." Annie Lee's voice trembled with feeling. "I really appreciate your kindness."

"Now, my purpose for coming here today is twofold. First, I wanted to offer you representation. And second, if you agreed, I wanted to start building my case immediately because your trial will probably start in about three weeks."

"Okay. What do I need to do?"

"Well, I need to ask you a few questions." Jonathan opened his briefcase and pulled out a yellow legal pad and a pen. "Annie, some of these questions might seem harsh, but I have to ask them. I have to prepare you for what the prosecutor might ask. Okay?"

"All right."

"Tell me about the evening of Friday, July 10 through Saturday, July 11. Tell me where you were. What you were doing. Who you were with. Don't leave out any details."

"Well, Otis had been in a real foul mood that Friday night. He accused me of having an affair with Jim Cunningham. We argued. I tried to calm him down, but he stormed out of the house in a rage. I needed to get out and get some fresh air, so I called my brother Earl. He came and picked me up around eight o'clock. We went to his place, played some records, and drank some gin—a lot of gin, almost a fifth of Seagram's. I passed out on his sofa. When I woke up, it was around seven o'clock Saturday morning. I had Earl drive me home. I got there around seven thirty."

"What's your brother's full name? He'll have to take the stand and testify for you. He'll have to corroborate what you just told me."

"His name is Willie Earl Price."

"Your husband, Otis, worked for the deceased. Did you know Jim Cunningham? And if so, what was your relationship with him?"

"He was my boss too. I did some light housecleaning for him, and I cooked for him, usually on weekends."

"How would you characterize your relationship?" he asked.

"What do you mean?"

Jonathan cleared his throat. "The prosecutor has suggested that your relationship was of a romantic nature, and therefore, your motive for killing him was vengeance after he rejected you while planning to marry later this year."

"Mr. Jim Cunningham was my boss and *only* my boss."

"So there was no romantic involvement?"

"No, there was not."

"Are you certain of that? This fact is extremely critical to the prosecution's case as well as my defense."

"As I said before, nothing was going on between me and Jim Cunningham. I worked for him… cooked and cleaned. That's all."

"For what period of time?" Jonathan asked.

"A little over one month, starting on June 11. He was one of the nicest people I'd ever met. I had no reason to harm him."

"To your knowledge, did Mr. Cunningham have any enemies?"

"To my knowledge, no. As I said earlier, he was one of the nicest people I ever met. I didn't know much about his personal life, but I do know that his fiancée had been pretty upset with him not too long ago."

"How long ago?"

"About a week before Jim died," Annie said.

"What happened?"

"They had a big blowout in his front yard. We'd gone to Greenville for the Fourth of July and got back home around two thirty in the morning. Otis and I had fought on the way. He lost control of the car, and we ended up in a ditch. When we finally made it home, we heard a commotion coming from Mr. Jim's house."

"Could you tell what they were arguing about?"

Annie Lee was silent for a moment. "I... I can't be sure. Wait, I just remembered something. I couldn't hear every word because of the distance. But whatever Jim Cunningham said must have ticked her off because her voice grew louder when she said to him, 'Don't be surprised if you wake up with a bullet in your skull!' Then she got into her car and sped out of his driveway, flying past our house. Jim Cunningham wasn't shot in the head, but he is dead."

"That's true. Do you know the fiancée's name?"

"Sarah... Sarah Bingham. I wonder if any of the authorities bothered to question her."

Jonathan scribbled some notes on his pad. "Well, that will be my second order of business after I confirm your alibi. I plan to ask my cousin Titus Jones to assist me as my investigator in your case. I'll have him give Ms. Bingham a call."

# Chapter 32

Sunday afternoon, Daddy came from Ms. Clara's house, seething with anger after talking to Momma on the telephone. She told him a big-time lawyer from Washington, DC, had read about her arrest in the newspaper and had come by the jail to talk to her about her case. I didn't understand why Daddy was so upset. He should have been happy. This lawyer might be the only hope we had for getting Momma out of jail and keeping her from going to the electric chair. I supposed Daddy could have been angry because he wanted to help her himself but couldn't, or maybe it was that age-old reason—jealousy. Either way, the lawyer, Jonathan Streeter, planned to come out to talk to Daddy later that day because Momma wanted to make sure Daddy agreed with Mr. Streeter taking her case.

Jo and I were sitting in the living room when Jonathan Streeter rolled up our driveway in a brand-new Oldsmobile Cutlass. I watched through the window with curiosity as he unfurled his tall, lean body out of the silver automobile. He shut the door and paused. As he buttoned his navy-blue suit jacket, he scanned the cotton fields that stretched for miles on every side. I wondered what thoughts had entered his mind. He was probably thinking how lucky he was to live in a big city like Washington, DC, rather than a remote no-man's-land surrounded by endless rows of cotton fields.

The lawyer grabbed a brown leather briefcase from the back seat and made his way up our rocky path. Within seconds, I heard a solid rap at the screen door. Jo and I bolted for the door.

She got there first. "Hi, can I help you, sir?"

"I'm Jonathan Streeter. I'm looking for Otis Connor," he said through the locked screen door. "Is he home?"

"Just a minute. Daddy!" Jo called over her shoulder. "Mr. Streeter is here."

Daddy came out of his bedroom, wearing a white short-sleeved button-down shirt, black pants, and a scowl. Exchanging places with Jo, he unhooked the screen door and pushed it open. "Come in."

The man stepped into the living room and extended his hand. Daddy ignored it. Mr. Streeter cleared his throat and placed his hand in his pants pocket.

"I'm Jonathan Streeter." He smiled, revealing straight pearl-white teeth. His deep, rich voice seemed to hang on the air, as did his cologne, which smelled of spice and wood. His smooth skin was the color of molasses. "I'd like to speak with you about your wife's case."

"Uh-huh." Daddy sized up the man.

The room seemed to shrink around Jonathan Streeter, and for an instant, an almost imperceptible look of surprise registered on his face. Perhaps he'd expected to see a younger man. After all, Daddy was seven years older than Momma. Or maybe he'd expected someone taller or more attractive, or perhaps it was something else altogether. Either way, as quickly as it appeared, it was gone, and I doubted Daddy even noticed. Jonathan's neatly trimmed Afro glistened like the men and women in the Afro Sheen TV commercials when *Soul Train* was playing. With his success, I'd thought he would be a much older man, maybe in his fifties or sixties. He was probably around thirty-four or thirty-five—closer to Momma's age.

"Have a seat." Daddy gestured toward the sofa as he ambled over and took a seat in his recliner, leaned back, and locked his fingers over his stomach. "Y'all kids go find somethin' to do while I talk with this man about yo' momma's situation."

Neither of us hesitated in leaving the room. I'd learned a long time ago not to test Daddy's patience by being disobedient, though

I was totally fascinated by this tall stranger with perfect posture and a confident demeanor. But I had to hear the conversation between Daddy and this man, so I went to our room, waited a few minutes, then walked into the kitchen, got a glass of tea, and sat at the table, pretending to read *Charlotte's Web,* though I'd finished reading the book two days prior.

"Now, what 'zackly is it you want to talk to me about? I understand you already been down to the jail and talked to my wife," Daddy said in a tone as sharp as a surgeon's scalpel.

"That's true. I saw the story of your wife's arrest in the newspaper, and I realized we went to school together. I went to see her to make sure she is being treated okay."

"When I talked to Annie Lee today, she told me you plan on takin' her case for free. Why? What do you 'spect to get out of it?"

"I expect to get a not-guilty verdict for your wife."

"I 'preciate you wantin' to take her case for free, but me and my brothers done already started raisin' the money. So you can just tell me what you gon' charge."

*Daddy, you really don't know what you're asking,* I thought. We'd all have to work the rest of our lives, die, come back to life, and work a second lifetime to pay Mr. Smooth-Talking Attorney, who was probably already rich.

"Listen, Otis, I grew up in Lowell. I know how tough it is for families like yours and mine."

"You growed up 'round here?" Daddy's voice softened a bit.

"As a matter of fact, I did. I grew up in the projects across the tracks just south of downtown Lowell. I was able to get a scholarship to go to college and then law school. I represent Black people whose civil rights have been violated or who have been falsely accused of crimes. That's what I do. All I want to do is see to it that Annie has a fair trial. I hope you want the same thing."

"'Course I want the same thang." The spring in the chair squeaked as Daddy leaned forward.

"I understand you and your brother have been looking for an attorney to represent Annie, but you're having a hard time finding one."

"Now, that's true."

"Well, there's not a lot of time left to do that. Annie's trial will probably start within the next three weeks. And we all need to be on the same page and moving forward to provide her with the best defense. She wanted me to talk with you to make sure you agreed with my taking her case."

There was a pause. Then Daddy said, "Well, bein' that we have been havin' a hard time findin' somebody we can afford and you offerin' up your service for free... I guess Um on board."

"Okay, great. Since time is short, I really need to kill two birds with one stone. Now that I have your agreement, I want to continue building Annie's case," Mr. Streeter said.

Daddy didn't agree or disagree, so the lawyer continued. But it seemed that each time Mr. Streeter said Momma's name, it conveyed a certain familiarity as it rolled off his lips. I wondered if Daddy felt the same way.

"Now, Otis, I need to ask you a few questions." Mr. Streeter opened his briefcase, closed it, and began flipping through pages like in a tablet. "You worked for the deceased, Jim Cunningham. Is that correct?"

"Yeah."

"How long did you work for him?"

"'Bout seven years."

"What was your relationship with Mr. Cunningham like?" Mr. Streeter asked.

"Normal, I guess. I didn't have no problem with him. He was okay."

"Now, Otis, the prosecutor has suggested that Annie's relationship with your boss was of a romantic nature and she killed him because he rejected her. How do you feel about that?"

"A lie! Gossip, plain and simple."

"So there was no romantic involvement?" Mr. Streeter asked.

"Naw, Annie Lee wouldn't do nothin' like that. She ain't that kind of woman."

"Otis, where were you Saturday, July 11, between the hours of one and two o'clock in the morning?"

"What?" Daddy's voice rose with indignation. "You thank I had somethin' to do with Jim's murder? Well, I didn't. I didn't have no reason to kill that man."

"These are routine questions, Otis. Everyone who's had recent contact with the deceased is a suspect until he or she can be eliminated as such."

Daddy was quiet for a beat. "Well, I guess I had a little too much to drank that night, and I passed out in my car on the side of Old Leland Road somewhere near the Mennonite church. When I woke up, I tried to drive on home, but the car was driving funny. I had a flat tire, so I slept there till daylight so I could flag somebody down and get some help."

"Did anyone see you while you were parked alongside the road?"

"Yeah, a stranger come by… a young man probably in his twenties, knocked on the window 'round six o'clock in the mornin', scared the hell out of me. He took me to get the tire fixed at Fred's tire service."

"Do you remember his name?"

"Naw… wait. Jimmy something. I don't remember his last name, but like I said, he work at the shop where I got my tire patched up."

"To your knowledge, did Mr. Cunningham have any enemies?" Mr. Streeter asked.

"Don't most rich people got enemies? Most of 'em their own family members scratchin'

and clawin' over money."

"Did you meet any of Jim Cunningham's family members?"

"No, but one of them spent a lot of time down there at his house doin' his books. See her speedin' past our house all the time. His cousin, Caroline Cunningham."

I looked up from pretending to read my book. *Yeah, that Ms. Caroline is evil all right, but would she kill her own cousin?*

I could hear Mr. Streeter shifting pages in his notebook again. "I'll have my investigator give Caroline Cunningham a call. Thank you for taking the time to speak with me, Otis. Annie's trial will start soon. I'll see you then."

# Chapter 33

Three weeks passed, and we all waited on pins and needles for Momma's trial to start. I had triple-dog dared Ray Martin to go down to the courthouse in downtown Lowell with me to sneak into Momma's trial. Ray wasn't my friend's real name. His real name was Benjamin Martin, but somehow, he'd gotten stuck with the name Ray because he wore horn-rim glasses with lenses as thick as Coca-Cola bottle glass. From first grade on, kids had teased him, saying his lenses were so thick he had X-ray vision. Over time, he went from being X-Ray to Ray-Ray to just plain Ray.

I could count on Ray to keep a secret. My problem had been convincing him to go. I tried to bribe him with some of my comic books, but that didn't work. In the end, I just had to turn it into a challenge—because of his highly competitive nature, I knew Ray would go for it. So I dared him to come. If he didn't, he'd have to do my history homework for a month. But if he did, I'd have to do his math homework for a month. Thank goodness he was terrible in math.

Momma's trial started at ten thirty, according to Daddy. Ray rode his bicycle to my house, and I told Jo that I was going to ride to the store with him. Jo was busy combing Tammy's hair, and Tammy was busy squirming and complaining, so Jo gave me a dismissive wave, and Ray and I were on our way. We lived about a mile and a half from the courthouse, roughly six blocks from our school. Ray pedaled, and I rode the handlebars the first half of the way. When it was my turn to pedal, my stomach started to rumble with anxiety as we drew closer to the building. It didn't help the situation that Ray began to glance over his shoulder like we'd escaped from Alcatraz.

"I don't know, Bailey. This might not have been such a good idea. If my momma finds out I went downtown without her knowing, she's gonna kill me."

"How's she gonna to find out? Are you gonna tell her? Look at the top of that building," I said, referring to the flag that hung listlessly in the gray sky atop the two-story building. "We're almost there. We only have two more blocks to go."

"No, I'm not going to tell her. But what if somebody in the courtroom recognizes me?"

"So, you're famous now? Just stick to the plan. We'll sneak in quietly and sit in the back row. If anybody asks, I'll tell them my mom told me to come."

The gloomy sky and damp air cast an ominous feel over my bright idea, but since the courthouse was so close, I decided we'd come too far to turn back. I pedaled along the cracked sidewalk speckled with bird poop and acorns. Ray bounced up and down on the handlebars.

As we drew closer to the courthouse, I tried to steady my nerves. If I started to panic, Ray would surely crumble and confess our plot to the first authority figure who looked at us too long or with the slightest probing. It was too late, but I started to think I should have chosen my sidekick a little more carefully.

"Bailey, look!" Ray said.

"What?"

"Isn't that a police car coming toward us?"

Sure enough, I could see the black automobile with a rack of lights on top gradually making its way up Third Street. Heat raced up my spine. A sick feeling swept over me. If the police caught us, Daddy would beat the stuffing out of me.

"There's our school marquee," I said, turning left to leave the sidewalk and riding on the marshy low-cut grass.

I pedaled with all the strength I could muster to get to the sign some fifty yards in front of us. When we reached it, I parked the bike behind it, and we hunkered down low, peering out from behind it to watch for the police car. Within a couple of minutes, the black-and-white car cruised by slowly. Neither of the two officers looked our way. Relief washed over me. We remained for a few minutes to regain our composure and make sure the car was gone for good. Then we set out for the last few blocks to get to the courthouse.

We finally turned onto Main Street, the location of the courthouse. After riding one block farther, we reached a tan two-story brick building with broad windows on both the first and second floors. Granite scrolls ran from the bottom to the top of the building on both sides of the dark metal door, giving it a look of grandeur. The ornate crest above it conveyed the seriousness of the business that took place within. We parked Ray's bike behind the building and raced back to the front. He grabbed the bronze handle and pulled the heavy door toward us. My knees suddenly felt like two wet noodles.

We stepped into the foyer, and I looked for the courtroom where Momma's trial was scheduled to take place. People moved about like they were on their way to someplace important, most of them carrying a stack of folders or a briefcase. All of them were white. The men were dressed in suits and the women in suits or dresses. Some of them shot us curious glances, but no one stopped us or asked why we were there. My mouth felt dry, and my tongue stuck to the roof of my mouth. Even if I'd wanted to speak, I couldn't have.

We were fortunate that there was only one courtroom in the building. We followed the arrow that pointed to the courtroom of the Honorable Ezekiel C. Boone III. The white marble hallway led to two wooden double doors at the end. The brass plate on the sign had the judge's name in impressive-looking black letters.

I pushed one of the heavy doors open just as the officer in the court crowed, "All rise. The Honorable Ezekiel Clayton Boone III presiding!"

The officer standing at the door peered down at us with squinting, questioning eyes. Spotting a vacant seat in the back row next to an old Black couple, I quickly ushered Ray to the right and followed him. I couldn't see the judge when he walked into the courtroom, because the people in front of me blocked my view, but I soon heard the loud rap of his gavel.

"You may be seated," he said.

I slid into the smooth wooden bench. My heart thudded hard against my rib cage. I stole a glance toward the officer at the door, half expecting him to be beckoning to me. But he wasn't. To my relief, he'd turned his attention to what was going on in the front of the courtroom.

When everyone had sat down, I could finally get a full view of the room. I'd never been inside a courtroom before. To my surprise, it actually looked a lot like the courtroom on *Perry Mason*, except this one was in color, and *Perry Mason* was in black and white. The judge, dressed in a black robe, sat high up with a big desk that surrounded him as he looked down at something through narrow wire-framed glasses. The American flag, on a silver pole, stood to his left. A wooden-framed picture of President Nixon hung on the wall to his right.

Then I noticed Momma sitting on the left side of the courtroom, across from the judge. Mr. Streeter leaned over and said something to her. Momma nodded. I couldn't see their faces. She wore a navy-blue jacket. There was a slender white man with curly brown hair seated between Mr. Streeter and Momma. I couldn't see his face, either, but I doubted I would have recognized him even if I could.

As I looked around, I could see that there were mostly white people in the courtroom. The few Black people sat in the last two rows, except Daddy, who was in the second row, behind Momma, with Uncle Lance and Uncle Earl.

A tense, uncomfortable silence hung in the air. I wasn't sure what it was—fear, hate, or anger—but it was palpable. Then the judge looked up, the crown of his bald head shining like the hood of a brand-new car. His chubby cheeks jiggled as he gave instructions to the jury while peering over his glasses. The jurors sat on the opposite side of the courtroom from Momma. It seemed like he talked for hours in his dry monotone. I understood some of the information but not most. He spoke at length, explaining the burden of proof. Then he rambled on with an explanation regarding reasonable doubt and best evidence. Overwhelmed by the legal jargon, my mind started to drift, and my head started to bob. As I felt myself slipping into dreamland, Ray's bony elbow jabbed me in the side, and I jumped.

"Who's that?" Ray whispered as the tall, lean white man from the table across the aisle from Momma and Mr. Streeter walked to the center of the room. "The judge said his name is Francis Sutton. Isn't Francis a girl's name?"

"Maybe. But he's the prosecutor. I remember Uncle Earl mentioning him. He goes by Frank, but Francis must be his real name."

With a steely glance, the old Black man next to me cautioned me to be silent. Obligingly, I leaned back in my seat.

Frank Sutton smoothed down his tie and buttoned his suit jacket with an air of self-importance. He looked at the judge, at Mr. Streeter, and then at the twelve people sitting together in the jury box.

"Your Honor, opposing counsel, members of the jury, I'm Francis George Sutton, and I'm representing the State of Miss-sippi in this case against Mrs. Annie Lee Connor in the capital murder of James Tanner Cunningham." Mr. Sutton pronounced Mississippi as though it had three syllables instead of four. "If you would allow me, I want to take you back to a sunny morning in July 1970. James Cunningham sat in his home office at his desk."

The prosecutor laced his hands in front of him. He eyed each of the jury members as he continued to speak. "He probably sipped a cup of coffee as he worked on his financial records for Cunningham & Son Plantation. I can imagine the coffee aroma waftin' in the air. There was a calendar on his desk, and I can envision him taking a red ink pen and drawing circles around a particular date. A special date. September 12, 1970. He drew circles around and around that date." The prosecutor mimicked a circular motion with a pen in his hand.

"Jim Cunningham, as his friends called him, was a man with a bright future. You see, at thirty-four years of age, Jim had everything. He had wealth, good looks, and respect in the community, and he was about to marry." He made the circle again. "On September 12, 1970, Jim Cunningham would marry Ms. Sarah Jane Bingham, the love of his life."

He pointed to the young woman with loose chestnut-brown curls, who sat one row behind the prosecutor's table. She dabbed her face with a white handkerchief. A woman with shoulder-length ginger hair sat next to Sarah Bingham, with an arm around her shoulder. I realized it was Ms. Caroline. Momma and Daddy had talked about how close she and Mr. Jim were. They'd grown up as kids together. Her dad was Mr. Jim's older brother, Beau Cunningham. Momma said Mr. Jim was sure Mr. Beau would become governor of Mississippi one day. I remembered hearing Daddy say Mr. Beau didn't become governor because they found out he liked to dress up in women's clothes.

"Jim Cunningham," Sutton continued, "was about to start a new life with his new bride. And I'm certain they had planned to start a family. But that day and that new life would never happen for Jim Cunningham because, in the early-mornin' hours of July 11, 1970, this woman..." He pointed to Momma. "This woman, Annie Lee Connor, sneaked into Mr. Cunningham's home while he was sleepin' and stabbed him forty-six times in the throat and chest area, severin' his carotid artery, killin' him instantly."

Mr. Sutton walked to his table and took some pictures from a folder. He walked back to the jury and handed the photos to a white woman sitting at the end. Her face became a twisted mask as she glanced at the photos. She looked at all of them then quickly passed them along to the other jurors.

"As you can see from these photographs, this was a most savage and brutal crime," the prosecutor said. "A most horrific display of brutality and debasement."

Shock registered on some of the jurors' faces as they looked at the photographs. Others covered their mouths as if to stifle an outburst. Some of the women wiped away tears that rolled down their cheeks. After the jurors had all looked at the photos, they handed them back to Sutton, and he placed them in his folder.

"Today, you are also gonna hear the testimony of Sarah Jane Bingham, the fiancée of Jim Cunningham, who is gonna to tell you about her discovery of a secret affair that her fiancé was havin' with another woman. That woman's name is Annie Lee Connor, the defendant.

"Later this week, you are gonna hear the testimony from Dr. Karl Edward Vincent, the medical examiner for Washington County and the city of Lowell, Miss-sippi, who will testify about the stab wounds. He will show that the depth of those wounds is consistent with someone of Annie Lee Connor's height and weight. He will tell you that the person who committed this horrific crime weighed between one hundred fifteen pounds and one hundred twenty-five pounds."

Sutton retrieved a single sheet of paper from a folder on his table. Again, he gave the paper to the first juror. "This is a recent copy of

Annie Lee Connor's driver's license. I want to call your attention to Mrs. Connor's weight when the license was issued one year ago. Her weight was one hundred twenty pounds."

The jurors each took a turn looking at the sheet of paper. Sutton walked back to his table and flipped through some documents in another folder as the paper made its way around to all of the jurors. The final juror looked at the page and passed it back to the first juror, who handed it to Sutton. The prosecutor placed it back into the folder on his table.

Sutton walked back over and faced the jury. "Later in the week, you are also gonna hear from Dr. Wesley John McCullough, a clinical psychologist, who will give you a profile of someone who could stab a person repeatedly in just such a violent manner. And he will testify that this kind of murder is a crime of passion. Based upon the testimony of these experts and witnesses, the state will prove beyond a reasonable doubt that Annie Lee Connor killed James Cunningham, in cold blood, committed an act of premeditated murder because of vengeance. Annie Lee Connor was having an affair with Jim Cunningham, and he rejected her because of his upcoming marriage to Sarah Bingham. And we will expect you, the jury, to return a verdict of guilty."

Frank Sutton strode back to the prosecutor's table with a satisfied look on his face and took his seat.

"An affair? What does that mean?" Ray's eyes were owllike behind the Coke-bottle lenses of his glasses.

"Shhh!" I admonished Ray as a couple of people sitting in front of us glanced over their shoulders at us before turning back around.

My stomach twisted into knots. *Was Daddy right about Momma and Mr. Jim? Momma a cold-blooded murderer? Can any of this be true?*

# Chapter 34

I shifted uncomfortably in my seat, having heard Mr. Sutton say all those awful things about Momma. The urge to run to the front of the room and shout at the top of my lungs that they were all lies nearly overwhelmed me. But I knew that would only bring shame to Momma. So I crossed my arms tightly over my chest, pressed myself against the back of the bench, and kept watching the proceedings.

Judge Ezekiel C. Boone III's blue eyes peered over his silver-framed glasses toward the defense table. "Are you ready, Mr. Streeter, to present your opening statement?"

"Yes, Your Honor." Mr. Streeter rose from his seat and, in a similar fashion as Mr. Frank Sutton, buttoned his navy-blue suit jacket and walked to the front of the courtroom. "Your Honor, opposing counsel, and members of the jury, murder is a terrible crime. Murder committed by stabbing a human being forty-six times is a most horrific crime. But this isn't just a trial about a horrific murder. It's a trial about life *and* death. It's about the life and death of James Tanner Cunningham and the life and potential death of Annie Lee Connor." Jonathan walked across the courtroom and stood in front of the jurors.

"I'm Jonathan Streeter, and I'm representing the defendant, Mrs. Annie Lee Connor. When I decided to take this case, I did so with both fear and apprehension. I was afraid then, and I'm afraid now that even with my degrees and the ten years of experience I have as a trial lawyer, I may be ill-equipped to save Annie Lee Connor's life because Mrs. Connor has already been put on trial. She's been tried and found guilty of the crime of being Black. That crime alone has earned many innocent Black men and women a death sentence. And so, as we approach this trial, I ask that you *not* try Annie Lee Connor for the crime of being Black but as an innocent woman fighting for her life—a life that's seen numerous hardships and injustices." Mr. Streeter pressed his fingertips together in front of him, almost prayerlike, and looked toward Momma. "A life that began in 1936 in Indianola, Mississippi. Born Annie Lee Price to parents Levi and Gloria Price, she lived on a plantation with her mother and father, who worked in the fields, picking and chopping cotton, from sunup to sundown.

"The oldest of ten children, Annie was required to drop out of school when she was in the seventh grade and care for the younger children while her parents worked. She worked in the cotton fields in Indianola until she moved to Greenville. In 1952, she was hired as a clerk for a small stationery company. Because of her high math aptitude, she later helped with their books and records. Annie became one of the company's most dependable workers.

"Annie met and married Otis Henry Connor in 1955. They have been married for fifteen years and are the parents of three daughters and a young son. Annie has never been arrested for any crime.

"Now, I'm not going to stand here and try to convince you that Annie is a saint. But she is a devoted wife and mother. On July 10, Annie consumed too much alcohol while she and her brother played records at his apartment. Annie passed out just before midnight and remained at her brother's place until seven o'clock the following morning. Later in the trial, you will hear the testimony of Willie Earl Price, Annie's brother, corroborating Annie's whereabouts and providing a solid alibi for Annie at the time Jim Cunningham was murdered.

"The prosecutor will have you believe that Annie Connor broke into Jim Cunningham's home around one thirty in the morning, stabbed him forty-six times out of vengeance, then sneaked out and disappeared into the darkness. That's what he wants you to believe.

"But what facts will show is there is not a single shred of evidence linking Annie Connor to this crime. There is no motive. There is no murder weapon, and there is no physical evidence of any kind linking my client to this crime. There is not a single eyewitness who can testify that Annie Connor was anywhere near Jim Cunningham's residence at the time of the murder.

"So, what we have, ladies and gentlemen, is a classic case of a rush to judgment. You will hear during the trial that there was no other suspect ever considered, only Annie Connor. No one else was even questioned or interviewed. Did Jim Cunningham have enemies? The sheriff's department didn't consider the possibility. They set their sights on Annie, and that was the end of the investigation rather than the beginning.

"Now, as the defense, we have nothing to prove. The burden of proof lies solely with the state. That means the prosecution has the burden of proving beyond a reasonable doubt the certainty of every piece of evidence they present to you. There can be no weak links. If there is a weak link, the prosecution has not proven its case.

"During our closing argument, we will establish for you how the prosecution has failed on every point to prove their case beyond a reasonable doubt. And we will ask you to do what the evidence demands, and that is to find the defendant, Annie Lee Connor, innocent of the capital murder of James Tanner Cunningham."

Mr. Streeter walked back to the defense table, where Momma sat, and took his seat. He didn't look worried, but neither did he have the same overly confident look that Frank Sutton wore on his face after concluding his opening statement.

The judge removed his glasses and glanced out toward the two lawyers, then the jurors. "We've been into this session for the better part of the morning. Why don't we break for fifteen minutes?" He slammed his gavel, pushed his seat back, and headed toward his chambers in the back of the courtroom.

"All rise!" the bailiff called.

# Chapter 35

"All rise! The court is now back in session. The Honorable Ezekiel C. Boone III presiding," the bailiff said in a gravelly voice.

Ray and I sneaked back into the courtroom after hiding out in the men's bathroom. Judge Boone reentered the courtroom from his chambers and took his seat behind the bench in a high-backed leather chair.

"You may be seated," the judge said. "Mr. Sutton, are you ready to call your first witness?"

"Yes, Your Honor. The state calls Ms. Sarah Jane Bingham."

Ms. Caroline, sitting next to Ms. Sarah, gave her a nod as though to assure her that she would do fine. After rising slowly, Ms. Sarah took unsteady steps toward the witness stand. Every eye in the courtroom was on her. Her light-blue tailored suit fit perfectly on her petite frame. She'd buttoned the ruffled white collar to the top of her neck, giving her the demure look of a true Southern belle. She stopped when she reached the bailiff.

"Place your left hand on the Bible and raise your right hand," he said. "Do you swear to tell the truth, the whole truth, and nothing but the truth, so help you, God?"

"I do."

Loose chestnut curls touched Ms. Sarah's shoulders. She had trimmed bangs and high cheekbones. Even with her puffy eyes and a red nose, I thought Ms. Sarah was very pretty.

"You may be seated."

Mr. Sutton rose from his seat and approached the witness. Standing in front of her, he rested an arm on the witness stand. "You are Sarah Jane Bingham, are you not?"

"Yes, I am." Her fragile voice carried a slight Southern drawl.

"Ms. Bingham, I know this is difficult to talk about, but I have to ask you: what was your relationship to James Cunningham?"

"Jim was my fiancé."

"And how long were the two of you together as a couple?"

"We dated for two years. We got engaged on Valentine's Day, and we were going to be married this September." She brushed away a stray tear.

"You had planned to get married on September 12 of this year. Is that correct?" he asked.

"Yes, sir."

"Ms. Bingham, can you think of anyone who would have a reason to harm Jim Cunningham?"

"Yes, sir."

"Is that person in the courtroom today?" Mr. Sutton asked.

"Yes, sir." She pointed at Annie Lee and shot a hateful glance in her direction. "That woman over there. She worked for Jim and enticed him into a sordid affair."

"Let the record show that the witness has identified Annie Lee Connor. I have no further questions, Your Honor."

"Mr. Streeter, your witness," Judge Boone said.

Mr. Streeter stood and buttoned his suit jacket. He walked toward Ms. Sarah Bingham, who dabbed at her cheeks with a tissue. He stopped several feet in front of the witness stand, lacing his fingers in front of him.

"Ms. Bingham, do you have any proof that my client had an affair with Jim Cunningham?" Mr. Streeter asked.

"No, sir, but a woman knows these things," she said, flicking her bangs from her face.

Mr. Streeter walked toward the jury then turned to face the witness. "You said a woman knows these things. Then were you aware, Ms. Bingham, that your fiancé was having a year-long relationship with an elementary school teacher named Rebecca Reed until three months ago?"

Ms. Sarah's mouth flew open.

Frank Sutton surged from his chair. "Objection, Your Honor. Jim Cunningham is not on trial here today."

The judge removed his glasses and gazed intently at Mr. Streeter. His words were edged with steel. "Counselor, you're out of order. I will not tolerate this kind of tomfoolery in my courtroom. The jury will disregard Mr. Streeter's last question."

"Withdrawn, Your Honor," Mr. Streeter said. "Ms. Bingham, were you aware that Jim Cunningham was sleeping with three other women in Washington county besides yourself during most of your courtship?"

"Objection, Your Honor!"

"How did that make you feel, Ms. Bingham," Mr. Streeter continued, "knowing that your fiancé was cheating on you with half the women in the county? Betrayed? Angry? Angry enough to kill him?"

Covering her face, Ms. Sarah broke into sobs. Loud chatter erupted in the courtroom.

Judge Boone pounded insistently with his gavel. "Mr. Streeter, in my chambers! Court will recess one hour for lunch. The witness may step down."

As people stood all around me, I knew it was time for Ray and me to make our move to leave the courtroom. I couldn't help but think that Mr. Streeter had been very mean to Ms. Sarah, who'd already been crying. Suddenly, he seemed like the bad guy. But how could that be when he was defending Momma? Court was very confusing.

## Chapter 36

"Come on!" I said to Ray as I scooted from the bench, hoping neither Momma nor Daddy had caught a glimpse of me.

I bolted for the exit, and Ray followed right on my heels. My heart pounded louder than that judge's gavel as we exited the courtroom. Our speedy escape was hindered by grown-ups who moved about as leisurely as a bunch of cats strolling down an alley. As we skittered around them, it seemed the hallway extended itself with every step. When we finally turned the corner and entered the lobby, I had a sudden urge to break for the door, but I knew running would be a telltale sign we were up to no good.

*Just be calm—only a few more steps.*

When I pushed the door open, I welcomed the burst of warm air, which graciously conferred the safety of the outside world upon us. Ray and I raced to the back of the building to retrieve his bicycle. We hopped on, and I pedaled as hard as I could to put distance between us and our adolescent antics.

"You can slow down, Bailey," Ray finally said after several blocks. He must have heard me huffing and puffing. "I think we're at a safe distance now."

"Okay." My heart still pounded, but this time, it was from the frantic pace of pedaling hard for two blocks.

"I'm thirsty. Let's go get something to drink," Ray said.

"Yeah, I'm a little hungry too. I know a place. It's in Black Dog, not too far from our school."

"Okay, let's go." Ray paused. "Bailey, I sure wouldn't want to be in your momma's place right now. You don't reckon she killed that Mr. Cunningham, do you? And what did that man say about your momma? The... affair. What does that mean? And is that true?"

I jammed the brakes hard. The momentum swung Ray around, and he jumped from the handlebars.

"No, she didn't kill him, and you keep my momma's name out of your mouth! You hear?" Locking eyes with Ray, I could feel my temples start to pulsate. "And you'd better not mention anything that went on in that courtroom today either."

"Yeah, all right." Ray pushed up his glasses. "I didn't mean nothing by it."

"Swear you won't say anything."

"Okay. Cross my heart and hope to die, stick a needle in my eye."

"All right. Let's go."

I got off the bike, too, and we continued to walk side by side up the sidewalk. After a moment, I broke the silence. "Momma's so lucky she's got Mr. Streeter as her lawyer. He's really smart, and he seems fearless. He doesn't believe Momma killed Mr. Jim either. That's why he took the case."

"That other lawyer sure thinks she done it. The white lawyer."

"Yeah, seems like it." As I looked ahead, I saw the beige brick of the school just two blocks away. "We're not too far from the restaurant now."

"Do you think your momma's scared? She's a Black woman on trial for killing a white man. And she's surrounded by nothing but white people in the courtroom. I know I'd be scared."

"I'm sure she's probably a little scared," I said. "You know, one time I heard Uncle Earl say that in America, the life of a negro ain't worth a whistle."

"What did he mean by that?"

"Did you ever hear of Emmett Till?"

"No, who is he?"

"He was the Black boy that a group of white men beat to death and cut off his privates because he supposedly whistled at a white woman. It happened around 1955 or '56, I think."

"For real? For whistling at somebody?" Ray asked.

"Yeah."

"And they think your momma actually killed a white man. That's a whole lot worse than just whistling."

"You know what else is bad? There is only one Black person on the jury. That lady sitting in the middle."

"So? What does that matter?" Ray asked.

"Weren't you listening to Mr. Streeter? He said since Momma was already tried and convicted of being Black, by the white people, she's automatically guilty of any other crime she's accused of."

"Boy, that's messed up. So, how many white people on the jury do you think will be on your momma's side?"

"I don't know."

"How many have to be on her side for her to go free?"

"All of them."

"All of 'em?"

"Yep. And the Black lady."

"I hate to say it, Bailey, but your momma is in big trouble."

"I know."

We finally reached the restaurant and hid the bicycle behind it. We walked up to the front of the yellow building and stepped inside.

# Chapter 37

Jonathan Streeter exited the courthouse, flanked by Titus Jones, his investigator, and Scott Jacoby, his law clerk. A media circus had erupted outside, with flashbulbs popping, cameras angled toward Jonathan, and microphones thrust in his face as reporters from local, national, and international news networks swarmed around him to get the first update of the sensational murder trial. A substantial crowd had formed in front of the courthouse, as well, creating an electric charge in the air.

Black people waved signs in the air, chanting, "Free Annie Lee! Free Annie Lee!"

The white crowd raised signs, waved Confederate flags, and shouted, "Fry, nigger, fry! Fry, nigger, fry!"

Law enforcement officers from the Greenville and Lowell police departments and the Washington County Sheriff's Department worked aggressively to keep the two highly agitated groups separated. Over the noise, reporters shouted a barrage of questions at Jonathan in rapid succession.

"Mr. Streeter, do you think a Black woman in Lowell can get a fair trial for killing a white man?"

"Mr. Streeter, what is your strategy for saving the life of a Black woman in the deep South?"

"Will Annie Connor go to the electric chair, Mr. Streeter?"

Jonathan stepped onto the sidewalk. He looked into the camera directly in front of him. Reporters thrust their microphones in all shapes and sizes near his face. Camera shutters clicked. He cleared his throat. As he began to speak, the noise of the crowd leveled.

"Today, a woman is on trial for her life. She is a Black woman being tried for killing a white man. My client is innocent of committing this crime, and we will prove her innocence. I believe in our country's justice system, and I believe Annie Lee Connor will get a fair trial in Lowell, Mississippi. When it's all said and done, she'll walk away a free woman. I have no further comments. Thank you very much."

Jonathan politely pushed the microphones from his face as he made his way past the throng of reporters and camera tripods. Several reporters followed him, lobbing more questions. He kept his same steady pace until he and his two companions reached his vehicle and climbed inside. He pulled away from the curb, leaving a throng of reporters behind.

Jonathan drove about a quarter of a mile east of downtown Lowell to a subdivision known as Black Dog. It occurred to him that when he was younger, he'd never thought to ask how the neighborhood got its name. Within a few minutes, he pulled into a parking lot next to a small yellow wood-framed building, with Freeman's Desserts and Exquisite Dining in bold, colorful, hand-painted strokes on the two large front-facing windows.

The owner and original cook, Evelyn Freeman, was around eighty-five years old and disabled. She and her husband, Ernest, had moved to Lowell from Baton Rouge in the late 1940s and opened the small restaurant. Ernest died from a stroke in 1958. Since the late sixties, the couple's son and daughter had run the restaurant and successfully maintained the high standard Evelyn and Ernest had established some thirty years prior.

When Jonathan, along with Titus and Scott, entered the cozy eatery with ten dining tables and chairs, bright-orange walls, and African artwork, he noticed the restaurant had changed very little since his last visit. As always, the sweet smell of freshly baked desserts and Southern fried chicken never failed to trigger hunger pangs. Jonathan sighed with relief, spotting a single open table near the back of the restaurant. He didn't have time for a long wait, nor did he have the inclination to dine elsewhere. A girl with honey-colored skin and perfectly round Afro puffs greeted them with a smile.

"Good afternoon, welcome to Freeman's. Three for lunch?"

"Yes," Jonathan replied.

"Follow me, please."

The three men walked across the checkerboard-tiled floor to the table. As he passed the glass dessert-display case, Jonathan glanced at scrumptious-looking pecan pies, sweet potato pies, a five-layer chocolate cake, and a flaky white coconut cake.

Most patrons talked quietly over Al Green's soulful crooning of "Let's Stay Together," not taking a second look at the newcomers, while others gawked at them. Two young boys sat at a table, sipping soft drinks through straws and sharing a rather large slice of coconut cake. They watched the trio pass, and Jonathan gave them a nod. He thought back to the last time he'd eaten at Freeman's—probably Christmas his senior year of high school. Since leaving Lowell, he'd compared every other soul food restaurant to Freeman's, and they'd always come up short.

"This food smells like heaven," Scott said. "How did you find this place?"

"You forget I'm from around here. This restaurant has been here for decades, but it's been a long time since I've been here—maybe twenty years."

"If the food tastes as good as it smells, I may never leave."

"Then you might want to figure out your sleeping accommodations," Titus said to Scott with a chuckle.

As a retired sheriff from the Washington County Sheriff's Department, Titus had gotten to know many of Lowell's citizens. After retiring from the department and opening his own private investigator agency, he'd gained a few extra pounds and was an imposing figure at six feet, four inches tall, with skin as dark as midnight. And at forty-two, he was in exceptionally good shape.

The waitress with the Afro puffs waited for the men to be seated. Jonathan shed his coat and draped it across the back of his chair. The other men did likewise. Titus sat across from Jonathan, and Scott sat to his right.

"I'm Tess, and I'll be serving you today. Can I start by taking your drink orders?"

"Go ahead," Jonathan said to Scott.

Scott Jacoby had started working on his law degree at Delta State University. He wanted to gain some experience as a trial lawyer, so he'd taken a year off to assist in court cases. With green eyes and curly brown hair, Scott would ordinarily stick out like a sore thumb in this part of town—an all-Black community—except that Freeman's was frequented by as many white patrons as Black. Scott was quite at home in a mixed crowd. His father, Harvey Jacoby, had been a prominent civil rights attorney who'd started his career serving with the Southern Christian Leadership Conference during the height of the Civil Rights Movement. He'd even participated in sit-ins and marches. He was almost killed in one of the demonstrations when an angry white mob attacked them. But it never weakened Harvey Jacoby's resolve to continue fighting for civil rights for Black people.

"I'll have a Dr. Pepper," Scott said.

"Coke for me," Titus added.

"The same," Jonathan said.

"I'll be right back with your drinks and to take your food requests."

"Thank you," Scott replied to the waitress. He turned to Jonathan. "Can I ask you a question?"

"Sure, Scott. What is it?"

"Why did you go after Ms. Bingham so hard in the courtroom earlier? I mean, since she's grieving and all, won't the jury be sympathetic toward her and maybe dislike you because of the way you... handled her?"

"Possibly." Jonathan paused when the waitress approached and placed a red plastic basket on the table, filled with fluffy biscuits, golden-brown hot-water cornbread, and two small dishes of honey butter. He picked up one of the biscuits and spread a generous amount of butter on it then took a bite, savoring the sweet and salty flavors. "As I was saying, there's a possibility I may have alienated the jury just a bit, but we have a long way to go. And I'm sure I can make up whatever ground I might have lost in the long run."

"So why even do it?" Scott asked, reaching for the cornbread.

"It was necessary. The battle lines had to be drawn right up front. Frank Sutton needed to know that we came to play hardball. Every witness. Every piece of evidence. We came to fight, and we came to win. I also wanted to offer the jury another possible motive for Jim Cunningham's murder—an angry fiancée who'd been cheated on several times. What's the saying? Hell has no fury like a woman scorned. Well, my intention was to plant a seed of doubt early. If necessary, I may have to make it sprout and grow into something the jury can see for themselves."

"That makes sense." Scott bit into the warm bread. He munched greedily. "My goodness, this is delicious. Can we get some more of these? One basket won't be enough."

Jonathan chuckled. "I'm sure we can get more."

He grabbed three of the single-page laminated menus stacked between the silver napkin holder and the salt and pepper shakers. After handing a menu to Scott and Titus, he perused the front and back of his. *Fried pickles. Fried green beans. Some things do change.*

"I think you ticked off Judge Boone too," Titus said, flipping the menu over after reading the front. "He must have given you *some* tongue-lashing when he called you into his chambers."

"Wasn't too bad. I've grown a pretty tough hide over the years. I'm not that worried about Judge Boone." Jonathan scoffed down the remainder of the biscuit. "I'm more concerned about the witnesses Sutton will place on the stand. We've got to discredit each one or find an expert in the same field who's equally or more qualified to counter their testimonies. And we need to find Jim Cunningham's enemies."

"You're assuming he had some," Titus said. "From everything I've heard, he was a pretty cool cat."

"A man with that much money always has enemies. Someone's always looking for a way to knock a rich joker like Cunningham off his perch *and* steal his money bag."

"Yeah, you're right about that." Titus reached for a piece of hot-water cornbread.

"We also need to look into his finances for any irregularities. Find out who will inherit his fortune. Could be another motive," Jonathan said.

"And here I thought Sarah Bingham was crying because Mr. Cunningham had been killed. Now I think she was crying because she won't be getting any of that Cunningham fortune. Shucks, I'd be crying too." Scott laughed, and so did the other men.

The waitress returned and placed tall plastic tumblers filled with sodas over ice in front of the men. "Are you ready to order?"

"Yes," Scott said enthusiastically. He read off his order. "And can we have some more of those cornbread thingies... whatever you call them?"

"Sure, I can bring some more hot-water cornbread." The waitress smiled as she took the other two orders without writing a single word then headed to the kitchen. After a few minutes, an older, heavy-set

Black woman brought out two plates. She had a short salt-and-pepper Afro and wore a white apron.

"Pork chops, turnip greens, and yams?"

"That's mine." Titus rubbed his dark hands together in anticipation.

"Fried chicken, macaroni and cheese, and cabbage?"

"Right here," Scott said.

"Mr. Streeter, I'll be right back with your meal. The meatloaf was just coming out of the oven," the woman said apologetically. She must have recognized Jonathan from the news.

"No problem," Jonathan assured her with an easy smile.

Moments later, the woman returned and placed a plate in front of Jonathan, piled high with meatloaf, a mound of mashed potatoes, and collard greens. "I'll be back with more bread. Enjoy." She turned on stubby legs and headed back to the kitchen.

Jonathan ate a forkful of meatloaf and allowed the savory dish to satisfy his taste buds. There was little talking as the men devoured their food. They'd almost finished eating when an engine roared loudly outside. A thunderous crash followed. Large shards of glass exploded inside the restaurant. High beams washed the back walls.

Shielding their eyes from the headlights as they emerged from the back, the two waitresses were struck by the eighteen-wheeler's cab, which crushed and pinned them against the dessert display. The cab came to a stop in the center of the dining room.

There was no driver.

Fluorescent lights flickered.

Chunks of sheetrock fell from the ceiling like giant snowflakes.

Loud screams erupted.

Jonathan leaped to his feet, scanning the horrific scene in disbelief. His heart raced a hundred beats per second. His mind switched to damage control. Tossing debris aside, he raced toward the truck. Titus surged from his seat, instinctively drawing his weapon. Scott stood frozen, his eyes bright and blinking rapidly. Patrons scrambled to their feet. Fear paralyzed them. Panic-stricken faces looked about.

"Everyone, out!" Jonathan waved frantically. His nostrils burned from the pungent smell of diesel fuel. His heart pounded rapidly. He threw the vehicle in reverse and hit the gas.

"Scott, get out of here! Titus, get those two boys out of here!" Exiting the vehicle, Jonathan flipped wood debris and metal pipes, stumbling toward the women.

A tall Black man in a stained apron emerged from the back. He recoiled, seeing the headlights and the devastation. Jonathan motioned for him.

When they reached the older woman, Jonathan checked for a pulse. *She's gone.* The younger woman lay next to her. Her eyes became huge and glassy. Her lips and chin trembled uncontrollably. Blood oozed from a cut on her forehead. Tears ran down her cheeks.

"Hold on. We're going to get you out of here," Jonathan said.

Titus lifted the two boys under his arms and made his way to the exit. "Jon, you need to hurry. This truck is going to blow."

The man in the apron helped Jonathan lift wood and metal pieces that trapped the young woman. One leg had been crushed, white bone exposed. The men carried the girl between them, stepping haphazardly on pieces of broken dishes, shattered glass, and twisted metal. They reached the street and continued to walk several blocks to distance themselves from the building, which had started to burn. Finally, they stopped and eased the woman onto the ground. Restaurant patrons looked on in horror as a red fireball ripped through the restaurant ceiling. The blast echoed violently into the sky. Plumes of smoke billowed, forming gigantic gray clouds. Flames shot from the gaping hole where the front door had stood. The wood frame erupted, splintering into a thousand pieces.

A single fire truck arrived with lights flashing and sirens blaring. The firemen descended quickly and began spraying a gush of water on the building. Jonathan looked down at the two boys standing near them. They looked visibly shaken, and one of them had started to cry.

He turned to the one who wasn't crying. "What's your name, son?"

"Bailey Connor."

"Do you live around here, Bailey? Did you say Connor? Are you related to Annie Connor?"

"She's my mother."

"How did you get downtown?" Jonathan asked.

"We rode my friend's bike. We left it behind the building."

"Were you at the trial?"

"Yes... yes, sir."

"Okay. I'll give you boys a ride home after the court proceedings end today. I've got to be back there within a matter of minutes, so you'll have to come with me. I don't know what condition your friend's bike will be in once the fire is extinguished, but I'll come back and get it."

Jonathan glanced at Scott. The color had drained from his face. He coughed into his fist. They'd all been inhaling caustic smoke fumes from the burning debris and charred rubber.

Titus stroked his goatee and locked eyes with Jonathan. "That calling card was for you, Jon."

Jonathan looked down at his hand. Blood flowed from a cut, dripping onto the sidewalk. He removed his tie and wrapped it around the wound. A heavy frown settled on his face, accompanied by the all-too-familiar clawing at the back of his throat.

He swallowed hard. "I know."

# Chapter 38

The firefighters put out the fire but not before Freeman's restaurant had burned completely to the ground. The older lady had died in the crash, and the younger one had to be taken to the hospital. Everyone else made it out okay thanks to the quick actions of Mr. Streeter and his cousin, Mr. Titus Jones, who carried Ray and me outside to safety.

What a day it had been. First, we'd watched Mr. Streeter in the courtroom performing like a maestro skillfully conducting an orchestra, and then we'd almost been trapped in a burning inferno. But my day wasn't over yet. I had to face someone who would be more frightening than a raging fire—my daddy. I was afraid if he found out I'd sneaked into the courtroom and later almost gotten killed in a fire, he would beat the life out of me.

The trial wasn't over for that day. Mr. Streeter had to return that afternoon to finish, and Ray and I had to go back with him because the bicycle was still behind the restaurant. The paramedics wrapped his hand in a white cloth to stop the bleeding from the cut he got from a piece of broken glass.

When we entered the courtroom, everyone had taken their seats, including the judge. He sat up high and looked down at Mr. Streeter as he walked to the defense table. "Awfully nice of you to join us, Mr. Streeter."

"My apologies to the court, Your Honor. There was a fire at the restaurant where we had lunch."

"A tragic incident, I'm sure, but we must be diligent about getting on with the court's business. Therefore, I expect you to be prompt when you enter my courtroom, Counselor."

"Yes, Your Honor."

"Is the prosecution ready to call your next witness?" Judge Boone asked.

"Yes, Your Honor. The state calls Dr. Karl E. Vincent."

Dr. Vincent rose and lumbered to the witness stand. His brown-and-beige glen plaid suit was loosely draped over his tall, lean frame. After being sworn in by the bailiff, Dr. Vincent sat as straight as a board. He swept a hand across his parted brown hair and watched through silver-framed teardrop glasses as Mr. Sutton approached.

He stopped several paces in front of the witness. "Good afternoon, sir. Would you please state your full name for the record?"

"I'm Dr. Karl Edward Vincent."

"What is your profession, Dr. Vincent?"

"I am the medical examiner for Washington County in the state of Mississippi."

"Dr. Vincent, how long have you been the medical examiner for Washington County in the state of Miss-sippi?" Sutton asked.

"For twenty-five years, sir."

"And what are your duties as the medical examiner, Dr. Vincent?"

"My duty is to determine the cause of death of victims, whether natural, accidental, or intentional."

"Doctor, when were you notified of James Cunningham's death?" the prosecutor asked.

"I was contacted by the sheriff's department on Saturday, July 11, at eight o'clock in the morning. I arrived at the decedent's home at eight thirty in the morning."

"Did you examine the body?"

"I did a preliminary examination at the scene and a thorough examination when the body was brought to the morgue."

"Would you please describe for the court the scene you found when you arrived at the decedent's home?" Mr. Sutton asked.

"Certainly. I found a deceased white male who appeared to be in his early- to mid-thirties, covered in a pool of blood, lying face up in his bed, with multiple stab wounds in his face, upper torso, and neck area."

"And could you determine the cause of death?"

"The deceased died from a loss of blood due to the severing of his carotid artery."

"Dr. Vincent, would you describe the nature of the injuries sustained by the deceased?"

The witness nodded. "As I said, the deceased was stabbed multiple times in his face, upper torso, and neck area. The wounds were made with a sharp instrument. More than likely, it was a hunting knife or similar, with a four- or five-inch blade."

"How many times was the victim stabbed, Dr. Vincent?" the prosecutor asked.

"Forty-six times."

Mumbling erupted in the courtroom.

"Order," the judge said, rapping with his gavel.

When the room was quiet, Sutton continued. "Did the wounds, Doctor, suggest anything about the killer, her height or weight?"

Jonathan pushed up from his seat. "Objection, foundational, Your Honor. No evidence has been produced that supports that the killer is a woman."

"Sustained," Judge Boone said.

"I'll rephrase the question, Your Honor. In your professional opinion, Doctor, what conclusions can you draw about the killer, based on the stab wounds?"

"Based on the deep thrust of the weapon and the depth of the wounds, in my professional opinion, the killer was more than likely a female between one hundred fifteen and one hundred twenty-five pounds."

Mr. Sutton walked to his table, pulled out a transparency, placed it on the overhead projector, and pushed a button. When the light came on, it projected the image of Momma's driver's license onto the screen. My heart started beating erratically.

"I will remind the court that this is the driver's license of Annie Connor, taken just thirteen months ago." Mr. Sutton took the pointer and pointed to Momma's weight then circled it on the transparency. "At the time this license was issued on August 9, 1968, Annie Lee Connor weighed one hundred twenty pounds."

Intense chatter arose in the courtroom. The juror who sat at the end scribbled notes in her notebook.

I wanted to scream, "Y'all leave my momma alone! She didn't do this terrible thing!"

Judge Boone rapped with his gavel several times. "Order. Order in the court." He waited for the chatter to subside. "Continue, Counselor."

"Based on the wounds, Doctor, can you tell whether the killer was right- or left-handed?"

"From the direction of the wounds, I'm almost one hundred percent certain the killer was right-handed."

"Dr. Vincent, compared to other victims you've examined who suffered a violent death, how would categorize this one?" Mr. Sutton asked.

"This is by far the most violent act of brutality I've seen. The attacker punctured the victim's major organs, including his heart and both of his lungs. If James Cunningham had not died from the severing of his carotid artery, he would have certainly bled to death within the hour from massive blood loss from the other stab wounds."

"Dr. Vincent, did you determine Jim Cunningham's time of death?"

"I did. I examined the body at eight thirty a.m., and I estimated that he'd been dead for approximately seven hours, making the time of death one thirty a.m. Allowing a half hour each way, for the fluctuations of temperature, this establishes his death within the time bracket of one to two a.m."

"Thank you, Doctor. Your witness, Counselor," Mr. Sutton said to Mr. Streeter.

"I have no questions at this time, Your Honor, but I reserve the right to recall the witness at a later time."

"Very well, the witness may step down. Let's take a fifteen-minute recess," the judge said.

"All rise," the bailiff said.

People filed out of the courtroom, undoubtedly exchanging comments about the doctor's testimony.

*How could anyone think Momma could do such a terrible thing as stab Mr. Jim all those times? They don't know her like I do. In fact, they don't know her at all.*

I swallowed a lump in my throat and batted away the tears that stung my eyes. Mr. Streeter scribbled something on his legal pad then turned to speak to Momma. I took that as the cue for Ray and me to make our escape before Momma looked back and saw me. I'd heard enough of the prosecutor and his witnesses bad-mouthing Momma.

# Chapter 39

Ray and I left the courthouse and waited outside on the curb near Mr. Streeter's car, which was in the courthouse parking lot. Mr. Streeter had said he'd give us a ride home because of the traumatic events of the day, and we no longer had the bicycle. He was right—I still felt nervous and a little sad about the restaurant burning to the ground. The owners had lost their family business, which they'd worked hard for. Even though I wanted to cry, I didn't. Ray, on the other hand, cried as though his family owned the restaurant.

After an hour or so, we watched Mr. Titus Jones climb into his sporty black Mustang and speed from the parking lot. Scott Jacoby left shortly after him, in his shiny candy-apple-red Volkswagen. Not long after that, Mr. Streeter exited the courthouse and made his way to where we were. He unlocked the car doors and told us to get in.

We dusted our pants off, and I sat in the front seat next to Mr. Streeter. Ray climbed into the back. For a time, no one said anything, just listened to the radio. I almost forgot how much trouble I would be in once I made it home. I simply enjoyed the smooth, comfortable ride and the delightful smell of a brand-new car. Mr. Streeter went back to Black Dog to pick up Ray's bicycle, which was covered in soot from the fire, and the tires looked like burned pieces of bacon. Ray had a terror-stricken look on his face. He'd probably be in a lot of trouble because his parents didn't know he would be anywhere near a burning building. His charred bicycle would give up his secret quicker than a dog could slap a tick. I felt really bad for Ray because it would be all my fault if he got punished.

Mr. Streeter dropped Ray off and placed his bicycle next to his front porch, then we headed toward my home. After a moment of silence, Mr. Streeter glanced over at me. "Bailey, are you okay?"

"Yes, sir."

"Did your mom know you'd be in the courtroom today?"

"No, sir."

"Did your dad know?" he asked.

"No, sir."

"When I drop you off, you do know your dad will probably figure it out."

"I know."

"How do you feel about that?" Mr. Streeter asked.

"Scared."

"You think he'll punish you?"

"He'll probably beat the stew out of me," I said.

"Maybe he won't be that upset."

"You don't know my daddy." We rode in silence for a while. "Mr. Streeter, can I ask you a question?"

"Sure, Bailey, what is it?"

"How do you know my momma?"

"We went to school together a long time ago. Fourth through the seventh grade. She was one of the smartest people I knew."

"Smarter than you?" I asked.

"Yep, smarter than me."

"Can I ask you another question?"

"Sure, go ahead."

"Why do people hate my momma and say all those mean things about her?"

"That's the twenty-thousand-dollar question, Bailey. People hate out of fear, jealousy, ignorance. Now, the question you should really ask is why they accused your mother of this crime. And the answer could be those three things—fear, jealousy, and ignorance. But there's also convenience. It was convenient for certain people to point the finger at your mother because she's a woman, she's Black, and they felt she would be defenseless. An easy target."

"But you're helping her, and you won't let her go to prison, right?"

"Bailey, I'm going to do everything in my power to see to it that your mother doesn't see one day in prison. You have my word on that."

For the first time since Momma's arrest, my breath didn't get caught in my chest when I talked about her. "Mr. Streeter, can I ask you one more question?"

"Sure."

"Are you rich?"

Mr. Streeter chuckled. "No, I wouldn't say that I'm rich. But I would say I have a good job that pays pretty well."

"Do you like being a lawyer?"

"Most of the time."

"Why not all of the time?" I asked.

"Because sometimes our justice system is manipulated to the advantage of some and the disadvantage of others. What I mean is that Black people go to prison for crimes they didn't commit more often than any other race, and our justice system should not allow that to happen. And that's why I became a lawyer—to make sure the Black people I represent get a fair trial."

"I have one last question."

"Bailey, you ask a lot of questions. You might consider becoming a lawyer when you grow up." Mr. Streeter chuckled.

I hadn't considered becoming a lawyer before, but since I'd never become a doctor, maybe I would consider it. "Mr. Streeter, do you dislike Mr. Sutton for what he's saying about Momma?"

"The prosecutor? No, I don't dislike him, Bailey. He's doing his job. I just have to do mine better."

As we turned into our driveway it was nearing six o'clock, and the sun still hung high in the evening sky.

Mr. Streeter turned to me. "Well, it's time to pay the piper. You want me to go inside with you and explain to your dad where you've been?"

"Um... no, I don't think so."

"Okay."

When Mr. Streeter parked behind Daddy's Volkswagen, my heart started to pound wildly in my chest. There was Daddy, sitting on the front porch, smoking a cigarette, with a half-full pint of liquor at his side. Mr. Streeter put the car in park, and I thanked him for giving me a ride home. As I stepped out of the vehicle on legs as weak as Kool-Aid, Daddy rose and stubbed his cigarette out on the bottom step with the toe of his shoe.

Before I could utter a word, he had made his way to Mr. Streeter's car. Fire blazed in his eyes. "What the hell you doin' with my son?"

Mr. Streeter opened his car door and stood facing Daddy. "I gave Bailey a ride home."

"Home from where? Jo said he went to the store. That was four hours ago."

"I... I... I went to the courthouse to see Momma's trial."

"You done what? Boy, have you lost your damn mind? Do you know how dangerous it is for a colored child to be ridin' a bike on the streets of Lowell?"

"I wasn't by myself though, Daddy. Ray Martin rode with—"

"Shut the hell up! Don't say another word, or I'll knock you into the middle of next week! I been everywhere lookin' for yo' li'l ass. Wit' white folk mad over Jim bein' kilt, you coulda been strung up just to make a point. If I ever hear of you goin' anywhere again without my say-so, you gon' be sorry you was born. Now, gone on in the house. I'll deal wit' you later."

"Otis, go easy on the boy, he—"

"Listen here, nigga—you in yo' high-dollar suit and fancy car. Just b'cause you helpin' my wife wit' her case, don't give you no right to tell me how to run my family. I didn't ask for yo' advice, and I don't need it. Now, get the hell off my prop'ty and stay the hell away from my boy."

Mr. Streeter threw up his hands, got back into his car, and backed out of the driveway. I prayed that when Daddy had said he'd deal with me later, that meant tomorrow, after he'd cooled off, and not within the next few minutes, while he was still hotter than a Fourth of July firecracker.

# Chapter 40

Titus Jones took the two-hour-and-fifteen-minute drive northeast on Highway 287 to Oxford, Mississippi, on Friday at around ten in the morning. He checked Caroline Cunningham's background and learned she'd attended Ole Miss in the fall of 1954 after graduating from Lowell High School. After college, Caroline returned to Lowell in 1960 but moved to Oxford permanently after her mother and father died in a car accident in 1962. She moved into the family estate and worked as an interior decorator.

Titus turned off Highway 287 onto Highway 7 and drove six miles before exiting onto Canyon Run Road, a winding two-lane road bracketed by towering trees. He drove a couple more miles before the two cups of coffee and glass of orange juice he'd consumed a few hours earlier forced him to think about the absolute necessity of relieving himself. There had been no homes, much less service stations, for over an hour, and not knowing how much farther it the Cunningham Estate was, he couldn't wait. He thought with amusement about what Caroline's expression would be if he asked to use one of the bathrooms in her mansion.

Titus eased the Mustang GT to the side of the road near a stand of tall oaks, glanced about, and decided to take a chance. He got out, walked around to the backside of the largest tree, and, satisfied he was shielded from view, took care of business. Back at his car, Titus took a towel from his glove box and wiped the dust off his black leather shoes, almost restoring them to their original shine, then he got back into the driver's seat and drove on. Eventually, he came to a circular driveway fronting an imposing two-story Greek Revival mansion. He cruised to a stop, shifted the car into park, and let out a low whistle.

"So, this is what old money looks like." He killed the Mustang's engine and stepped out.

After retrieving his navy-blue suit jacket from the back seat, he slipped it on and ambled toward the imposing off-white structure, admiring its beauty. The eight thick white columns flanking the entrance, ornate banisters, and tall windows with dark-green shutters reminded him of the antebellum plantation houses customary in the South.

As he walked, the heels of his black leather wing tips click-clacked against the polished brick pavers leading to the front door. He adjusted his tie then rang the doorbell. A petite woman with short salt-and-pepper hair combed neatly away from her face answered the door. She wore a black dress and a white apron. A touch of pink lipstick complemented her ebony skin. Her expression was one of brief confusion that quickly changed to delight as though she'd made the connection as to who the cocoa-brown hulk of a man was.

"May I help you, sir?" Her expression remained pleasant.

"I'm Titus Jones, a private investigator working with Attorney Jonathan Streeter. I'm here to see Ms. Caroline Cunningham."

"Pleased to make your acquaintance, Mr. Jones. I'm Ruthie Nettles, Ms. Cunningham's housekeeper." She extended her hand, and Titus's huge hand enveloped hers like a catcher's mitt over a baseball. "Ms. Cunningham is expecting you. But would you be so kind as to go around to the side entrance, please? I'll meet you there."

"Yes, ma'am." Titus smiled as he turned and retraced his steps back to the circular driveway, which curved around to the left side of the house, facing a detached three-car garage.

Even dressed in his Sunday best, Titus was not surprised he wasn't allowed entry through the front door of the house of a white person. He understood he was a Black man in the deep South, but it stung. Reaching the side entrance, he rapped on the door and was greeted by Ruthie Nettles.

"Please come in, Mr. Jones, and follow me." Ruthie led him across a white marble entry, past a curving staircase, and into a cherry-wood-paneled library. "May I get you something to drink?"

"No, ma'am. I'm fine."

"Ms. Cunningham will be right with you."

"Thank you." Titus marveled at the richness of the furnishings. He knew just enough to know that while the oriental rugs, marble-topped bar, massive oak desk, and leather chair weren't new, they were definitely expensive. Ornately framed pictures of family members, dating back to the turn of the century, accented the walls. Hearing the click of approaching heels, he turned his attention to the doorway.

"Good afternoon, Mr. Jones." Caroline Cunningham held a half-full whiskey glass in one hand and a lighted cigarette in the other. Her green-eyed stare was unflinching as she took a long drag of her cigarette and slowly blew out the smoke. "Please, have a seat." She crossed the room, ground her cigarette into a crystal ashtray on the oversized maple coffee table, then sank into a nearby Queen Anne chair and crossed her legs at the ankles.

"I appreciate you taking the time to see me." Titus took a seat on the sofa facing Caroline's chair.

"What can I do for you, Mr. Jones?" She took a sip of her drink and set the glass on a gold monogrammed coaster. "I must warn you that I may not be much help, considering you work for the man who's representing my cousin's killer."

"Accused killer, and yes, ma'am, I do understand your position. We're only trying to get at the truth. I'm sure you can appreciate that."

"Certainly, but from where I'm sitting, it appears the woman who killed my cousin has already been found."

"You said 'appears.'" He pulled a small notepad from his jacket pocket. "You don't sound as convinced that Annie Connor killed your cousin as so many others in your community seem to be."

"If you mean white folk, Mr. Jones... I don't just go along, mindlessly following the crowd. And I'm not sure I can accept the prosecutor's motive. To think that my cousin would sink to such depths of depravity as having any kind of relationship with that ni..." Caroline lifted her glass and took a long drink of her whiskey. "Let's just say, Mr. Jones, that my cousin was a man of great dignity and self-respect. He was a proud Cunningham, and I don't believe for one second that he would disgrace our family by having a sordid relationship with that cotton farmer's wife." She drained the glass as though there had only been a drop in it.

"I see." Titus made notes on his pad. "So it definitely sounds like you're not convinced Annie Connor had a motive to kill your cousin. If there was no affair, there was no motive. Did I understand you correctly?" As he looked at Caroline, with her ginger tendrils cascading to her shoulders, her delicate features, and her perfectly placed freckles, he couldn't help but wonder why she was still single at thirty-two.

"Jim would never embarrass the family that way. Never in a million years. It's totally asinine to think that he would."

"If you don't think Annie Connor killed Jim, who do you think killed your cousin?"

"Isn't that your job, Mr. Private Investigator? Besides, I didn't say she didn't have a motive, nor did I say she didn't kill him. I said Jim would never disgrace himself by having an affair with her."

"I just thought you might have a theory. I tell you what—why don't we go over what we know from the beginning."

"Go right ahead." Caroline stood and walked to the bar. She opened a silver ice bucket, dropped several cubes into her glass, then poured a generous amount of dark liquor from a crystal decanter.

"I understand that you and Jim were very close."

"As close as brother and sister." She walked back to the chair and sat, crossing one shapely leg over the other. "Neither of us had siblings, and our parents vacationed together every year during the summer."

"Did you maintain that same closeness as adults?"

"Mr. Jones, I have no motive to kill my cousin, if that's what you're getting at. We were close. I loved Jim very much. I even helped him keep his books up until about four months ago."

"What happened four months ago?"

"He no longer wanted me to keep them." She waved a dismissive hand. "Said he was hiring an accountant to make sure everything was in order before he and Sarah got married. But he never hired anyone. He was my cousin, so I still visited Jim from time to time. And after his maid became ill, I'd take him a nice cooked meal every so often. My Ruthie is an excellent cook, you know."

Titus nodded. "Did you doubt your cousin's explanation that he was going to hire an accountant?"

"Of course not." She paused. "Not at the time. I had no reason to until…"

"Until what?"

"Until Jim started acting… different, secretive."

"How so?" Titus asked.

"About a year ago, he started hanging out with an old high school friend, drinking, and going up to Tunica."

"What were they doing in Tunica?"

"Who knows? There's absolutely nothing in Tunica but cotton fields and a few honky-tonks. He said something about buying land and investing in some casinos. I thought in Tunica, sure, the money would just roll in." She laughed.

"What's his friend's name?"

"Kade Wiley." She took a sip of the whiskey.

"Of Wiley Luxury Cars in Greenville?"

"That's the one. He'd been trouble all through high school. A bad seed. I warned Jim about hanging out with him. He was white trash then, and just because he inherited some so-called luxury-car outfit doesn't make him any better now. Just plain lucky his uncle left that car business to him, if you ask me. Like my momma used to say, once white trash, always white trash."

Titus scribbled a note on his pad. He waited, not uttering another word. He remembered something his grandmother always used to say: "Loose lips sink ships." And if Caroline was in a talkative mood instigated by the gods of alcohol, he was going to let her steer the boat. He didn't judge her for her heavy drinking. He figured it was her way of coping with the loss of her cousin. And it might work to his advantage.

"Jim had so much potential," Caroline continued. "Although I think he was altruistic to a fault. He must have had a Messiah complex, always trying to save the strays. Even when we were kids, he would try to save this stray animal or the next. I tried to convince him to go into politics like my father..." She took another sip then opened a drawer in the chair-side table and retrieved a silver cigarette case. "Do you have a light?"

"No, I quit eighteen months ago. Doctor's orders."

"Good for you." She searched the drawer until she found a lighter, lit her cigarette, took a long drag, and blew a smoke funnel toward the ceiling.

Titus looked down at his notes, trying to ignore the allure of an old habit beckoning him like a wayward mistress. "Your father was the former mayor of Lowell." It was more of a statement than a question.

Caroline swirled the ice cubes in her glass, looking at them as they chased each other. "The one and only Beau Cunningham, Cinderfella, the cross-dressing mayor of Lowell, Mississippi, who apparently preferred the company of young men to his own wife." She took a generous gulp of her drink before placing it on the coaster. "Like my father, Jim had no aspiration to go into politics. But my mother..."

Caroline smiled, but her eyes went cold. Titus felt a chill race up his spine.

"Strong-willed and determined," Caroline continued, her words slurring. "She encouraged my father to run for mayor and, after his two successful terms, convinced him to run for lieutenant governor of our fine state. His opponent started digging into his private life and discovered... well, you know the rest."

"That must have been very difficult for you."

Caroline threw her head back in a guttural laugh. "Learning to ice skate, Mr. Jones, is difficult. Being publicly humiliated during your junior year of college while running for homecoming queen and preparing to pledge Kappa Kappa Gamma is more than difficult." She forcefully snuffed her cigarette out in the ashtray. "It was devastating."

"So, if your father's political career was so devastating, why would you want your cousin to follow in his footsteps?"

"Redemption, Mr. Jones. He would have risen above my father's mistake. He would have restored the Cunningham good name, which was sullied by my father."

"But he wasn't interested," Titus said.

"No, he was content running that damn cotton plantation."

"It provided him with a good, respectable living, did it not?"

"That's not the point. He could have sold that plantation, invested the money in the stock market, and made millions more. Now, with Jim being gone..." Tears settled in her eyes. Biting her bottom lip, she blinked them away.

After a moment, Titus said, "Ms. Cunningham, I understand you will inherit your cousin's entire estate."

"I didn't hear a question." Her gaze narrowed.

"Did you know he'd willed everything to you?"

"His lawyer contacted me the day after Jim was murdered." She paused, her glassy eyes scanning the room casually. "As you can see, Mr. Jones, I have no need of Jim's money. Again, if you're trying to find a motive for why I would kill my cousin, whom I loved dearly, you are barking up the wrong tree."

"I didn't mean to offend, Ms. Cunningham. We have to consider every possibility and eliminate each one until we find the killer." Titus made a note and then rose to his feet. "Well, thank you, ma'am. I believe I've taken up enough of your time. I appreciate your hospitality." He stood and began walking toward the door.

Caroline didn't answer, nor did she look up. She took another cigarette from the case, placed it between her lips, and lit it.

Titus turned to face her. "One more thing, Ms. Cunningham."

Drawing on her cigarette and blowing out a long trail of smoke, she glared at him with an almost predatory look. The hairs on the back of Titus's neck stood on end. He cleared his throat.

"I found records that indicate you graduated from Lowell High School in May of 1956 and entered Ole Miss in the fall of that year. But I found no record of you graduating from Ole Miss."

"Is that germane to your investigation, Mr. Jones?"

"Not at all. Idle curiosity."

"Well, if you must know," she said matter-of-factly, her features softening, "I left Ole Miss during my junior year after my father's indiscretions made national news. I traveled abroad for a year, spending time with my aunt Meagan, and when I returned to the States the following year, I completed my undergraduate studies at Mississippi State. Is there anything else?"

"No, that's all. Thank you again for your time."

Right on cue, Ruthie Nettles returned and escorted Titus to the side entrance. He walked swiftly to his car. Sliding into the driver's seat, Titus Jones swept a hand over his smooth head and wondered what it was about Caroline Cunningham that caused an unsettled feeling in the pit of his stomach.

# Chapter 41

When the court reconvened Friday morning, Frank Sutton called his third witness to the stand. Aided by a wooden cane, Dr. Wesley John McCullough hobbled to the stand with a decided limp. His dark-navy suit had a tailored look, as did his neatly starched white dress shirt with silver monogrammed cuff links. His dark hair with a touch of gray at the temples had deep cowlicks and was neatly trimmed. He stopped in front of the bailiff, leaning his cane against the witness stand. He raised his left hand after placing his right hand on the Bible.

"Do you swear to tell the truth, the whole truth, and nothing but the truth, so help you, God?" the bailiff asked.

"I do."

"You may be seated."

Dr. McCullough took his cane, limped around to the chair, and sat. He rested his cane across his lap.

"Dr. McCullough," Sutton said, rising from the prosecutor's table and walking toward the witness stand, "would you please state for the record where you are currently employed and the specialized area of medicine that you practice?"

"I am a board-certified doctor of psychiatry. I've been employed at the Whitfield State Hospital for the past thirty-two years. I diagnose and treat patients who have mental health problems, emotional issues, or behavioral disorders. I also counsel patients and analyze their medical history to determine the best course of treatment."

"Thank you, Doctor. Now, Dr. McCullough, have you ever treated patients at Whitfield who have committed violent crimes, including murder?"

"Yes, sir, I have. Over the past thirty-two years, I have treated exactly 31,440 patients who have committed violent crimes. Five hundred seventy-six of those patients committed murder."

"Dr. McCullough, please share with the court the profile of a person who would commit a murder as violent as Jim Cunningham's."

"Certainly. In my professional opinion, based upon the study of human behavior and human psychology and the thirty-two years of practice at Whitfield, the person who committed this brutal act is someone who has a very violent nature. This person takes pleasure in causing others physical pain. This individual is someone who lacks a conscience and feels no remorse for the victim."

"Doctor, does the manner in which the victim was killed suggest this was a random act?"

Dr. McCullough shook his head decisively. "Oh, no, sir. Not by any means was this murder a random act. With the violent nature of this crime and the sheer number of stab wounds, this suggests a crime of passion—an act of revenge or extreme hatred. The killer knew the victim and wanted him dead."

"Thank you, Dr. McCullough. No further questions." Sutton glanced toward the defense table, his lips curled in a sneer, obviously pleased with Dr. McCullough's testimony. "Your witness, Counselor."

Jonathan glanced at the note Scott had slid to him. *Have something important to do this afternoon. Should be back before the evening session ends.* He nodded as Scott slid out of his seat and exited the courtroom.

"Counselor," Judge Boone said, peering over the rim of his glasses, his flabby jowls dangling, "do you have any questions for this witness?"

"Yes, Your Honor. My apologies. The defense would like to cross-examine the witness." Jonathan approached the witness stand. "Dr. McCullough, you stated that the murder of Jim Cunningham was a crime of passion, is that correct?"

"Yes, that is correct." He shifted in the chair.

"In your treatment of the 31,440 patients who have committed violent acts and the five hundred seventy-six who committed murder, did you have the occasion to treat a patient named Bonnie Marie Potts?"

"Why, yes, I did."

"Doctor, would you please share with the court your diagnosis and treatment for this patient the media dubbed Unlucky Seven?"

"I believe it was the fall of 1959. A twenty-seven-year-old woman named Bonnie Marie Potts was admitted to Whitfield after she'd been found not guilty for reasons of insanity in the stabbing death of her fiancé."

"Continue, Doctor," Jonathan said.

"Ms. Potts stabbed her fiancé thirty-seven times then set his body on fire because she thought he wanted to end their relationship to date another woman. During my treatment of Ms. Potts, I diagnosed her as having a multiple personality disorder. At various times, due to certain types of external stimuli, one of seven personalities would emerge."

"Why did she murder her fiancé, Dr. McCullough?"

"She murdered her fiancé because one of her seven personalities told Ms. Potts that her fiancé wanted to end the relationship and start a new relationship with one of the other six personalities."

A collective gasp swept through the courthouse.

"So, Doctor, would you say that Unlucky Seven killed her fiancé out of jealousy?"

"Yes, I would."

"Then would you consider the murder she committed a crime of passion, Doctor?"

"Yes, I would, but..."

"Thank you, Doctor. Now, tell me, out of the five hundred seventy-six patients you treated who committed murder, can you tell me the number of those who killed their spouse or lover?"

"One hundred sixty-five."

"Almost thirty percent of your patients who committed murder killed their spouse or lover, is that correct, Doctor?"

Dr. McCullough shifted almost imperceptibly in his seat. "Y-Yes, that's correct, but..."

"Would those murders be considered crimes of passion, Doctor?"

"Yes," he mumbled.

"Could you please speak a little louder, Doctor?"

"Yes, they would be considered crimes of passion."

"Now, Doctor, you stated previously that Jim Cunningham's murder was a crime of passion, did you not?" Jonathan asked.

"Yes, I did."

"Then is it possible that Jim Cunningham was murdered by *his* fiancée, a woman scorned, who found out that he was sleeping with half the women in Washington County?"

"I vehemently object, Your Honor." Sutton pushed up from his chair. "Counsel is calling for baseless, unwarranted speculation."

"Sustained," Judge Boone said.

"The question is withdrawn. I have no further questions for Dr. McCullough."

"The witness may step down," the Judge said.

Dr. McCullough left the witness stand and, with the help of his cane, limped hurriedly down the aisle toward the exit, without so much as a glance at the prosecutor's table.

"You may call your next witness, Mr. Prosecutor," Judge Boone said.

Sutton's face was beet red. "The prosecution rests, Your Honor."

"This has been a long week. Therefore, this will conclude today's session. Thank you, jurors. Court's adjoined until ten a.m. Monday morning."

"All rise."

## Chapter 42

"They're here! They're here!" Tammy jumped up and down in her white patent leather shoes and worn dress that had once been purple but had faded to lavender. Her two ponytails clipped with purple butterfly barrettes bounced up and down. The full measure of her glee was revealed in her wide grin with two missing front teeth.

Even though a dark cloud hung over the horizon, threatening to release a torrential downpour, it could not quell the excitement in our house that Saturday afternoon, which had taken on the feel of Christmas day. Sweet aromas from the cake Jo and I had baked floated from the kitchen and made my stomach growl. We'd cleaned the house from top to bottom—mopped, dusted, and shined. I'd sprayed air freshener throughout the house to eliminate the stale scent of cigarette smoke so the baby would be able to breathe better.

Finally, the wait was over. Uncle Earl had just arrived, bringing Priscilla home with Matthew Jordan, her baby boy. Now she was back, and everyone was excited except Jo—and Daddy, who was nowhere to be found. He'd left when Uncle Earl called and said he was about to bring Priscilla home.

After Pricilla went to stay with Big Momma, Jo became the oldest child in the house, and now that Priscilla had returned, Jo would become second all over again. Not that it really garnered her any special privileges. Momma and Priscilla seemed more like sisters than mother and daughter. Momma had never had that same relationship with Jo. She must not have been quite mature enough.

Hearing the car doors slam, I rushed out of the front door and practically flew down the steps. Tammy was right on my heels. Priscilla got out of Uncle Earl's car and stepped carefully over the rocky driveway, balancing five-month-old Matthew on her hip.

Priscilla's hair was pulled back in a long ponytail with a white ribbon to match her white button-down sweater. Her long bangs were swept to one side and pinned behind her ear, perfectly framing her oval face. She smiled broadly, revealing perfect white teeth—the teeth she swore were as big as Mr. Ed's. I took Matthew out of her arms and whirled him around. Tammy rushed over and hugged Priscilla around her slender waist.

Priscilla planted a kiss on Tammy's cheek. "Tammy, look at you. You're getting to be a big girl."

Tammy cupped Priscilla's face with her hands. "You so preddy."

"And you're pretty too." She took Tammy by the hand and walked up the steps.

Jo stood on the porch, watching the rest of us with a look of detached interest as though we were some kind of freak show and she was the only sane person among us.

Uncle Earl took Priscilla's suitcases from the trunk of his Ford LTD and made his way up the steps. "What's up, Jo? Why you not getting in on all of the action? Not glad to see your big sister?"

"I mean, I don't know what all the fuss is all about. She's been gone less than six months. They're acting like she was gone forever."

"To them, it probably seemed like it." Uncle Earl pulled open the screen door and went inside.

"Humph!" Jo folded her arms defiantly.

A low rumble of thunder echoed at a distance, followed by a streak of yellow lightning that zigzagged across an ominous gray sky.

"Y'all come on—everybody better get inside," Uncle Earl said. "It looks like this storm is gonna finally get here."

I climbed carefully up the steps with Matthew.

When she stepped onto the porch, Priscilla smiled. "Hi, Jo."

"Hey, Priscilla." Jo's face was expressionless.

"Come on inside, Jo. It's about to storm," Priscilla said.

Just as everyone entered the house, thunder rumbled loudly, shaking the small frame house to its cinder block foundation. Lightning flashed through the open curtains. Lights in the house flickered off but came back on. I was glad Uncle Earl was there. The house always seemed safer when a grown man was in it.

"Y'all got a flashlight? We might need one if these lights go out. And make sure it's got a good battery too," Uncle Earl said.

Checking the kitchen-sink drawers, I found a flashlight. I clicked it off and on to make sure it was working. "I found a flashlight, and it works!" I yelled.

"That's good, Bailey!" Uncle Earl yelled back. "Bring it in here, and put it on the coffee table."

"I hope you plan to stay for a while, Uncle Earl. At least until the storm passes," I said.

"I'm gonna stay long enough to eat some of that cake—that's for sure." Uncle Earl chuckled. "And it better be good."

A low grumbling rolled above the house, growing steadily louder, erupting into a loud clap of thunder, causing the house to vibrate. Lighting flashed through the thin curtains, and a driving rain pelted the tin roof. Howling, whistling winds blew so hard they rattled the front windowpanes.

Another peal of thunder, followed by a bright flash of lightning, caused everyone to freeze like statues. Talking ceased. Then Tammy ran to Uncle Earl and wrapped her arms around his legs. Matthew started crying. Priscilla and Uncle Earl exchanged looks of concern.

"The Lord's just doin' his work," Uncle Earl said, his voice a little unsteady. "Let's just wait a few minutes for the storm to pass, and then we'll dive into that cake."

As the storm raged on, lightning continued to flash through the curtains, and thunder sounded like a gigantic bowling ball rolling in the heavens. I was afraid a bolt of lightning might strike the house if we did anything to disrespect what Uncle Earl called the Lord's work, so I stayed on the floor at the end of the sofa closest to the wall. Priscilla sat on the sofa, bouncing Matthew on her knee and patting him on his back to console him. Uncle Earl sat next to her. Tammy was next to Uncle Earl, gripping his arm, while Jo pulled the curtains tight in a vain attempt to block out God's lightning show. Then she sat on the floor with her back to the window, facing me. I closed my eyes tightly, bowed my head, and prayed silently.

*God, it's me. It's Bailey. I'm terrified right now. I believe Uncle Earl and my sisters are scared too. Even little Matthew is scared. God, please don't let the storm blow our house down, because we won't have any place to live. And last thing, God, please don't let this storm be a bad sign for Priscilla coming back home. In Jesus's name, I pray. Amen.*

# Chapter 43

Scott's windshield wipers whipped back and forth against the unrelenting rain like metronomes gone mad. The driving rain, which looked like translucent sheets in his headlights, reduced his visibility to less than thirty yards as gusts of wind buffeted his Volkswagen. Scott downshifted to second gear, bringing the Beetle to a virtual crawl over the pooling water on the highway. With his hand, he wiped away the condensation fogging his windshield, then he turned on the defroster. He'd started to regret his decision not to wait until the storm had passed before heading to the club to meet with Jonathan and Titus.

With the windshield practically clear, Scott turned the defroster off because the interior of the car had started to feel like a sauna. As he wiped the beads of sweat from his forehead with the back of his hand, he glanced in the rearview mirror. The sudden appearance of headlights gave Scott's heart a jolt. He tried to rationalize that it was probably nothing but decided he needed to get off that stretch of deserted highway as soon as possible. He shifted the car into third gear, accelerating up to thirty-five miles per hour, plowing through the buckets of water. The vehicle behind him sped up to match his speed. Scott swallowed hard, and his heart pounded like a drum in his chest. Emerging out of the darkness, a tan pickup truck closed the distance between them. Scott could see a Confederate flag flapping wildly from the truck's antenna. A knot tightened in his stomach. Hot mercury raced up his spine. There was no convenience store or other building he could duck behind and hide. Scott pushed the car into fourth gear and punched the accelerator. Walls of water splashed high from underneath his tires. The truck accelerated and raced up behind him.

Scott pressed the accelerator to the floor. The truck shot forward. It slammed into the Volkswagen.

Scott skidded off the highway and onto the shoulder. His heart thudded. He wrestled with the steering wheel, bringing the vehicle back onto the road. The truck rammed the Volkswagen once more, metal scraping metal. The Beetle swerved.

With a white-knuckle grip, Scott jerked the car back onto the road, staring straight ahead, afraid to take his eyes off the road, afraid to look into the other vehicle—afraid of what he might see. Just before the truck rammed him again, Scott glanced over. Terror seized him. Two hooded faces with holes for eyes, grinning like distempered hyenas, leered back at him. The truck slammed Scott's Bug again. The Beetle was no match for the larger vehicle and began to swerve and hydroplane. The Bug skidded off the road and then flipped and landed on its side in a waterlogged ditch. As the Beetle's wheels spun, the truck sped ahead and disappeared into the darkness.

# Chapter 44

Friday evening, Jonathan Streeter walked into Club Casablanca right before the ominous gray skies opened up and unleashed a furious thunderstorm onto the city of Greenville. Lightning flashed, illuminating the dimly lit bar, followed by a boom of thunder that rocked the foundation of the single-story off-white brick building. Patrons chatted at small chrome tables, seemingly oblivious to the looming threat. A small flame danced wistfully in the clear votive candle in the center of each table.

Cigarette smoke mixed with the smell of stale beer greeted Jonathan with each creaky step he took on the dark wooden floors. Bright neon lights glowed from the walls, creating a festive vibe, advertising Miller High Life and Winston cigarettes.

The owners—rotund identical twins Carl and Jesse Peterson, who looked to be in their mid-forties—sat behind the bar, engaged in an animated conversation. Had it not been for their different clothing—Carl in a dark tailored suit and a gold watch and Jesse in an ultra-suede rust jacket and khaki pants—it would have appeared as though one man was looking in the mirror at himself.

Jonathan glanced around and spotted a table near the back, not far from the two empty pool tables, and decided it was the best location, being the farthest from the other tables. And from that vantage point, he had an unobstructed view of the entire place. A jazzy ambience infused the air as the jukebox softly played the Jackson 5's "Never Can Say Goodbye." He chose a seat facing the door so he could see Titus and Scott when they entered. As a rule, he never sat with his back to the door, knowing it was the easiest way for someone to sneak up behind a fellow and split his wig.

Jonathan removed his trench coat, draped it over the back of the chair, and sat. He pulled out a pack of Benson & Hedges 100s from inside his suit jacket pocket, lit one, took a long drag, then blew a stream of smoke through his nostrils. From the corner of his eye, he saw a girl with mocha-colored skin approaching, wearing black leather hot pants and black leather boots. Her purple silk sleeveless blouse, with the top three buttons undone, showcased her ample cleavage.

When she reached his table, she smiled, revealing deep dimples in both cheeks and pearl-white teeth. She was stunning. Large gold hoop earrings dangled from her swanlike neck, complementing her perfectly shaped Afro. She was totally out of place in a small town like Greenville. Jonathan pitied her a bit, knowing that for a girl with her extraordinary looks, opportunities to legitimately garner the type of notoriety she deserved were limited.

"Hi, handsome. I'm Diamond. I'll be taking care of you tonight. Can I get you something to drink?"

Jonathan's smile met hers. "Sure, Diamond. I'll have a double Hennessy on the rocks, please."

"You're not from around here, are you, sugar?"

"What gave me away?"

"Your walk. Your style—your drink. Everything." She laughed.

"I actually grew up in Lowell, but for the past twelve years, I've lived in Washington, DC."

"Well, you don't say." She allowed her eyes to rove slowly over Jonathan. "The big city looks good on you. I'll be right back with your drink."

It was impossible not to notice the curves of Diamond's perfectly shaped hips or the tantalizing musk that lingered as she turned and sashayed from the table. Taking another pull of his cigarette, he shifted his glance to the silver lighter in his hand, trying to suppress the primal urge stirring inside. Oddly enough, he felt the same way when he was close to Annie Connor—only more protective.

Diamond returned and placed his Hennessy on a white cocktail napkin in front of him. "Here you are, sugar." She leaned in close enough for him to get a good whiff of her perfume and catch a peek of her full cleavage, which glistened with tiny flecks of gold. "Can I get you *anything* else?"

"Not right now, thanks." Jonathan smiled politely after taking a swig of the cocktail.

Diamond sauntered away, casting a seductive glance over her shoulder that seemed to say, "You know where to find me."

Jonathan took another sip, closing his eyes and letting the cool liquid slide down his throat. Just as the muscles in his body started to relax from a strenuous week of litigating, he heard the creak of footsteps getting closer. He hoped they were Titus's or Scott's. They weren't.

"Hey, don't I know you? Ain't you that lawyer who's representing Annie Connor? Yeah, yeah, you the one."

Jonathan opened his eyes to see a man in a fedora and a rain-dampened khaki overcoat. With his pockmarked skin, he looked as if he'd been beaten in the face with a bag of nickels. At first glance, he looked like a gangster, but he gave a gap-toothed grin that made him look more like a cartoon character. When he removed his hat, his receding hairline aged him by ten years. He looked close to fifty, though he probably wasn't.

"Yes, I'm Jonathan Streeter." He extended his hand. "And you are...?"

"I'm Sam Jones. I'm a supervisor on the shipyard over on the levee. I'm pleased to make your acquaintance, sir." He shook Jonathan's hand enthusiastically. "We don't see many big-time lawyers like yourself around Lowell, or Greenville for that matter. I saw you on TV the other day. You sure know how to handle yourself. It's good to meet you in person."

"Thank you, Sam. It's a pleasure meeting you as well."

"Say, look-a-here." Sam glanced over his shoulder then leaned in close enough for Jonathan to smell the onion on his breath. "Do you *really* think that Connor chick is innocent of killin' that fat cat she worked for out in Lowell? 'Cause, I don't know... if it was me, and my ole lady was creepin' around with some peckerwood, I would've busted a cap."

"Listen, Sam." Jonathan raised a hand. "I don't mean to be rude, but I'm waiting for a couple of my associates, and actually, I can't discuss the case with you—or anyone else for that matter—so if you would excuse me, please..."

Sam chuckled as he stood straight. "I understand. I didn't mean no harm, I just..."

Jonathan rose from his seat, towering over the man by half a foot. He extended his hand. "No harm done. Have a good evening."

Sam hesitated then shook Jonathan's hand. He sucked his teeth, turned, ambled over to the bar, and took a seat. Before Jonathan sat back down, he saw Titus's massive frame darken the door. He gave a quick wave and watched his cousin make his way over to the table.

Titus shook Jonathan's hand then shed the drenched black leather bomber jacket and draped it over his chair. "This storm is pretty nasty."

"Yeah, I got in here just before the skies opened up." Jonathan signaled for the waitress to come over as the two men sat down. "Timing is everything."

"Where's Scotty boy? I expected him to get here before me. You know, white people are always on time or early. Wish our people adopted that philosophy." Titus laughed.

"Yeah, I thought he'd be here by now too. The storm's probably holding him up. He probably decided to wait for it to pass. I'll give him a couple more minutes, then I'll call him."

Diamond strutted back over to the table, wearing her perfect smile, ignoring the ogling of the male customers as she passed their tables. "What can I do for you, sugar? Another Hennessy?"

Jonathan nodded.

"And what about you, doll?" Diamond asked, looking at Titus.

"Chivas Regal, neat. Thank you."

"Coming right up." Her sultry stare lingered on Jonathan. Then she walked away.

"Gorgeous, isn't she?" Titus's eyes followed Diamond. "Looks like she's got the hots for you, Jon, but be careful, now. Girls like that are usually looking for one thing—the almighty dollar—and they are magnets for thugs and criminals with deep pockets and no moral compass."

"A word to the wise is sufficient." Jonathan took a final draw from his cigarette, blew a funnel of smoke, and stubbed it in the ashtray. "Besides, I'm focusing on one thing right now—this case. I can't afford to get distracted—even if distraction comes wrapped in what appears to be a perfect package."

After a few minutes, Diamond returned with their drinks. "Here ya go, sugar. Let me know if I can get you two anything else." Diamond lightly caressed Jonathan's shoulder before walking away.

Titus took a swallow of his Scotch. "So, what do you think?"

"About what?"

"About everything. How the trial is going. The witnesses, their testimonies—all of it."

"All things considered, I think it's going pretty well. Although we might have taken a hit with Dr. Vincent's testimony, as well as the prosecutor tying Annie's height and weight to the description of the killer. I watched the jurors' expressions, particularly the lead juror, who was intensely taking notes during that portion of the testimony. She latched onto it like a dog with a bone. But what we've got working in our favor is that no murder weapon has been found, and there's no eyewitness to the crime. So the prosecution's case is purely circumstantial."

"Yeah, those factors certainly point in your favor," Titus said. "But with an almost all-white jury, how much weight will that really carry? I'm sorry, Jon—I'm just playing devil's advocate."

"I can dig it. Our case has to be rock-solid so even if the jurors want to find Annie guilty, they don't have a choice but to exonerate her." Jonathan's brow furrowed as he looked at his watch. Scott was more than thirty minutes late. "Let me find a pay phone and give Scott a call. I'll be right back."

Jonathan pushed away from the table and walked past the pool tables at the back of the bar to find a pay phone. He dropped a dime and heard the soft clink when it hit the other coins. He dialed Scott's number and listened as the phone rang and rang, but Scott didn't answer.

Finally, Jonathan hung up the receiver and ambled back to the table, a feeling of concern darkening his mood. "There was no answer."

"Maybe something else came up, and he didn't get to call," Titus responded.

"Yeah, I hope so. He slipped me a note indicating he had something important to do and that he'd be back before we adjourned for the day, but he didn't return."

Titus took another swig of his drink. "Well, I've got some good news. I talked with Willie Earl Price this afternoon."

"Willie Earl's alibi for Annie is crucial. It can make this case for us. What did he say?"

"The same thing as Annie. They drank half of a fifth of gin and passed out until the next morning. Willie Earl can meet you tomorrow evening at four o'clock so you can prep him for cross-examination. You guys can meet at my office."

"Solid. I want to put Willie Earl on the stand first thing Monday morning." Jonathan took a sip of his cognac. "Now, were you able to find the young man named Jimmy, who Otis claimed as his alibi?"

"His name is Jimmy Lee Jenkins. He confirmed what Otis said. Told me Otis was asleep in his car when he rode past around six fifteen that morning. He stopped to see if he was okay and found that Otis had a flat tire. So he drove Otis to his uncle's body shop to get the tire fixed and then took him back to his vehicle."

"Something is nagging at me about Otis and his alibi," Jonathan said. "He nearly leaped from his chair when I asked him his whereabouts on the morning of Jim Cunningham's murder. And besides that, he strikes me as being a real mean son of a gun with a serious jealous streak."

"A real prize, huh?" Titus said. "What is it about his alibi that bothers you?"

"Jimmy Lee confirmed that Otis was parked by the road asleep at six thirty that morning. But how long had he been there?"

"You're saying he could have killed Jim Cunningham around three or four in the morning and then had the flat tire on his way home."

"That's a possibility."

"You might be on to something, Jon. He certainly would have a motive—insanely jealous husband. But is there any way to prove it?"

"I don't know. We might need to circle back to Otis. But for now, did you find anything useful on Vincent?"

"Nothing yet."

"Keep digging, Titus. We need something to counter his testimony."

"Okay. I'll keep looking."

"What about Cunningham's life insurance policy and the beneficiary of his estate?" Jonathan asked.

"Hold on to your wig—it's his cousin."

"Caroline Cunningham?"

"You got it."

"You don't think—"

"People have killed for less."

Jonathan nodded. "Yeah, a whole lot less. It's a long shot. But let's focus on Caroline Cunningham for now and see where that takes us. If we run into a dead end, we'll circle back around to Otis. Now, tell me about Ms. Cunningham." Jonathan drained his cognac glass and signaled for another.

"Man, that broad is a piece of work. Let me start by saying she is *loaded*. She lives in this huge mansion on thirty-five acres inherited from her parents when they died in a car accident about eight years ago. Beautiful, I mean beautiful, like right out of a magazine. When I stepped inside, I didn't know whether to shit or go blind." Both men chuckled.

"I hear ya. So, you don't think money would be a motive for her to kill her cousin?"

"Couldn't have been. Caroline's probably richer than Jim Cunningham was. He was rich, but she inherited a fortune."

"Are you saying we should scratch her off our list as a possible suspect?" Jonathan asked.

"I didn't say that."

"If money isn't a motive, is there any other reason she'd want to kill her cousin?"

Titus threw his hands up. "Could be hundreds of reasons. I just can't tell you one right now. Listen, I don't know how to explain it, but something's not right with that woman. There's something dangerous about her. It's in her eyes. They're cold and calculating."

"Are you sure that wasn't sadness or grief you saw?"

"Jon, I've looked into the eyes of more than a few men and women who've done some pretty horrific things, and I'm telling you, what I saw in Caroline's eyes was pure evil."

"Did you ask her if she killed her cousin?"

"Didn't have to." Titus turned up his Scotch. "When I asked her about their relationship as adults and about the inheritance, she knew what I was getting at, and she volunteered that she didn't kill him. Said she loved him like a brother and had no reason to kill him."

"But you're not convinced."

"My gut says there's a lot more to Caroline than we know right now."

"Then keep digging," Jonathan said.

"I plan to, but in the meantime, she put me on to another lead, someone else who may have been involved with Jim and possibly got him killed. Jim Cunningham had started hanging out with an old high school chum. A guy named Kade Wiley—not exactly high society, if you know what I mean."

They were quiet as Diamond placed a fresh drink in front of Jonathan and strutted away. "Yeah, I get your drift," Jonathan said.

"Well, Caroline had been keeping Cunningham's books up until about four months ago. He told her he was hiring a CPA, but he never did. She said about a year ago, he started acting different—secretive—after he began palling round with this Wiley fellow."

"And you don't think she offered Wiley up to you to get you off her trail?"

"She's cagey enough, but I'm not sure. I think it would be worth my time to keep a close eye on both of them," Titus said.

"All right. Start tailing Wiley to see what he's up to, and check his criminal record. I'll get a court order to get the bank records for Cunningham and Wiley. If there's anything fishy, it'll turn up there." Looking at his watch and beginning to feel a bit anxious, Jonathan pushed up from his seat. "I'm going to call Scott again."

Titus drained the contents of his glass. "I'm going to head over to the Elks Lounge on Alexander, where the music is loud and the women are hot. Wanna join me?"

"Naw, I'm going to have a couple more," Jonathan said and emptied his glass. "Then call it a night if I can't reach Scott."

"A couple more? You sure about that? Why don't you come with me, and I can drive you home afterward."

"I'm a big boy, Titus. I can handle my liquor."

"Okay. Well, be safe, my man. I'll see you Monday morning." The two men shook hands, then Titus grabbed his jacket and headed for the door.

# Chapter 45

Jonathan Streeter resisted being pulled out of a deep sleep by the telephone's persistent ringing. When it continued, he willed his eyes open. The neon hands on the bedside clock told him it was eleven thirty-five.

*Who'd be calling at this hour?*

A rush of panic made him sit upright. *Is it the jail? Has Annie been attacked—or killed?*

He groped in the darkness and grabbed the receiver. "Hello."

"Mr. Streeter, I'm sorry to disturb you at this hour. This is Scott's father, Harvey Jacoby. I thought you'd want to know that Scott was in an accident tonight."

"What?" Jonathan lurched forward. He grabbed his head as the room started to spin. "What kind of accident? Is he all right?"

There was a long pause on the other end of the line. "He's in ICU. He was driving in the heavy downpour. His Volkswagen flipped. The doctors don't know if he's going to make it." Harvey's voice cracked.

Jonathan threw the covers back and clicked on the lamp. With the receiver tucked under his ear, he scrambled to pull on his pants and slip back into his white dress shirt. "Where is he? What hospital?"

"Delta Medical Center."

"I'm on my way."

With his heart racing, Jonathan slammed down the receiver and dashed into the bathroom. He splashed cold water on his face and swished Scope mouthwash in his mouth. Then he grabbed his keys off the table, stepped into his shoes, and raced to his rental, which was parked in the hotel parking lot.

A myriad of thoughts cluttered his mind. *What if Scott doesn't make it? What will I say to his father? How will I bear to look into his mother's eyes, knowing I was responsible for whatever happened to him? How will I ever be able to forgive myself?*

Jonathan swung the car out of the parking lot and punched the accelerator as he raced up Highway 82. His chest tightened, and a lump rose in his throat. The dark, deserted streets provided the perfect driving conditions... until out of nowhere, a car appeared, flashing its high beams. The bright lights were reflected in Jonathan's rearview mirror, blinding him. He squinted, shielding his eyes with his hand. His heart pounded. He remembered with clarity the explosion at the restaurant. And now something had happened to Scott.

*Could I be the target—again?*

The car switched lanes.

*What is this fool doing?* Flashing red and blue lights rotated back and forth on the roof of the black-and-white vehicle as it zoomed past Jonathan.

He exhaled. *Greenville's finest. The high beams were a warning to slow down.* If the police hadn't had bigger fish to fry, they would have pulled him over for speeding. Jonathan reduced his speed and cruised the remainder of the way to the Delta Medical Center.

When he walked through the sliding glass doors, he found the hospital to be as quiet as a cemetery and just as deserted. The lights were dim, and two women in white nursing uniforms and caps sat behind a circular desk with a sign that read Nurses Station. An elderly Black man pushed a bucket on wheels, mopping the white-tiled floors.

As Jonathan approached the desk, one of the women looked up at him over wire-framed glasses. "May I help you?"

"Scott Jacoby's room, please."

"Are you family?"

"No, I'm a friend."

"Sir, it's way past visiting hours, so you won't be able to see him now." She reached for a set of stapled pages and scrolled through the list of names. "Jacoby, Scott. He's in ICU. Even if it were visiting hours, only family members can see him."

"The family called and asked me to come down. Where would they be if not in his room?"

"There's a visitors' room on the third floor where the ICU is located. Perhaps you'll find them there."

"Thank you." Jonathan turned and headed for the elevator. He stepped in and pressed the button.

A minute later, the bell chimed, acknowledging his arrival on the third floor. It seemed loud and intrusive in the still quiet of the hospital. There was no movement on that floor, and no one attended the desk positioned across from the elevator.

Jonathan looked around for signs pointing in the direction of the waiting room. When he saw the white sign with black letters, his mouth became as dry as the delta soil, and he had a sinking feeling in the pit of his stomach. Though he didn't want his words to sound rehearsed, he began going over in his mind what he would say to Scott's father, feeling small and defenseless, not at all like the high-powered attorney everyone claimed he was. He had the sudden urge to turn and bolt from the hospital. But he knew, of course, he couldn't run and hold his head up later. Propelled by an inner strength, he kept walking until he reached the waiting room midway down the hall. Peering through the single glass pane in the door, he saw a teenager he guessed to be Scott's younger brother, tucked in a fetal position, asleep under a blanket. When Jonathan eased the door open and stepped into the room, the boy's eyes opened, and he sat up.

"Mr. Streeter?"

"You must be Aaron."

"Yes, sir."

"Where's your father?" Jonathan asked.

"I'll go get him." Aaron wrapped the blanket around his shoulders and lumbered past Jonathan, with his white socks softly tapping the tile floor.

Within minutes, a man with a slight build and curly dark hair, gray at the temples, entered the room. He wore a crumpled white dress shirt and wrinkled black slacks, and his green eyes were hollow and exhausted looking.

"Jonathan, I'm glad you came." Harvey Jacoby extended his hand, and Jonathan shook it.

"Mr. Jacoby, I am so sorry. Do you know what happened to Scott?"

"The details are rather sketchy, but based on the accident report prepared by the police, the damage to Scott's car indicated someone forced him off the road. It flipped and landed in a ditch."

Jonathan covered his mouth with his hand. Remorse filled him. "Sir, I didn't anticipate that anyone would come after Scott. Me, yes, but not Scott."

"Listen, son." Scott's dad placed a hand on Jonathan's shoulder. "This is not your fault. The fault lies with the cowards who tried to kill him. The blame lies with them as well. I warned Scott, before he joined your team, about what was at stake and what the inherent risks would be. He didn't go into this situation blindly. A lot has changed since the sit-ins in the '50s and early '60s, but a lot *hasn't* changed. He was fully aware of the dangers, but he still wanted to participate in the trial because he knows something bigger is at stake than just representing a Black woman. This is about an opportunity for achieving social change and equal justice under the law. It's about putting our legal system on trial and demanding that she rise to what the constitution mandates—a fair trial for every American regardless of his or her race, creed, or color. Even a Black woman accused of killing a white man."

"Thank you, sir. That means a great deal to me, knowing how you feel about this situation. Did the police find the people responsible?"

"No. There were no witnesses, and Scott has been unconscious since they brought him in. They induced a coma to keep his brain from swelling." Jacoby's eyes became bright with fresh tears. He cleared his throat. "He has a concussion, a broken leg, a crushed sternum, and several broken ribs. The doctors said he's lucky to be alive."

"Mr. Jacoby, is there anything I can do?"

"Yes—pray for my son and keep doing what you're doing, Jonathan. Don't stop because ignorant people out there want you to stop, hoping it will impede change. If we had stopped the freedom rides and sit-ins because a man had been lynched or beaten to death, or dogs had been released to attack protesters, or protesters had been sprayed with fire hoses, this country would not have experienced the change benefiting minorities today, including you, Jonathan. But be very careful. These people mean business, and they'll stop at nothing to have their way, because they are still fighting vehemently against equality for Blacks, and they don't want Jim Crow laws to be dismantled."

"I'll be careful, sir."

"Now, go on back, and get some rest. You've got a mighty big challenge facing you in the courtroom in the days to come. I'll let you know when there's a change in Scott's condition. And I'll certainly let you know when he's out of the coma."

"Did the doctors say how long that might be?" Jonathan asked.

"Optimistically, it could be a week. Could be longer. Right now, it's too early to tell."

"All right, Mr. Jacoby," Jonathan said, extending his hand. "I'm going to head on back to the hotel, but please let me know the moment Scott is awake."

"I will, Jonathan. Good night."

Jonathan left the waiting room with the burden of guilt not as heavy as before, though he still felt responsible for Scott's condition. He hoped Scott would recover completely. Otherwise, Scott's attack would be an albatross Jonathan would carry for the rest of his life.

# Chapter 46

Sunday evening, right after the sun went down, everyone gathered around the television in our living room to watch *Gunsmoke*, including Priscilla and Matthew, which I thought was particularly odd given that Priscilla only came out of our bedroom when Daddy wasn't home. Out of fear, she tried to avoid contact with him. As usual, I was sprawled comfortably on a rug on the floor.

A knock on the door gave us all a start. We looked toward the door then at Daddy. Judging by his puzzled expression, he was as mystified as we were.

Daddy peered out the window and scratched the back of his head. "Who knock?" he asked, slurring slightly from polishing off a pint of bourbon.

"Open the door, Otis. It's me, Annie."

"Annie Lee?" Daddy looked as though he'd heard a ghost.

"Yeah, it's me. Open the door."

My heart soared. I couldn't believe Momma had come home. Jo looked at me, excitement filling her eyes. Once Daddy regained his composure, he hurried to open the door. Momma rushed inside, and Daddy swept her up in his arms and spun her around. He kissed her on the lips and then on the cheek before letting her go. She had on the same navy-blue suit she'd worn in the courtroom.

"Annie Lee, what happened?" Daddy asked. "How did you get out? The trial ain't over."

"That Jonathan Streeter is one bad son of a gun. He asked the judge to lower my bail because of my good behavior and the death threats I'd been getting. Willie Earl came up with the bail money. So they let me out." Momma looked over at us. A bruise under her left eye was partially covered with makeup. "How are my children doing?"

We rushed over, grabbed Momma, and hugged her like we hadn't seen her in twenty years.

"We're fine, Momma," I said. "Now that you're home."

"Yeah, we're fine now," Jo said, wrapping Momma and me in a tight embrace.

"Guess what, Momma?" Tammy said, tugging on her skirt.

"What is it, Tammy?" Momma smiled down at her.

"Look, Momma, Priscilla came home." Tammy grinned, pointing toward Priscilla, who sat in the chair by the window, with Matthew on her lap. "Her and little Matthew, they came back."

The smile on Momma's face couldn't mask the fear in her eyes. She stole a glance at Daddy, biting her bottom lip. Heat rushed up my spine. Suddenly, I felt nauseated.

"Priscilla, I'm... I'm so glad you're back," she said.

"Me too, Momma." Priscilla smiled absentmindedly while stroking Matthew's hair.

"Your momma thought Priscilla ought to be here to help the other kids out since you was gone," Daddy said. "But now that you back, I think it's time for that little tramp to leave for good." Daddy drew a knife from his pants pocket. He popped a seven-inch blade. "I'm gon' see to it right now!"

Priscilla's eyes widened as she pulled Matthew to her chest. She rushed out of the room and into our bedroom, slamming the door behind her.

"No... no... no, Otis. That's my child. Don't talk like that. My God, what are you doing?" Tears formed in Momma's eyes.

Jo and I clung to Momma. Tammy started to scream and cry. My heart thumped so hard I thought it would leap right out of my chest and onto the floor.

"Don't hurt Priscilla, Daddy!" I yelled, hot tears streaming down my face. "Please don't hurt her!"

"Daddy, please don't hurt Priscilla!" Jo screamed.

"Go get her! Go get her now!" Daddy's red eyes sparked with rage, and spit flew from his mouth. "Never mind—Uma get her myself!"

Momma moved quickly, stepping in front of Daddy, blocking his way to our room. "Otis, no! I'll take her back to Momma's tomorrow. I promise. Otis, please, please don't do this."

With a hard backhand, Daddy sent Momma flying against the wall. As he headed toward our room, Momma regained her balance and leaped onto Daddy's back with a stranglehold around his neck. He flung her off like a dog shaking off a flea. Momma fell to the floor but quickly scrambled to get up.

I couldn't move. My feet felt glued to the hardwood floor.

Daddy reached the bedroom.

He kicked open the door.

Priscilla stood there. The double-barreled shotgun was aimed at Daddy.

With the knife in his hand, Daddy lunged at Priscilla. The shotgun blast knocked him back. He fell backward onto the floor. The gaping hole in his stomach spilled out blood and guts, turning his white T-shirt dark crimson.

Screaming, wailing, and loud sobbing engulfed the entire house. I collapsed to my knees, crying uncontrollably. Suddenly, Daddy sat bolt upright, his red eyes glaring at me. He reached for me. I shrieked and fell backward.

Someone grabbed my shoulder. "Let me go! Let me go!" I screamed.

"Wake up, Bailey. Wake up," Jo said, shaking me.

I jerked upright, wildly looking around for Daddy, expecting to see him sprawled in the middle of the floor with an enormous red hole in his chest. Wiping the tears from my eyes, I saw the credits to *Gunsmoke* scrolling across the TV screen.

"You must have been having a bad dream. You fell asleep right after Daddy went across the road to Ms. Clara's to talk to Uncle Earl on the phone. Are you okay?"

"Yeah, I'm okay," I said, allowing relief to wash over me.

"Good. You scared the daylights out of me with all that screaming." Jo patted me on my head then walked toward the kitchen.

I got up and went into our room and saw Priscilla and Matthew asleep on their bed. I'd never been so happy to see two people in my life. I went over and snuggled close to Matthew's warm little body, inhaling the sweet scent of baby shampoo in his hair. The slow rhythm of his breathing gave me some comfort. But knowing that what had happened in my dream could happen in real life left me with an overwhelming feeling of sadness and dread. I got very little sleep that night.

# Chapter 47

Butterflies fluttered in my stomach as I slipped into the courtroom Monday morning. Jo wouldn't come with me because Matthew had been crying a lot, and she wanted to stay with Priscilla to help her take care of him. I didn't want to go downtown alone, but I didn't dare ask my friend Ray to come with me, because of the incident with the fire and his bike being burned to a crisp. He had been punished after that happened, and I knew he'd be too afraid to sneak downtown again.

So I asked my friend Leo Ware instead. Leo had apologized for the things he'd said about Momma that led to the fight we had the day we played basketball. He must have felt guilty, and going with me to the trial was his way of making it up to me.

We rode Jo's bike downtown, and Leo followed me as we sneaked into the courtroom and eased into the back row. This would be the day things turned around for Momma. The judge would have to let her go free after hearing Uncle Earl's testimony. Uncle Earl would be Mr. Streeter's first witness this morning, according to Daddy, who'd talked to Uncle Earl Friday night. He'd said Uncle Earl felt good about testifying because he knew he could prove Momma didn't kill Mr. Jim because she was with him the entire time.

The courtroom was packed. The jury had filed in and taken their seats. Everyone waited for the judge to enter—everyone except Mr. Streeter, who checked his watch and glanced back at the door as he waited for Uncle Earl to arrive. It wasn't like Uncle Earl to be late for anything. He said he believed what white people did about being on time—that if a person was ten minutes early, he was fifteen minutes late.

Momma sat to Mr. Streeter's left, in the middle seat where Scott Jacoby usually sat. The seat to Momma's left was empty. I'd heard on the news that his Volkswagen had been forced off the road. He seemed nice enough, so I prayed that he was all right.

The bailiff, standing at the front of the courtroom, looked toward us and said in a loud voice, "All rise. Court is now in session, the Honorable Judge Ezekiel C. Boone III presiding."

We all stood until Judge Boone entered the courtroom from his chambers and took his seat on the bench.

"You may be seated," Judge Boone said. "Good morning, members of the jury, Mr. Streeter, and Mr. Sutton."

"Good morning, Your Honor," replied a chorus of voices.

"Mr. Streeter, I understand a member of your team was involved in a terrible accident. The court extends its deepest sympathy over the matter and hopes Mr. Jacoby has a full and speedy recovery."

"Thank you, Your Honor."

"With that being said, are you ready to proceed by calling your first witness?"

"I am, Your Honor."

Mr. Streeter had planned to call Uncle Earl as his first witness to establish Momma's alibi, but because he hadn't arrived, he would have to call someone else to the witness stand. I strained my neck to see who he would call.

"The defense calls Caroline Cunningham to the stand."

Ms. Caroline rose from her seat and strutted to the witness stand with an air of confidence, wearing an expensive-looking black suit and black high-heel pumps. It appeared that if she commanded time to stop, it would obey her. The single string of pearls and pearl stud earrings contrasted with her wavy ginger hair, which cascaded down to her shoulders, giving her a look of royalty.

"Ms. Cunningham, you were previously sworn in by the court. Therefore you are still under oath," Judge Boone said.

"Yes, Your Honor."

Ms. Caroline took the witness stand, crossing one leg over the other. She glared at Mr. Streeter in a way that would probably have intimidated most men. But I was sure Mr. Streeter had grown accustomed to dealing with witnesses and prosecutors who thought they were smarter, better, or craftier than he.

As Mr. Streeter approached the witness, he smoothed down his royal-blue pin-dot silk tie and buttoned his navy-blue suit jacket. "Your Honor, the defense requests to treat Ms. Cunningham as a hostile witness."

"Permission granted. You may proceed, Counselor."

"Ms. Cunningham, would you remind the court what your relationship was with the deceased, James Cunningham?" Mr. Streeter asked.

"Jim was my cousin."

"Would you say you had a close relationship with your cousin?"

"Yes."

"How often did you visit your cousin or vice versa?" Mr. Streeter asked.

"When I was keeping Jim's books, at least twice a month."

"Ms. Cunningham, with you keeping your cousin's books and becoming familiar with his business practices, would it be fair to state that he was a man of integrity?"

"The highest."

"Would it surprise you, then, that your cousin, a man of the highest integrity, was a philanderer?"

I glanced around the courtroom to see if anyone else looked as baffled as I was concerning the word Mr. Streeter had called Mr. Jim. But no one seemed to be confused at all.

"Jim was a man like any other red-blooded man in America. He wasn't married. So if he were still sowing his wild oats, I wouldn't be surprised or concerned."

"So you are aware he was having romantic relationships with several women at the same time."

"Objection, Your Honor!" Mr. Sutton pushed up from his seat. "Jim Cunningham is not on trial here today."

"I request leniency, Your Honor, to establish another possible motive for Jim Cunningham's murder," Mr. Streeter said.

"Get to the point quickly, Counselor."

"Yes, Your Honor. Now, Ms. Cunningham, the prosecution has based their entire case on the unsubstantiated rumor that Jim Cunningham, your cousin, was having an affair with Annie Lee Connor. As someone very close to the deceased and who spent a considerable amount of time with him, do you think there was a romantic or sexual relationship between your cousin and Mrs. Connor?"

"Absolutely not!" Caroline's cheeks bloomed crimson. "Jim would never stoop to such depravity."

"In other words, Ms. Cunningham, you don't believe the prosecution's theory?"

"Objection, Your Honor. Leading the witness," Sutton said.

"Sustained."

"Ms. Cunningham, do you understand that by stating you don't believe your cousin had an affair with Annie Connor, it negates the prosecution's motive for Annie Connor killing Jim Cunningham? In other words, if there was no affair, Mrs. Connor had no basis to kill your cousin."

"What I'm saying is I don't believe my cousin slept with that woman. You can draw whatever conclusions you will from that."

"Ms. Cunningham, did your cousin have any enemies that you were aware of?"

"Can you be wealthy without enemies, Mr. Streeter?"

"Are you personally aware of any enemies Jim might have had?"

"One or two."

"Can you name them?" Mr. Streeter asked.

"One moved to California about three years ago. His name's not worth mentioning. The other is that troublemaker from high school that Jim started back to hanging around with... that snake Kade Wiley."

"Is this the same Kade Wiley who is the owner of Wiley Luxury Cars in Greenville?"

"The same."

"According to your testimony, Ms. Cunningham, you stated that your cousin hung around with Kade Wiley in high school, which would suggest they were friends. Why would you think Mr. Wiley became your cousin's enemy?"

"Because they'd gotten into some business deals together that became contentious."

"And in your opinion, do you think those business deals were contentious enough for Mr. Wiley to kill your cousin?"

Mr. Sutton leaped to his feet. "Objections. Calls for speculation."

"Sustained."

"I have no further questions. Your witness, Mr. Sutton," Mr. Streeter said.

Frank Sutton fastened his suit jacket and walked toward the witness. "Ms. Cunningham, did you ever have the occasion to witness an argument between Jim Cunningham and Kade Wiley?"

"No, I did not."

"Did you ever hear Mr. Wiley threaten Jim Cunningham?"

"No, sir, I did not."

"Thank you, Ms. Cunningham. Now, let's move on. You stated that you visited your cousin at least twice a month when you were keeping his books. Did you ever have the occasion to see the defendant, Annie Connor, at your cousin's residence when you were there?"

"Once or twice."

"Would you say their relationship was friendly?" Sutton asked.

"I would say..."

"Yes or no, Ms. Cunningham?"

"Yes."

"Friendlier than the relationship between a boss and an employee, Ms. Cunningham?"

Mr. Streeter pushed up from his chair. "Objection, Your Honor. The prosecutor is asking the witness to psychoanalyze the relationship between Jim Cunningham and Annie Connor."

"Sustained."

"I'll rephrase the question. Ms. Cunningham, did you ever see your cousin and Annie Connor interacting inappropriately for an employer-employee relationship?"

Caroline stared at Sutton with daggers in her green eyes.

"The witness will answer the question," Judge Boone said.

"No," she hissed.

"Your Honor, I'm done with this witness." Frank Sutton turned and walked back to the prosecutor's table without even a glance back at Ms. Caroline. She must not have answered the questions the way he wanted her to.

"You may step down, Ms. Cunningham." Judge Boone looked toward the defense table. "Counselor, you may call your next witness."

Mr. Streeter looked at his watch and then at the door. Uncle Earl still hadn't shown up. "The defense requests a recess, Your Honor," he finally said.

"Fifteen minutes."

"All rise!"

When Mr. Streeter stepped into the hallway, Leo and I followed him and hid around the corner. I saw Mr. Jones coming toward him. Judging by the grim expression on Mr. Jones's face, Mr. Streeter wasn't going to like the news he brought. The men stepped away from the crowd, which spilled out of the courtroom. We tiptoed closer so we could still hear them.

"What is it? Where's Willie Earl?" Mr. Streeter asked.

"He's not coming."

"What do you mean he's not coming? Why not?"

"Willie Earl is dead. He was shot execution style in his apartment late last night."

Shockwaves exploded in my brain. "No, no, no! Not Uncle Earl! It can't be true!" I bolted down the hall, toward the exit. Blinded by tears, I zigzagged through a blur of people.

"Bailey, Bailey!" Mr. Streeter called. "Bailey, wait!"

# Chapter 48

With Bailey and Leo at his side, Jonathan strode back into the courtroom, feeling as though he'd been kicked in the gut by a stallion. He'd had one heck of a time calming Bailey down after the boy had overheard that his favorite uncle had been killed. Jonathan steeled his emotions to break the news to Annie Lee, Bernadette, and Walter, though his first inclination was to bolt for the door to find a dark-brown bottle of liquor to climb into.

Annie Lee stared at him intently when he walked in with Bailey. She stood. "What is it, Jonathan? What's wrong? Why is Bailey here?"

"It's your brother Willie Earl."

"What about Willie Earl?" Bernadette asked, rising from the seat. Walter stood at her side. "Where is he? He was supposed to testify."

Jonathan hesitated. "I'm so sorry. Willie Earl has been killed. He was shot to death last night in his apartment."

"Oh, Lord, tell me that's not true! Not my baby brother!" Tears filled Annie's eyes then cascaded down her cheeks. "It can't be true. Jonathan. Tell me it's not true!"

Bailey rushed to her, held her tight around her waist, and sobbed.

"I'm so sorry, Annie," Jonathan said, holding her and Bailey as they wept.

Bernadette buried her face in Walter's chest, crying. "Willie Earl. Not Willie Earl."

"Who did it, Jonathan?" Walter asked over mournful sobs.

"The police don't know."

Jonathan watched as a guard eventually led an inconsolable Annie Lee out of the courtroom with Bailey hanging on to her. He was distraught with grief and pleading for the officer not to take her away. Walter and Bernadette agreed to take Bailey and Leo home and share the news of Willie Earl's death with Otis and the girls before it appeared on the evening news.

When court resumed, Jonathan stood with his fingertip pressed against the polished defense table. Two tragic things had happened—an innocent young man had been killed, and his client no longer had an alibi. He needed time to rethink his strategy and consider what his best options were, going forward, for winning the case. Annie's agonized look after hearing the news that Willie Earl had been murdered stirred within Jonathan. He'd seen the hope fade from Annie's eyes. She'd finally allowed herself to feel confident that Willie Earl's testimony could free her. She understood the weight and significance of her brother's testimony. With Willie Earl gone, she had nothing to hold onto.

*And what do I have to hang my case on?*

"Your Honor, the defense requests to meet in chambers."

"Permission granted." Judge Boone swung his high back chair around and headed to his chambers.

Jonathan followed the judge, with Frank Sutton close behind him. The room was spacious, with law books of every kind lining built-in bookshelves. Positioning himself behind an enormous mahogany desk with ornate carvings, Judge Boone removed his glasses and stared up at Jonathan.

"Mr. Streeter, what's going on? What's the nature of this request?"

"Your Honor, I was just informed that my key witness, Willie Earl Scott, was murdered late last night, shot execution style in his apartment."

"I'm very sorry to hear that, Counselor. That is indeed a tragedy. But how does this affect the court?"

"Your Honor, the jury will never hear the testimony of a credible witness whom I believe was crucial in vindicating my client. And due to this unfortunate circumstance, the defense respectfully requests a continuance so that I can reassess my defense strategy."

"Now, Your Honor…" Sutton stepped forward to protest.

Judge Boone held up a stubby hand to silence him. "Mr. Streeter, if your defense was based solely upon the testimony of one witness, I'd say you have a mighty weak case to begin with, and time is not going to do a thing to remedy that. Now, the state expects due process to be carried out in an expedient manner, and because of this fact, I'm going to deny your request for a continuance. However, the court is not unsympathetic to your plight. Therefore, we shall reconvene Thursday afternoon at one p.m." The judge leaned back in his chair, lacing his fingers across his ample stomach. "Is there anything else, Counselor?"

"Thank you, Your Honor. Nothing further."

"Any objections, Mr. Prosecutor?"

"No objections, Your Honor," Sutton said with a smirk.

Jonathan walked back into the courtroom and began gathering his papers as the judge dismissed court for the day. He looked up as Titus approached.

"What now?" Titus said.

"Let's talk outside." Jonathan led the way out of the courtroom.

His previous confidence that he could free Annie Lee had started to ebb away, causing a sick feeling in the pit of his stomach. He had to come up with a new strategy, and he'd have to do it quickly. But what? Caroline's testimony was strong and might have created some doubt in the minds of the jurors. She'd pointed to another possible suspect, Kade Wiley. But was it enough? Of course not. It was only a start. To convince the jury, he'd have to show that Wiley had a motive, the means, and the opportunity to kill Jim Cunningham. Jonathan and Titus waited in the lobby for the crowd to clear out.

"I've got a new angle that could potentially be solid. But in all honesty, Titus, it's going to be an uphill battle."

"What's the angle?"

"Caroline Cunningham testified that Jim had hooked up and was doing business with his old chum Kade Wiley—the guy you told me about last Friday when we met."

"The cat who owns Wiley Luxury Automobiles in Greenville."

"Yep. The very same." Jonathan rubbed his chin. "Well, Caroline testified that their business dealings had become contentious. And she seemed rather passionate in her mistrust of Wiley. So I'd say he's definitely worth looking into, especially since we lost Willie Earl's testimony."

"How can I help?"

"Lorenzo has a contact down at the county clerk's office who pulled some strings to get the subpoenas for Wiley and Cunningham's bank records expedited. I should have the subpoenas signed later today. Can you go down to their banks and retrieve the records first thing in the morning?"

"Consider it done," Titus said.

. "If those two were in business together, and I mean monkey business, it has to show up in their financial transactions, especially if they were dealing with large sums of money."

"Time and place to go over the records once we have them?" Titus said.

"Your office at five o'clock tomorrow evening."

"Solid. I'll be there."

"By the way, I had Wiley served today," Jonathan said.

"To testify?"

"That's right."

"Jon, don't you think that's a little premature? We haven't gotten his bank records yet. To put him on the stand now would be like going down a blind alley."

"I don't think so. We have Caroline's testimony that he and Cunningham had business dealings that had gone south, and I'm betting after I dig into his records tomorrow, I'll have a few pointed questions to ask Mr. Wiley on Thursday."

"Okay, you're the boss man. I see you have everything under control."

"I'm not so sure about that. But I'll see you at five tomorrow, and we'll go from there."

"Right on. See you at five." Titus shook Jonathan's hand then walked away.

Jonathan left the courthouse feeling exhausted—but hopeful. If he found questionable transactions between the two men, he could tie it back to Caroline's testimony, giving Wiley a possible motive for killing Jim. His objective was to create doubt in the minds of the jurors regarding Annie's guilt, knowing most of them were already convinced Annie should go to the electric chair.

# Chapter 49

On the ride home, I cried myself to sleep in the back seat of Aunt Bernie's car. When we pulled into our driveway, I heard her calling my name. I tried to open my eyes, but they felt tight and swollen and pricked by a thousand needles. With my heart shredded, I dreaded our having to tell Priscilla, Jo, and Tammy the horrible news about Uncle Earl.

When we walked inside the house, Jo looked up from where she sat opposite Tammy, getting ready to start a game of checkers. David Ruffin's new solo album, which Uncle Earl had bought for us, played on the console turntable he'd given Momma over a year ago. It must have been close to one thirty in the afternoon—too early for Daddy to be home from work, especially since he'd started working on a plantation in Hollandale. Most of the time, it would be after dark when he got home, and he'd be too drunk to do anything except stumble into the bedroom and fall across his bed.

Jo scanned Aunt Bernie's face, then Walter's, then mine. "What's wrong, Aunt Bernie? What are y'all doing here on a weekday?"

"Where's Otis?" Aunt Bernie asked.

"Still at work. What's wrong? Did something happen?"

"We have some news to share with you girls, but we wanted Otis to be here too."

Jo stood. "What kind of news?" Her voice rose with alarm. "Did something happen to Momma?"

"No... no, Jo, nothing happened to your mom. Would you go get your sisters, please?"

Jo hurried into our bedroom then returned with Priscilla and Tammy and stood facing Aunt Bernie.

"What is it, Aunt Bernie? What's happened?" Priscilla asked.

"It's your Uncle Earl. He's... he's been killed."

"Uncle Earl!" Jo screamed. Shock and disbelief filled her eyes. "There must be some mistake. He... he... he can't be... dead. He was just here a few nights ago."

"There's no mistake, Jo. Honey, I'm so sorry," Aunt Bernie said.

"What happened to him?" Priscilla's voice cracked as tears flowed down her face.

"Someone shot him. We don't know yet who did it." Tears tumbled down Aunt Bernie's face. She wiped them with the back of her hand. Walter stood at her side, gently rubbing her back.

Priscilla covered her face with both hands and ran out of the room, sobbing. Tammy followed her, trying to console her. Jo rushed into the bedroom, slamming the door behind her. Their mournful sobs echoed through the thin paneled walls. I stood there. Fresh tears stung my eyes. A lump rose in my throat, restricting my breathing. I wailed, coughing and convulsing.

Aunt Bernie tried to console me. "It's okay, baby. Let it out."

In the background, David Ruffin crooned "My Whole World Ended (The Moment You Left Me)."

# Chapter 50

Aunt Bernie said she was almost certain the police had notified Big Momma of Uncle Earl's death, with him being her youngest son and next of kin. When she called Big Momma on Ms. Clara's phone, Aunt JoAnn answered and told Aunt Bernie that Big Momma had become so upset that no one could calm her down. Aunt JoAnn called the paramedics because they were afraid Big Momma's blood pressure would shoot up and she'd have a stroke. The paramedics sedated Big Momma and took her to Delta Medical Center.

"Why would anyone want to hurt Uncle Earl?" I asked Aunt Bernie between sniffles. "He never hurt anybody his whole life."

"Yeah, he was nice to everybody," Priscilla said, wiping away tears as she walked back into the living room. Jo was a few steps behind her.

"Aunt Bernie," Priscilla asked, "did Uncle Earl get killed because he was gonna testify for Momma?"

Bernadette and Walter exchanged knowing glances. "Earl was a good guy," Walter said. "He didn't have no enemies. This might be hard for y'all kids to hear, but me and your aunt Bernadette do believe Earl was probably killed to keep him from testifying for your momma."

I felt sick to my stomach. With a deep ache in my heart from losing Uncle Earl, I'd never once thought the reason he'd been killed had anything to do with Momma's trial. But it made sense. Killing

Uncle Earl would prevent him from testifying for Momma. And he was the only person who could give her a solid alibi.

"What is Mr. Streeter going to do now to save Momma?" I asked.

"We don't know, Bailey," Walter said. "But Mr. Streeter is a real smart man. He'll figure out something."

"Something like what?" Jo asked. "Uncle Earl was it. He was the one sure thing Momma had for her case."

"Kids, don't do this," Aunt Bernie said. "Let Mr. Streeter figure it out, okay? Now, me and Walter need to leave. I want to get to the hospital to see how Momma is doing before visiting hours are over. Everything's gonna be okay."

"Thank you for bringing me home, Aunt Bernie," I said as she wrapped me in a tight embrace. Then she hugged Jo.

"Y'all kids lock up," Walter said. "I'm sure Otis will be home soon."

I walked Aunt Bernie and Walter to the door and locked it behind them, then I slumped back onto the sofa next to Jo. My head ached from crying all day. Priscilla walked into the room, holding Matthew. She sat in the blue floral chair next to the window.

"It's hard to believe Earl is gone, isn't it? He wasn't too much older than me," Priscilla said.

"I still can't believe it," I said, feeling tears well in my eyes. "Losing him could mean we lose Momma too. We've got to do something to help Mr. Streeter."

"Like what?" Jo asked.

"I don't know, but I overheard Mr. Titus saying to Mr. Streeter that he believed Ms. Caroline is hiding something that could be important to the case. And I wouldn't doubt it one bit. That woman is pure evil. I know it."

"Well, that ain't proof," Jo said.

I nodded. "We have to find the proof."

"Wait a minute," Priscilla said, bouncing Matthew on her knee. "I remember several years ago there was something in the news about Ms. Caroline's parents being killed."

"So?" Jo asked. "How can that help Momma's case?"

"I don't know. That's all I remember." Priscilla shrugged. "There might have been more to the story than that."

"Maybe we can go to the library tomorrow to see if we can find something on Ms. Caroline to help Mr. Streeter," I said. "Maybe something bad was reported in the news about that ole green-eyed she-devil."

"Oh, I remember now." Priscilla's eyes brightened. "Ms. Caroline's dad was named Beau Cunningham, and he and his wife died in a car wreck."

"Well, that won't get us anywhere," Jo said, standing and walking into the kitchen.

"So, we're going to the library tomorrow, right, Jo?" I called after her. "To see if we can find anything evil Ms. Caroline might have done?"

"Yeah, bucket head, we're going. You're right for once. Somehow, we've gotta help Mr. Streeter win Momma's case."

# Chapter 51

After eating a delicious ham-and-egg breakfast Priscilla had fixed, Jo and I jumped on her bicycle and headed for the Lowell Library. Uncle Winston had given Jo the bike after we stayed with him those two weeks back in May. It had belonged to his son, Joel, who had grown up and moved to Texas. It was a good thing I hadn't asked Jo if I could ride her bike the day of the restaurant fire. Otherwise, it would have been destroyed along with Ray's bicycle.

Dad had already left for work, so we didn't have to explain where we were going. Jo and I reached the library parking lot sometime after ten o'clock in the morning. I pulled the heavy glass door open, and we stepped onto the dark-green Berber carpet. Fluorescent lights buzzed in the large room lined with rows of wooden shelves, which were filled with volumes of books in various sizes and colors. The air smelled of mildew and damp newspaper.

We headed to the information desk, where a middle-aged woman sat organizing card-catalog index cards. She wore a floral-print purple-and-yellow dress, with a periwinkle cardigan draped around her shoulders. Her short jet-black hair, dark drawn-on eyebrows, and ruby-red lipstick gave her the distinct look of a 1920s B-movie actress. The nameplate on her desk said Emma Perkins. She didn't lift her head as we approached, so Jo cleared her throat.

"Excuse me, Ms. Perkins," Jo whispered.

"Oh, I'm sorry. I didn't see y'all standing there. How can I help you, hon?"

"I'm working on a project for summer school, and I'm looking for newspaper articles on the former mayor of Lowell, who died in a car accident a few years ago."

"I know precisely who you're talking about. Mr. Beau Cunningham was the former mayor of Lowell who ran for Mississippi lieutenant gov'nor. He was a fine-looking man, and smart too. Would have made a wonderful lieutenant gov'nor." Chatty Cathy folded her hands on the stack of cards and prattled on. "It's such a shame people ruined that man's fine career with all those terrible rumors. His wife must have been so disappointed." Ms. Perkins exhaled. "Oh, let me hush. You didn't come here to listen to me natter on about Mr. Cunningham. You came about a newspaper article, didn't you, hon?"

"Yes, ma'am," Jo said, shooting me a side glance.

"I'll have to go into the back and look through our microfiche to see if we still have any records on the Cunningham family. Why don't y'all go over yonder and have a seat at one of them there tables, and I'll see what I can find?"

"Thank you," Jo said. "Oh, Ms. Perkins, if you have any other newspapers that printed the family's stories besides the *Lowell Times Herald*, I'd like copies of those too, please."

"Of course, hon. I'll be right back with those papers." Emma pushed up from her chair and waddled toward the back of the library.

A young woman with her blond hair pulled back in a ponytail took Ms. Perkins's place at the front desk. Jo and I sat at one of the small square wooden tables and waited.

Reappearing twenty minutes later, the woman carried several sheets of paper and wore a triumphant smile. "In addition to finding the *Lowell Times Herald* article, I was pleased as puddin' to find copies of the *Delta Democrat Times*, the *Jackson Clarion-Legend,* and the *Memphis Daily News*."

Jo smiled and reached for the papers. "This is much more than I was hoping for. I might get an A on my report. Thank you for taking the time to find all of these articles."

"If there's anything else I can do to help you with your research, hon, you just holler."

"I will. Thanks, Ms. Perkins."

Jo divided the pages between the two of us. She read the *Lowell Times Herald* article first. There were details regarding the crash that had killed Mr. and Mrs. Cunningham and a significant amount of coverage concerning Mr. Beau's rise and fall in the political arena. But there was nothing to suggest anything evil or out of the ordinary about Caroline.

The *Delta Democrat Times* was similar to the *Lowell Times Herald*. I read the Jackson and Memphis newspaper articles out loud, and they had less coverage than the two local papers but carried the same information. And neither of them mentioned anything that could have been considered suspicious or even questionable about Caroline.

Sliding the papers aside, Jo let out a sigh. "I really thought we'd find something. This is like looking for a needle in a haystack. Only worse."

"How is it worse?" I asked. "We didn't find anything."

"With the haystack, you know you're looking for a needle. But we don't know what we're looking for. And maybe there *ain't* nothing to find. Maybe you're wrong about Ms. Caroline."

"I'm not wrong, Jo. You haven't been face-to-face with that woman. You haven't looked into her cold green eyes. I think she's capable of doing something horrible, like stabbing somebody to death."

"Okay, Inspector Clue-Slow. Grab those papers, and let's go home."

# Chapter 52

The trip to the library had been a bust, so Jo and I rode back home, hardly uttering a word. Sadness and disappointment set in after the failure of our big idea. We had nothing to offer Mr. Streeter to help him win Momma's case. When we got home, we headed to the kitchen for a cool drink of water. We were both thirsty and tired after riding the bike back from downtown Lowell. We had taken turns pedaling and riding the handlebars. I didn't feel much like watching TV or reading, so I filled my water jar a second time and headed back outside. Soon after, Jo came out and sat on the porch beside me.

"What are you thinking, Bailey? Nothing crazy, I hope."

"The same thing. We have to find something that will help Mr. Streeter with Momma's case. Now that Uncle Earl can't testify for her, we have to do something."

"Okay, smart guy, what do you want to do now?"

"Well, I was thinking if Ms. Caroline does have some deep, dark secrets, we have to find them."

"You mean we ride my bike to her home in Oxford, Mississippi, to look for these secrets?" she asked.

"No, Jo, think about it. Ms. Caroline was at Mr. Jim's house every other week. She was there a lot. Maybe she left something down at his house."

"You want to go snooping around in a dead man's home?"

"I don't want to, but we have to. What else can we do?"

"We can let Mr. Streeter figure it out, like Aunt Bernie said."

"Or we can do nothing and let him lose Momma's case," I said.

"Boy, you are insane."

"So, you're not going to go with me—to help Momma?"

"You are determined to do this, aren't you?" she asked.

"Time is running out, Jo. Mr. Streeter had planned to put Uncle Earl on the stand yesterday. And now he can't." My voice cracked with emotion.

"Okay, Bailey, I'll go with you, but only to help Momma. When do you want to go?"

"In the daytime—that's for sure."

"There might be nosy people coming to peek inside the house during the day because of what happened down there."

"I'm not going to Mr. Jim's house at night. It's too spooky."

"Okay, we'll go tomorrow morning after Daddy leaves for work. We just have to keep our fingers crossed and pray that nobody comes to peek inside the house while we're snooping around."

"Thanks, Jo." I grabbed her and gave her a big hug. A sense of relief washed over me, knowing we were going to do something to help keep Momma from going to the electric chair.

# Chapter 53

When court resumed Thursday afternoon, Kade Wiley walked to the witness stand with an easy gait. A custom navy-blue suit draped his tall, lanky frame like a wet flag on a rainy day. With a steady hand, he smoothed down his green-and-blue-striped silk tie. Gold cuff links gleamed from the wrists of his monogrammed white shirt. His hazel eyes scanned the courtroom like those of a cagey animal mapping out an escape route. After being sworn in by the bailiff, Wiley took his seat. He ran a hand through his neatly trimmed brown hair, which had fallen into his narrow face. He tugged at his stiff collar and adjusted the sleeves of his suit jacket.

"Your Honor," Jonathan said, rising from his seat. "Defense requests to treat Mr. Wiley as a hostile witness."

"So noted."

Jonathan walked toward the witness stand, stopping several feet in front of the witness. Jonathan assessed the man, who clearly considered him an adversary. In his years of practicing law as a civil rights attorney, Jonathan had opposed Wiley's type before. Raised in abject poverty, Wiley most likely had been taught by his parents and grandparents to despise Black people, especially Black men, who exceeded the Wiley family standard of living. The more successful a Black man was, the greater their hatred, believing that Black men who excelled deprived them of something they were entitled to. The entire Wiley clan was dirt-poor, except Wiley's uncle Gus, who had gone into the used-car business at a very young age and, through a few shrewd business deals, had bought into a new car business. Gus eventually became the owner of a luxury car dealership, which Wiley had inherited. In the past eight years since his uncle had passed, Kade Wiley had become a man of considerable wealth, running the Wiley Luxury Car dealership.

Jonathan was aware Kade would not willingly give him any information that would be beneficial in acquitting Annie. He could see the disdain in Wiley's eyes and knew the man despised him more than he hated the woman accused of killing his friend. Doing a direct examination of Wiley was a risk for Jonathan but one he had to take in order to offer the jury another possible murder suspect and thus create reasonable doubt for Annie Lee.

"Mr. Wiley, would you please state, for the court, your occupation?"

"I don't have to answer none of your questions, nigger!" Wiley spat.

"Mr. Wiley," Judge Boone said, peering down at the witness. "Need I remind you that you are in a court of law? You will refrain from using racial epithets, and if you do not answer Mr. Streeter's questions, I *will* hold you in contempt. Do you understand?"

"Yes, sir, Judge, but only because you said." Wiley shifted in his seat and adjusted the knot in his tie.

"Continue, Mr. Streeter," Judge Boone said.

"Do I need to repeat the question, Mr. Wiley?"

"That ain't necessary. I'm no retard." Wiley swept his hair from his face. "I own Wiley Luxury Cars in Greenville."

"How did you come to know Jim Cunningham?"

"I met Jim in the ninth grade."

"Were you close friends?" Jonathan asked.

"We became close in high school. We played football together."

"Now, after high school, Jim went on to college, and you stayed home and went to work for your uncle at his car dealership and eventually took over his dealership after he passed. Is that correct?"

"Yeah, that's right."

"That's the Wiley Luxury Car dealership in Greenville. Is that correct?"

"I think I said that before."

"Mr. Wiley, I understand from previous testimony that you and Jim Cunningham were involved in some business deals together. Now, with Mr. Cunningham being a cotton plantation owner and you being a luxury car company owner, would you explain to the court the type of business deals the two of you were involved in together?"

"Your Honor, do I have to answer all these dang questions?"

"You'll answer the questions, Mr. Wiley, or be held in contempt," the judge said.

"It was for future investments."

"Would you please elaborate on the kind of investments?" Jonathan asked.

"We were plannin' to invest in some gamblin' casinos to be built up in Tunica."

"I see. Now, did these investments require the accumulation of a significant sum of money?"

"Of course they did."

"And how were you acquiring the money?"

"Through investors."

"Now, Mr. Wiley, did you and Jim Cunningham have to invest a certain percentage of the money as well?"

"Of course."

"What was the source of your money which you planned to use for building the casinos, Mr. Wiley?"

"My income and my savings."

"Your personal earnings?" Jonathan asked.

"Ain't that what I said?"

Jonathan walked to the defense table, picked up several sheets of paper, and handed them to Judge Boone. "I'd like to enter Jim Cunningham's bank records as Defense Exhibit A. Now, Mr. Wiley, an analysis of Jim Cunningham's banking records revealed several large deposits of cash between February 12, 1969, and July 2, 1970. Cash deposits in the amounts of between five thousand dollars and eight thousand five hundred dollars were deposited into Mr. Cunningham's bank account every single month during the aforementioned timeframe. Since you and Mr. Cunningham were close business associates, can you tell me the source of these deposits?"

"How would I know? I didn't follow the man around everywhere he went."

"Mr. Wiley, are you familiar with the Pictet Group?"

"Never heard of it."

"For the record, the Pictet Group is a Swiss bank in Geneva, Switzerland—one of the oldest Swiss banks on record, established around 1905. Transfers were made from Jim's C&S Plantation business account to his Swiss bank account, with the Pictet Group each month matching the deposits made to Jim's business account. Mr. Wiley, is your name on this Swiss bank account as one of the drawers?"

"Of course not! I don't know nothin' about a Swiss bank account," Wiley said.

Jonathan walked back to the defense table, pulled several more sheets of paper from a manila folder, and handed them to Judge Boone. "Your Honor, I'd like to enter, as Defense Exhibit B, the bank records of Mr. Kade Wiley officially obtained through a court order."

Wiley whipped around in his seat to face the judge. His ears and neck blossomed a shade of beet red. "My bank records are private, Your Honor. Are you gonna let this... this person expose my private business in this courtroom? I ain't on trial."

"I object, Your Honor." Sutton sprang from his seat. "This line of questioning is immaterial and has no bearing on these proceedings whatsoever."

"If it pleases the court," Jonathan said, "the defense asks for latitude, Your Honor, so that the connection between this witness and Jim Cunningham's murder may be established."

"Get to your point quickly, Mr. Streeter."

"Yes, Your Honor." Jonathan turned back to the witness. "Now, Mr. Wiley, are you familiar with Wildlife Defenders, Americaid, and Waterway International?"

Wiley shifted in his seat. "Those are nonprofit organizations that I created. Wildlife Defenders help save certain endangered species of birds and fish. Americaid and Waterway International provide help and clean water to people in the Mississippi Delta caught up in natural disasters."

"Mr. Wiley, there have been deposits made to these nonprofits ranging from five thousand to twelve thousand dollars each month since they were created in January 1968. To date, each of these entities has a balance that exceeds one million dollars. Mr. Wiley, where is all of this money coming from?"

"Private donors mostly."

"Now, Mr. Wiley, you previously testified that you were not familiar with the Pictet Group, is that right?"

"That's what I said."

"Then would you please explain to the court the large transfers that were made to each of these entities from Jim's Swiss bank account with the Pictet Group, in the amounts ranging from twelve thousand five hundred dollars to twenty thousand dollars, for the last fifteen months?"

Wiley cleared his throat. "Well, I... uh... I plead the fifth."

"Isn't it true, Mr. Wiley, that these entities are not real companies but rather shell companies that were created for the sole purpose of being cash repositories to finance your casinos?"

"I object, Your Honor," Sutton said. "This witness is not on trial, and Mr. Streeter has failed to show the relevance of this testimony and how any of it relates to Jim Cunningham's murder."

"Sustained." Judge Boone peered over his silver-framed glasses at Jonathan. "Mr. Streeter, you are wearing the court's indulgence mighty thin."

"Yes, Your Honor. I only have a few more questions for this witness to establish my point."

"Then get to it quickly, Counselor."

"Mr. Wiley, in your earlier testimony, you stated that you and Jim Cunningham had partnered to open several casinos in Tunica. Is that correct?"

"Yes." Wiley raked an exasperated hand through his hair.

"According to the sworn testimony of Caroline Cunningham, Jim Cunningham's cousin, your business dealings with Mr. Cunningham had become contentious. Mr. Wiley, were the disagreements over money?"

"No!"

"And because these agreements had become so contentious, involving millions of dollars, you killed Jim Cunningham, didn't you, Mr. Wiley?"

The courtroom buzzed like an active hornet's nest. Judge Boon tapped with his gavel to silence the chatter. "Quiet in the courtroom."

"Are you crazy?" Wiley's face had become flushed as he glared at Jonathan with unvarnished contempt. "I didn't kill Jim. He was my friend. You've got your murderer right over there!" He pointed at Annie Lee.

"Mr. Wiley, where were you between the hours of one and two o'clock a.m. on Saturday, July 11 of this year?"

"Home asleep."

"Can anyone corroborate that?" Jonathan asked.

"Yes, my wife."

"I have no further questions, Your Honor, but I reserve the right to recall this witness. Your witness, Counselor."

Sutton glowered at him. "I have no questions, Your Honor."

# Chapter 54

The crowd had lessened, but many of the reporters outside the courthouse had waited for Kade Wiley. With microphones and cameras hoisted on their shoulders, they rushed him when he exited the building. But he pushed the cameras and microphones aside, strode to his silver-gray Mercedes Benz 280SL Coup, slid inside, and sped from the parking lot. Wiley cruised down Main Street through downtown Lowell and turned right onto Highway 82, headed west toward Greenville.

Titus Jones had been waiting in the parking lot, watching for Wiley. His assignment was to tail Wiley and report back on where the man went, what he did while he was there, and with whom he did it. At this stage in the game, Jonathan wasn't convinced Kade Wiley wasn't Jim Cunningham's murderer.

Because it was near the noon hour, Titus figured Wiley was headed for lunch—perhaps a liquid lunch, considering his demeanor when he left the courthouse. Halfway along the seven-mile stretch between Lowell and Greenville, Kade signaled and moved into the left lane. Titus followed three cars back in his 1968 Monaco blue GMC pickup. When there was a break in the oncoming traffic, Wiley turned left and swung into Ming's Garden Restaurant parking lot. After exiting the car, he took a draw from his cigarette, flicked it onto the concrete, and entered the restaurant.

Titus signaled and moved into the left lane. After allowing the oncoming traffic to pass, he downshifted and turned into the K-Mart's lot some fifty yards away and parked at an angle that allowed him to see who entered and exited Ming's Garden. Knowing he'd be there awhile, Titus reached into the glove box and retrieved a brown paper sack and the black leather case holding his thirty-five-millimeter camera. He opened the paper sack and pulled out two bologna sandwiches and a bottle of orange juice. The PI wolfed down the two sandwiches and took a few sips of juice as he affixed the zoom lens to his camera and waited to see who would arrive at the restaurant—and more importantly, who would exit with Kade Wiley.

An elderly couple drove up and then entered the restaurant, followed by a younger couple. Then two men in business attire arrived. Titus snapped several pictures. A few minutes later, two more men arrived—sharp dressers, in expensive black business suits and dark shades. One was tall and lanky with dark hair. The other was as wide as a tank with medium-brown thinning hair. *Snap. Snap. Snap.* Titus watched and waited as other patrons entered and exited the restaurant.

An hour later, Wiley came out, followed by Lanky and Stumpy. They walked over to Wiley's car and continued to talk. Stumpy puffed on a fat cigar, and Lanky stood wide-legged with his hands pushed down into his pants pockets. Titus wasn't close enough to hear their conversation, but their posture and facial expressions suggested they weren't planning a church picnic. He snapped multiple pictures of the trio—close-ups of each man's face and wide shots of the men standing together.

Fifteen minutes later, the men shook hands and went in separate directions. Wiley slid into his Mercedes, and the other men climbed into a black Cadillac Fleetwood Eldorado. Both cars headed west on Highway 82. The Eldorado turned left on Interstate 1, headed in the direction of Vicksburg, Mississippi. Titus followed Wiley until he turned into the parking lot of his car dealership. He watched Wiley drive around to the back of the building. Titus parked across the freeway in the parking lot of Western Auto. He camped out hunched down in his seat, fighting to stay awake, until he saw the headlights of the silver-gray Mercedes pop on at eight thirty that evening. Jumping erect, Titus switched on the ignition.

Wiley pulled onto the freeway and made a left turn, heading east toward Lowell. After traveling four miles, he turned right and continued down a gravel road a quarter of a mile to the parking lot of Kelley Joe's Bar & Grill. Neon lights of Budweiser and Camel glowed in the windows of the doublewide trailer that had been enlarged and converted into a bar. Titus was familiar with Kelley's. He and his partner had served a warrant to the owner, Kelley Joe Motte, when Titus had worked for the sheriff's department. Motte was as mean as a rattlesnake, having a particular disdain for people who looked like Titus, so it had given Titus great pleasure to arrest Motte on the charge of assault and battery of his girlfriend.

Rather than drive down the gravel road to park near Kelley's, Titus settled across the freeway at a feed store that had closed for the evening. He switched off his lights and adjusted his six-foot, four-inch frame to get comfortable for a long wait. He wasn't concerned about what Kade would do there. He already knew. Kelley's was the kind of place where good ole boys went to get drunk, and no one cared because everybody there got drunk. At Kelley's, Wiley was in his element. It was a far cry from the Greenville Country Club, where the high society of Greenville hobnobbed.

At eleven forty-two, Titus spotted the silver Mercedes turning left onto Highway 82, heading west. He started the engine, turned on the headlights, and pulled slowly onto the highway. He followed Wiley for ten minutes and watched as the man turned off the freeway onto Fairview Lane, a tree-lined street with custom two-story homes. Wiley pulled into the carport, which was covered with pink flowering vines. Titus waited for Wiley to go inside. The lights blinked on inside the house, and then within a few minutes, they went dark again. Satisfied that Wiley was in for the night, Titus pulled away from the curb three houses down, where he'd parked, then headed back east on Highway 82 toward Lowell.

As he changed lanes, Titus glanced in his rearview mirror. For the second time, he noticed that three cars back, another vehicle changed lanes as he did. *Probably nothing*, he thought. But his instincts from being in law enforcement for seventeen years told him it could be something. To validate his suspicion, Titus shifted gears, increased his speed, and changed lanes again. The car did likewise.

*Shit! I've got a tail.* Titus felt his mouth go as dry as the Delta soil. *Who is it? The Klan? The men who rammed the restaurant? Scott's attackers? Willie Earl's killers?*

Hammers of fear tapped lightly at his heart, but Titus continued to drive at the same rate of speed, not wanting to alert his pursuers that he was on to them. Spotting a twenty-four-hour gas station, Titus pulled up to the pump, though his tank was half-full. Entering the gas station, Titus furtively glanced outside while pretending to peruse the snack aisle. A late-model Buick Regal slowly pulled into the parking lot and parked near the air pump. The headlights blinked off. Three men were inside.

Titus continued to the back of the store and found a pay phone affixed to the wall near the restrooms. He dropped a dime and heard it clink as it hit the other coins. If there was one person Titus knew he could count on in a pinch, it was his high school friend Levi "Slick" Edwards. Levi had possessed a keen intellect and natural charm that set him apart from the other students his age. In junior high, he'd had a reputation as a smooth talker with a knack for getting out of tight situations, earning him the nickname Slick. By the time Slick entered Lowell High School, he'd mastered the art of influence and persuasion.

Slick earned an academic scholarship and attended college for two years, but after his sophomore year, he became bored and dropped out. Shortly thereafter, he moved to New York City and lived with an older cousin, quickly learning how to navigate the urban landscape, teetering on the boundaries of ethics and morality, perpetually dancing on the edge of danger. Operating on the fringe of society, Slick carved out a niche for himself as a freelance information broker, trading secrets and favors with anyone willing to pay the price.

After being shot three times when a deal went sideways, Slick returned to Lowell twelve years later for a slower-paced lifestyle. Before he settled into his profession as a barber, Slick experienced a few run-ins with the law. One particular incident took place when Titus, employed as a sheriff's deputy, responded to a call from a bar owner. Utilizing the same finesse with a straight-edge razor that he'd shown years before with his business pursuits, Slick had sliced and diced a man like a Thanksgiving turkey. Titus had arrested Slick but subsequently posted his bail. Slick had avoided serving any jail time as it was determined he hadn't initiated the altercation.

Titus dialed the number. "Answer, man!" Titus whispered.

"Hello," said a voice as deep as the Mississippi.

"Slick, it's Titus. I need your help, man. I've got a tail on me. A dark-colored Buick Regal's been trailing me for a minute."

"Where you at?"

"In Greenville on 82 headed toward Lowell, about four miles out. I need you to call Carl Lee, Tank, June Bug, and Tommy, and y'all meet me out in Strike City. Bring some heat. We're gonna lead these fools straight into a trap."

"We'll be there," Slick said. "You know I got you, brotha, and we'll light 'em up if we have to."

"Right on!" Titus hung up, paid the attendant for gas, and exited the gas station.

# Chapter 55

Titus's demeanor reflected composure, but every neuron, synapse, and sinew in his body registered hyperalertness. Shadows seemed darker, every sound sharper. With a trained eye, he assessed his surroundings, glancing about for the dark-colored Buick Regal. The sedan was no longer there, but Titus knew with certainty it wasn't far away. After pumping his gas, Titus slid into the cab of his truck. He turned the ignition, and the engine roared to life. Titus shifted the gears and eased back onto the highway. As he changed lanes, he glanced in the rearview mirror, but he didn't see a tail. He started to think his pursuers had abandoned the chase, but then he spied a black two-door Buick Regal parked at a service station ahead of him on the right side of the highway, with no lights on. Titus passed the vehicle then watched in his rearview mirror as the sedan slowly entered the highway three cars behind him.

*Sneaky son of a gun, I see you. Just follow me. I've got something for you.* Titus kept to the speed limit, allowing his crew time to arrive at the designated location. He maintained the same speed after reaching Lowell's city limits. He drove past the business-district exit and continued toward the rural area. Titus exited to the right and merged onto I-61, heading south. He cruised for a quarter of a mile then turned left onto Tribett Road, traversing a steep, winding curve. Emerging from the curve, Titus hit the clutch, shifted into fourth gear, and punched the accelerator. All two hundred fifty horses under the hood of his GMC pickup reared up. Adrenaline coursed through Titus's veins like quicksilver as he ripped down the blacktop road toward Strike City. The Buick raced behind Titus, matching his speed. Tall stands of trees and a small grouping of houses whizzed by as shadows. Titus's headlights bounced off the dark pavement, providing the only illumination under the pitch-black canopy of night. The other pair of headlights shone bright in his rearview mirror.

Reaching Strike City, Titus flew past Tent City, with its thirty or so makeshift tent houses. With his heart pounding ferociously, Titus continued speeding down Tribett Road, gripping his steering wheel. He stole a glance in his rearview mirror. Out of the darkness appeared four pairs of headlights falling in line behind the Buick. *The cavalry has arrived.*

When he reached Dunleith Road, Titus made a sharp left turn, hit the clutch, downshifted, then slammed hard on the brakes. His tires squealed like a pig being slaughtered. The truck fishtailed then stopped crosswise in the middle of Dunleith Road. Jumping out of his truck, Titus slid his weapon from his shoulder holster and aimed it across the hood at the oncoming car. With all four tires screaming against the asphalt, the Buick skidded to a stop fewer than ten feet from Titus's truck. Acrid fumes floated in the air from the burned tire rubber. Four vehicles pulled behind and alongside the Buick, boxing it in. Titus could hear his heartbeat gushing in his ears.

Positioned behind his truck, he called out. "You, in the Buick, as you can see, you are completely surrounded. Throw out your weapons, and step out of the car slowly." Titus's baritone echoed, silencing the mirthful singing of the night critters.

After a beat, the men inside the vehicle tossed their handguns to the ground from the two front windows. Titus's crew moved in quickly and collected the guns, keeping their own weapons trained on the passengers in the sedan.

"Now, step out of the car, place your hands over your head, and kneel on the ground in front of your vehicle. Don't try no funny business unless you want this to be your last joyride."

"Be cool, man. We're coming out."

The driver swung his door open. The passenger-side door opened almost simultaneously. Three men climbed out of the automobile and slowly walked around to the front of it. They knelt with their hands behind their heads as the headlights illuminated their frames. Relief washed over Titus. From their appearance, these weren't Klansmen. They didn't wear hooded sheets, and one of them was Black.

"Who the hell are you guys?" Titus asked. "And why have you been following me?"

"We're federal agents," the driver said. "My name is Martin Fortini. I'm with the FBI. My colleague to my right is Agent Reid Perkins. Next to him is Special Agent TJ Walker. He works for the Internal Revenue Service. You can check our credentials." He held his identification over his head.

"Slick, check their credentials. You and Tank frisk them to make sure they're clean."

Slick moved in quickly and checked the men's credentials in the car's headlight. Tank had the men stand, and they frisked them from head to toe, finding weapons in the two FBI agents' ankle holsters, which they confiscated as well.

"They're clean now, and their credentials look solid," Slick said. "Should we rough 'em up a bit for chasing you all the way out here? I mean, can I nick one or two of 'em with my straight edge on general principle?"

"Not yet. Let's hear what they have to say first," Titus said, approaching the three men as he holstered his weapon. "They might be legit."

"We are legit," said Fortini, a man of slight build with dark shoulder-length hair and a full beard. He wore blue jeans, a short-sleeved shirt, and a brown buckskin vest. "And our credentials are solid. We were following you not because you are of particular interest to us but because of the person you were tailing."

"You're interested in Wiley? Why?"

"My question to you is why are you interested in him?" Fortini said, crossing his arms and rocking back on the heels of his brown cowboy boots.

"I asked you first, and I believe I'm holding all of the trump cards, you dig?" Titus said.

Fortini glanced around at the four weapons trained on him and the other agents. "I guess you have a point. About six months ago, we got a tip regarding Wiley and Cunningham. And since that time, we've been working a joint task force, watching both men and building a case to bring charges against them for drug trafficking, money laundering, and tax evasion."

"You jivin' me!" Titus said, running a hand over his bald head.

"I'm as serious as a heart attack. Wiley has quite an operation going. He's smuggling in large quantities of cocaine, shipped inside those fancy new automobiles coming into his dealership. His operation is extensive, expanding as far east as Georgia and as far west as Texas, including Mississippi, Arkansas, and Tennessee. It's a multi-million-dollar operation."

"Where did Jim Cunningham come into the picture?"

"Wiley has been cleaning his dirty money through Cunningham's C&S Plantation, and they'd been meeting investors from Las Vegas, planning to build several casinos in Tunica. Actually, they were planning to break ground in a couple of months."

"This is getting more bizarre by the second," Titus said. "Now I understand why Wiley met with those fat cats today at Ming's Garden. They looked like mobsters."

"Yeah, they were. So, here's the kicker. We made a deal with Jim. He was going to be our star witness, turning state's evidence against Wiley for drug trafficking and tax evasion. We were poised to make an arrest when Jim turned up dead. We held off to ensure our case was still airtight without Jim's testimony."

"All of this drug activity is going on right under our noses." Titus shook his head incredulously. "So what does any of this have to do with you tailing me?"

"We need you to back off Wiley. We are this close to arresting him." Fortini gestured with his index finger and thumb. "We don't need him spooked by some local jock screwing up what we've worked our tails off to build for the past six months."

"Listen, Agent Fortini, you have a job to do, and I have a job to do. I'm a private investigator, working for Jonathan Streeter, who's litigating Jim Cunningham's murder case. Wiley is being considered as a possible murder suspect. Jonathan asked me to tail him to get the goods on him to prove there was bad blood between the two men."

"You've got a good theory, but let me save you some time on your investigation. We know for a fact Kade Wiley did not kill Jim Cunningham. We've had him under constant surveillance, watching his every move, since we started this investigation. At the time of Cunningham's murder, Wiley was shacked up at the crib of one of the waitresses from Club Casablanca. What's her name, TJ?"

"Crystal Davis, but she goes by her nickname—Diamond."

"Shit! The dude lied on the witness stand. I would have lied too." Titus chuckled. "Married but gettin' it on with a Black broad. I bet that wouldn't go over well with the boys over at the dealership, let alone the wife."

"So, you know Diamond?" asked Fortini.

"The hottest number in town."

"Well, do you think that's enough information for Mr. Streeter?" asked Fortini.

Titus sighed, crossing his arms. "Yeah, I think so."

"So, if we're done here," Fortini said, "I'd like to collect our weapons and head back to civilization."

"Fellas, give Agent Fortini and his colleagues back their weapons so they can head back to civilization," Titus said. "You think you can find your way back, or do you need an escort?"

"I think we'll manage," Agent Fortini said as he and the other two agents grabbed their weapons and climbed back into the Buick.

Titus's friends shook hands with him and made their way to their vehicles. He watched the headlights swing around, washing over the cotton fields, as his friends headed back toward Lowell. He sat there for a moment with his engine humming, contemplating the new revelation about Kade Wiley and knowing that it wasn't good news for Jonathan's case.

# Chapter 56

The alarm clock buzzed at seven o'clock a.m., rousing Titus from a deep sleep. Jerking upright, drowsy and confused, he had no idea of his whereabouts. Then he remembered. He'd made it home after two in the morning, having led three federal agents in a game of "catch me if you can" out into the middle of Lowell's no-man's-land.

Falling back onto his pillow, Titus stared at the ceiling, replaying in his mind everything Agent Fortini had told him about Kade Wiley and his drug-trafficking exploits. Fortini's account was almost too fantastic to believe—small-town Greenville, Mississippi, with a population of thirty-five thousand people, having a highly sophisticated level of criminal activity. Titus's next thought made him jerk upright in his bed again. He had to call Jonathan and tell him what Fortini had said about Kade Wiley. Jonathan could no longer consider Wiley a possible murder suspect because Wiley had a solid, unimpeachable alibi.

A hot shower and two cups of coffee later, Titus dialed Jonathan's number.

"Hello."

"Morning, Jon," Titus said in an even tone, trying to conceal his angst.

"Good morning, Titus. I hope you've got some good news for me. Did you find anything that puts a bull's-eye on Wiley's back?"

"Well, I tailed Wiley all day yesterday, as you requested, and the only thing out of the ordinary he did was meet with two fat cats at Ming's Garden restaurant, who looked like they could be gangsters."

"That could be something. Is there any way you can determine who those men were?"

"I already know who they are. They're casino bosses from Las Vegas who are planning to invest in gambling casinos in Tunica with Wiley. Cunningham was involved, too, of course."

"You work fast, man." Jonathan chuckled. "I'm impressed."

"Don't be. You see, a couple of FBI agents and an IRS agent tailed me yesterday while I was tailing Wiley. I noticed them last night as I was heading home. I didn't know who they were or what they wanted, so I led them out to Strike City with a few of my boys in tow. We boxed them in and had ourselves a come-to-Jesus meeting right in the middle of Dunleith Road."

"Sounds like quite a night. So, the feds told you Wiley was in bed with the casino bosses to build the casinos. That could be a legitimate business. Why are the FBI and IRS involved?"

"Get this—Wiley's been running a drug operation through his car dealership to the tune of millions of dollars. He's peddling drugs through Mississippi, Arkansas, Louisiana, Georgia, and Texas."

"You're kidding me," Jonathan said.

"No, sir, I'm not."

"So, the FBI has been watching Wiley and Cunningham?"

"Had them under surveillance for the last six months. They were about to arrest Wiley when Jim was murdered. The reason they held off on the arrest is because Jim agreed to be their star witness, turning state's evidence against Wiley. They'd made him a plea deal on his money-laundering charges for washing Wiley's dirty money through Jim's C&S plantation."

"All of this is going on in Greenville?" Jonathan asked.

"Can you believe it? But you know, it's almost the perfect setup. Who would have thought anyone would ship drugs into the country inside brand-new luxury cars—and of all places, to small-town Greenville, Mississippi?"

"You make a good point. And with that much money exchanging hands, there actually might have been bad blood between Wiley and Cunningham. Especially if Wiley found out Cunningham was going to turn state's evidence against him."

"There might have been, but it's a moot point."

"Why would you say that? If we can find a way to establish that there was bad blood between the two men because of their drug operation or that Wiley found out Cunningham was going to flip on him, then we'd certainly have a plausible motive for murder."

"It's moot because Wiley has an airtight alibi."

"Sure, he testified on the stand he was home with his wife," Jonathan said. "That was probably a lie. Witnesses lie on the stand all the time to cover their backsides. And Wiley probably knows that by law, his wife can't be ordered to testify against him."

"You're right—Wiley did lie on the stand. He wasn't home with his wife. But get this—he was shacked up at the crib of a certain waitress I warned you about, who works at Club Casablanca."

"Diamond?" Jonathan asked.

"You got it. The FBI has been watching Wiley and documenting his every move from the time the investigation started six months ago after they got a tip. Of course, their surveillance included the time Jim Cunningham was killed."

"Damn! We're back at square one."

"Sorry I didn't have better news, Jon. What now?"

"Maybe we should turn our attention back to Caroline. You said yourself there was something not right about her. Something disturbing. It's worth looking into, especially with the whole Wiley thing crumbling like day-old bread."

"So, what do you want me to do?" Titus asked.

"It's a long shot, but you could talk to the one person who knows where all the Cunningham bones are buried."

"Caroline's maid, Mrs. Ruthie Nettles. I met her when I interviewed Caroline at her home in Oxford."

"Wasn't she also Caroline's parents' maid? Yeah, why don't you give Mrs. Nettles a call?"

"It's your dime. I'll spend it however you want me to. I'll get right on it," Titus said.

"Hey, Titus, before you go, have the police found anything on Willie Earl's murder?"

"Other than calling it a professional hit, they don't have anything else—no leads, nobody heard or saw anything."

"Probably a Klan hit."

"You're probably right. I'll get started on the Caroline thing. Catch you on the flip side."

"Catch you later, man." Jonathan ended the call.

# Chapter 57

Jonathan ran a hand through his coarse hair and drew a line through Kade Wiley's name on his legal pad. He circled Caroline's name several times, knowing she was the longest of long shots. *What the hell have I gotten myself into?* His case had fallen apart right before his eyes. Annie Lee's brother was dead, and Annie was certain to die in the electric chair unless he came up with a Hail Mary—something solid to present to the jury that clearly established reasonable doubt.

He squeezed the rubber basketball in his hand with intensity then hurled it toward the trash can. A heaviness settled in the pit of Jonathan's stomach. His throat began to itch. He trekked over to the minibar, but each of the tiny bottles of liquor was empty. Jonathan grabbed his suit coat and headed for the door.

The sun cast a warm golden glow across a clear azure sky just before ten o'clock a.m., when he pulled into the parking lot of BJ's Lounge on Nelson Street in Greenville. The smell of stale cigarette smoke and chlorine bleach filled the dark, dank establishment that seemed the size of a shoebox. A lone customer, an old man with scraggly gray hair and beard and tan weather-worn skin, nursed a half-full mug of beer. He sat at the end of the white Formica bar. Jonathan took two steps in and glanced around, considering whether he should stay. Deciding it was just as good as any other place for what he needed, he strode to the bar and sat on a stool at the midway point.

"What'll you have?" asked the bartender, a man with smooth ebony skin and salt-and-pepper hair. Chewing on a toothpick, he tossed a white dish towel over his left shoulder.

"Hennessy, double, on the rocks," Jonathan said.

"That kind of day already?" The bartender reached up to the top shelf for the single one-liter bottle of Hennessy and poured a generous amount over ice in a glass. He placed the top back on the bottle and started to move it back to its original spot.

"Leave it." Jonathan slid a one-hundred-dollar bill across the bar. "Keep the change."

"You got it. Thank you, sir."

Jonathan nodded and took a sip of the dark liquor. The old man got up from his barstool and staggered to the jukebox. The single coin he dropped clanged when it hit the others inside the machine. After he punched in a number, a 45 record dropped, and the jukebox thumped out Joe Simon's ballad "Too Weak to Fight."

Jonathan shook his head. *That old man must have read my mind.* He took another gulp of his liquor. Dread consumed him. Soon, he'd have to face Annie Lee and tell her about her future—or the lack of one if she was found guilty and sentenced to the electric chair. He thought about the girls she'd be leaving behind and her young son, Bailey, who would no longer have the mother whom he loved deeply. A lump rose in his throat, and Jonathan drained the glass of its contents and poured another. He took a pack of Marlboro cigarettes from his jacket pocket and tapped one out.

The bartender appeared with a lighter and lit Jonathan's cigarette. He slid a silver ashtray in front of him. "You might want to slow down just a little bit, Mr. Streeter. It's still early in the day."

"Noted." Jonathan nodded, took a long draw of his cigarette, and blew out a white funnel of smoke. He took another swig of the dark liquor and watched as the bartender finished cleaning a glass with a white dishcloth.

They both turned toward the door when they heard it squeak on its hinges. Two white men walked into the bar. One whispered something to the other, and they approached the bar and stood next to Jonathan.

"Is this seat taken?" A tall, slim man with eyes the color of a thundercloud stared down at Jonathan as he gestured toward the seat next to him.

The man looked to be in his mid-thirties, with greasy dishwater-blond hair. His companion was short and stocky, with shaggy dark-brown hair and pockmarked skin. Jonathan looked up at the man but didn't utter a word. He took a nip of his cognac and took a long, slow draw from his cigarette.

"Mister," the bartender said, "there are twenty other empty seats in this bar. Why don't you take one of them?"

"His name ain't Mister. His name is Jedd."

"Shut up, Elroy! Dang it! Now they know both our names. It don't matter no-how." Jedd sucked his teeth. "As I was 'bout to say, I don't want to take one of them other seats. I want to sit next to the high-and-mighty lawyer from Washington, DC. I wanna know what money smells like." Jedd and Elroy cackled like two mental patients.

"Listen, Jedd," the bartender said, "it's too early to be starting trouble, so why don't you just take another seat, please?"

"I ain't startin' no trouble, boy. I just want to know what it feels like to be up close and personal with a bona fide superstar nigger attorney." Jedd chuckled, revealing crooked yellow-stained teeth, but the laughter didn't reach his cold gray eyes. He pulled the barstool back and sat next to Jonathan.

Elroy sat on the opposite side of Jonathan. "We'll have what he's drinking."

"You can't afford what he's drinking," the bartender said.

"Now, how do you know that?"

"Okay. It'll be twelve fifty for both of you."

"Just pour the damn liquor, boy."

"My name ain't boy. It's BJ."

The bartender made a three-finger pour of the cognac into two glasses and placed them in front of the two men.

Jedd drank the liquor in two gulps. "Another."

The bartender poured the second drink. The man gulped it down.

"Ooo wee, that's some smooth shit! I see why it costs so damn much." Jedd eyed Jonathan, who stared into his drink as though he hoped to find an answer for his client's fate swimming in the dark liquor.

"That trial must not be goin' too good... you hangin' out over here, drinkin' by yourself at this shit hole." He grinned. "Serve you right. You ought not to be tryin' to save that stinkin' slut after she kilt a white man anyhow. Let her fry in the electric chair."

"Hey," Jonathan snapped. "Shut your mouth."

"Oh." Jedd laughed. "I believe I just struck a nerve. What you gon' do if I don't shut my mouth—shut it for me, boy?"

Jonathan took another drag from his cigarette and then stubbed it out in the ashtray. "I might have to."

"Okay, let's find out." Jedd pulled a hunting knife with a six-inch blade from a sheath affixed to the back of his belt. He pressed the razor-sharp blade against Jonathan's neck. "Now, what you gone do?"

Something hot raced up Jonathan's spine. His heart pounded against his ribcage. His life flashed before his eyes. He saw his father being dragged through the streets of Indianola by a murderous racist mob. He saw this mother's grief-stricken face. He saw his client, Chauncy Jackson, shot in the head after he'd been acquitted of murder. He saw Annie being led to the electric chair, her feet and hands bound. Random thoughts of escape collided in his brain. But there was no escape.

*Have I met my fate? Will this be how it all ends for me—in a run-down bar in Greenville, Mississippi?*

"Put the knife down, and I'll show you," Jonathan said, keeping his voice steady.

"I kinda like these odds right here. I should just slit your throat open right now. But that would be too easy. Too easy, like runnin' that nigger-loving patsy of yours off the road and killin' that Price boy. Too easy, like rammin' that restaurant and settin' it afire. Dewey missed killin' you that time, but we gonna take care of you right now to make sure that Annie Lee Connor fries up like some crispy bacon in that electric chair for killin' one of our own. Now, I want you to beg. I want you to get down on your hands and knees like a dog and beg for your life. And you know what? I might just let you live."

Elroy stood beside Jonathan, nodding and grinning.

Jonathan didn't move.

"Didn't you hear me, boy? On your goddamn knees!"

"If you're going to kill me, you'll have to do it looking me in the eye." Jonathan turned his barstool to face Jedd.

"On your knees, nigger!" Jedd drew the knife back and sliced Jonathan across the chest. A thin red line of blood oozed across Jonathan's white shirt.

Jonathan surged from the barstool. Jedd pressed the point of the knife against his throat.

"That's enough!" BJ raised his double-barrel shotgun and cocked it. "Mister, you and your friend need to get the hell out of my bar right now before I blow a hole in you big enough for me to crawl through."

Elroy pulled a .38 revolver from his waistband. He fired three rounds at BJ, striking him in the chest. The bartender staggered back against the bar wall then dropped to the floor, blood spewing from his chest.

"Shit!" Jonathan scrambled over the top of the bar to get to the bartender. He grabbed a handful of white dishtowels and pressed them against the bloody gunshot wounds in the man's chest. The towels turned a deep red. When he looked at the man's eyes staring toward heaven, he knew the bartender was dead.

Jedd and Elroy burst into laughter. "He don't look so tough now with blood gushin' from his chest," Jedd said.

"No, he sure don't," Elroy said with a loud cackle.

With his heart beating wildly in his chest, Jonathan eased close to where the bartender's shotgun had fallen. He grabbed the gun and cocked it. Elroy fired two shots. Jonathan ducked back behind the bar. The rounds shattered the liquor bottles, spewing alcohol onto the floor. Jonathan rose and fired back. The blast hit Elroy in the abdomen, who staggered back then dropped to his knees and fell face down.

"You son of a bitch!" Jedd flung his knife. It struck Jonathan in the chest.

Jonathan stumbled back, cocked the shotgun again, and fired. The blast hit Jedd in the midsection, blowing him backward. Blood poured from his wound. Jonathan dropped the shotgun and fell onto his back with the knife plunged into his chest.

# Chapter 58

"Jo, wake up."

Jo pulled the covers over her head and turned toward the wall. "Go away, Bailey. Can't you see I'm sleeping?"

"Jo, get up! We have to go down to Mr. Jim's house. You promised."

Priscilla walked into the room from the kitchen, holding Matthew on her hip as he sucked on his pacifier and played patty-cake with Priscilla's cheeks. "Why are y'all going down to Mr. Jim's house?"

Jo threw her covers back. "Bailey has a bright idea that we may find some deep, dark secret that Ms. Caroline's been keeping that could help Mr. Streeter win Momma's case."

"Well, I'm glad y'all are going and not me. That house looks so scary now that nobody lives in it. And to think that good-looking man was killed down there." Priscilla shivered.

"We need to go now while it's still early," I said.

"Aren't y'all worried somebody will see you going down to that house in broad daylight?" Priscilla said.

"We'll go through the cotton field," I said. "Nobody will see us."

"What if the doors are locked?"

"I don't know, Priscilla." I threw my hands up in exasperation. "We'll figure it out when we get down there. Come on, Jo."

"Shoot!" Jo swung her legs from the bed and stumped toward the bathroom.

I went out back and waited anxiously on the steps for her to get dressed. Ten minutes later, Jo bounded down the steps.

"Let's go, bighead, since you're in such a hurry."

As planned, we hunkered down, cut through the cotton fields, and trotted between the rows. We reached the back of Mr. Jim's house and stayed low as we crept into his backyard. No vehicles were parked where his pickup truck and fancy sports car had once been. Jo and I sneaked across the backyard and up to the back of his house. I climbed the steps and twisted the knob. Just as Priscilla had predicted, the door was locked.

"Shoot! What do we do now?" I asked.

"Let's try that window over there." Jo pointed to the back side of the house on the left.

I found an old five-gallon paint bucket and placed it underneath the window. But being taller than me, Jo climbed onto the bucket and pushed upward on the window.

"It's locked."

"What do we do now?" I asked.

"Let's try that one on the right." Jo pointed to a second window at the back of the house. It was also locked. Jo jumped down off the bucket. "Hand me that big rock over there."

"You're not going to break the windowpane, are you?"

"You got any better ideas? Besides, no one lives here anymore. We came this far—we have to go all the way. And don't forget, we're doing this for Momma."

I knew breaking the window wasn't right, but I also knew we were doing the wrong thing for the right reason, as Momma had once explained to me. So I grabbed the rock and handed it to Jo. She stepped back several paces and then hurled the rock, which struck the center of the windowpane and shattered it.

"Yes!" Jo pumped her fist and sprinted back to the paint can.

Reaching carefully through the hole, she unlocked the window. Once she'd pushed the window up, she climbed inside and stepped delicately over the broken glass. It crunched beneath her sneakers.

"Come on, Bailey."

I looked around to see if someone would come and rescue me from this insane idea. But no one did.

"Come on, boy! We don't have all day. This was your bright idea, so don't go all yellow-bellied on me now."

I inhaled and stepped up on the bucket, my blood pulsating in my ears.

Jo grabbed my hand and helped pull me inside. I tumbled in headfirst. When I stood, I found myself in Mr. Jim's office, which looked the same as when I'd first seen it but felt eerie and melancholy. The hairs on the back of my neck stood on end. I remembered being there with Momma the day Ms. Caroline caught her looking at one of Mr. Jim's books, and I remembered the look in her cold green eyes.

"Let's start right here, Bailey. This must be Mr. Jim's office." Jo searched through the papers on the desktop. "I don't know what I'm looking for, but all I see are books with a whole lot of numbers, and these envelopes, I suppose, are bills. Nothing that will help Momma."

I went around the desk and started searching the drawers. The top drawer had a scattering of notepads, paper clips, and ink pens. I looked through the files in the side drawers and found nothing but records for C&S Plantation.

"Dang! I was so sure we'd find something here." As I plopped down in the high-backed leather seat, a thought occurred to me. "Hey, Jo when Ms. Caroline stayed here, she probably had her own room. She would've slept in one of those other bedrooms, right?"

"And you think she might have left something there?"

"Maybe. We should at least look."

"After this, we're leaving. Which room?" she asked.

"I don't know. There were two."

"Let's divide and conquer."

"What? You mean split up?"

"Yeah, Bailey. I'm ready to get out of this creepy house, and the sooner we check both rooms, the sooner we can go. Don't wimp out on me now. Remember, this was your bright idea."

"I'm no wimp!" I said.

"Then let's go."

Splitting up made sense, but it didn't stop me from getting the willies. We started up the hall toward the living room, tiptoeing as though we expected someone to hear our squeaky footsteps. We passed Mr. Jim's bedroom, and I refused to look in that direction. I kept my gaze straight ahead, but the metallic smell of blood, mixed with Mr. Jim's cologne and some type of cleaning solution, made my stomach lurch.

Midway down the hall, a knock on the front door stopped us in our tracks. Jo's eyes became like saucers. The second knock was louder. The third knock was louder still. I thought I would wet my pants.

"Shhh!" Jo placed a finger to her lips.

We waited. The knocking stopped.

"Whoever it was, they're gone now. I'll take the first room we get to, and you take the next one."

We continued up the hall past the living room, crossed the foyer, and climbed the stairs to the second floor. Jo took the first bedroom on the right, and I took the one across the hall. I tiptoed to the dresser, where a silver mirrored tray held a pink brush with stands of fine red hair. Seven or eight bottles of fingernail polish and a bottle of Chanel No. 5 perfume adorned the tray.

"Jo," I whispered, unsure whether she could hear me. "I'm sure this was Ms. Caroline's room."

I pulled open the top dresser drawer. It held Ms. Caroline's lingerie. Her pajamas were neatly folded in the next drawer. The other drawers contained a few tops and shorts.

Jo tiptoed into the room. "Find anything?"

"No," I whispered.

Jo walked to the chest of drawers and looked through them. "Nothing," she said, letting her arms flap to her side. "Okay, let's go."

"Wait, Jo, there's a closet." I ran to the closet and swung open the door.

Dresses and sweaters hung neatly. The scent of vanilla and rose drifted from them. A few shoe boxes had been stacked on the floor.

"Bailey, there's nothing here. Let's go."

"There's got to be something." I looked to the left then to the right. "There's just got to be."

"We tried. There's nothing here." Jo shrugged. "Now we really do have to leave it up to Mr. Streeter."

My heart dropped to my stomach. I swallowed hard. I couldn't disagree with Jo. We'd searched the house and found nothing.

*What would Mr. Streeter do now? And what hope does Momma have?* As we headed toward the door, something pink underneath Ms. Caroline's bed caught my attention. I kneeled and pulled it out. It smelled of vanilla and rose.

"What is it, Bailey?"

"It's a letter."

"A letter... from whom?"

"From Ms. Caroline... to Mr. Jim."

"Read it," Jo said.

My armpits started to itch. I felt I'd be violating Ms. Caroline's privacy. But out of desperation, I had to do the wrong thing for the right reason. The crumpled envelope had been opened, so I unfolded the letter and started reading. When I finished the four pages, Jo and I stared at one another, unable to speak.

"Let's go, Bailey," Jo finally said. "I think you found what we came for."

# Chapter 59

Jonathan heard the machines beeping. When he opened his eyes, he stared at off-white walls and dull fluorescent lights, confused as to his whereabouts.

"Welcome back to the land of the living," Titus said with a wide grin.

Jonathan turned and looked at his cousin. "Where am I?"

"Delta Medical Center. You were brought here yesterday a little past noon."

"Yesterday? Who... how...?"

"Apparently, you got into an altercation with a couple of good ole boys at BJs. You ended up with a knife in your chest, and they ended up dead. Unfortunately, so did BJ. An old-timer who was at the bar called the police after everything was over. Said he knew the men were trouble when they walked in, so he hid under a table in the back by the jukebox."

"Thank God he had the presence of mind to hide," Jonathan said.

"According to my source at the FBI, the two men who attacked you were Jethroe 'Jedd' Hess and his cousin Elroy Clayton. They are known members of the latest resurgence of the KKK that started about six years ago down in Adams County, near Natchez. The .38 caliber Smith & Wesson Clayton used to kill BJ is the same caliber gun used to kill Willie Earl Price. Ballistics will undoubtedly confirm it was the same weapon. The old-timer said he overheard one of them say the truck that rammed Freeman's Diner was driven by someone named Dewey. That lines up with the registration of the truck. A man named Dewey Bigler owned the big rig. My contact at the Lowell Police Department said Bigler filed a police report the day before the incident at the restaurant, indicating that it was stolen."

"Of course he did."

"Obviously, the Klan has been planning to get rid of you from the start to prevent you from defending Annie Lee. You might have guessed that Bigler is also a known member of the KKK." Titus sighed, folding his massive arms. "I'm hoping that because the Feds are looking into these crimes, it will be enough to deter these guys from trying again. And with Clayton and Hess dead, that might also send a message to them. Now for the good news: the doctor said they got to you just in the nick of time. You lost a lot of blood, but the knife didn't sever any major organs, so you'll be able to go home tomorrow."

Jonathan gripped his forehead. "Tomorrow... the trial. Titus, I honestly don't know what I'm going to do. I went to that bar to drown my sorrows because I'm all out of options for getting an acquittal for Annie Lee, and I just don't know how to tell her."

Titus stroked his goatee, allowing the sobering information to sink in. "Well, speaking of the trial, I ran into Harvey Jacoby in the elevator on my way up, and he said he needed to talk with you as soon as possible. He said it was urgent."

"Okay. Is he in Scott's room?" Jonathan said, leaning forward, trying to get out of bed.

"Whoa... wait a minute." Titus took Jonathan by the shoulders and gently guided him back to his pillow. "Let's get the doctor in here to see if you should be walking around. You've been heavily sedated since the surgery to repair that knife wound. But in the meantime, I can get Mr. Jacoby on the line if that would work."

Jonathan nodded. "Sure, that will work. Can you call him now?"

"Sure thing." Titus picked up the receiver, dialed the hospital operator, and was connected to Scott Jacoby's room. "Mr. Jacoby, this is Titus Jones. Jonathan is awake and would like to speak to you."

Jonathan took the phone. "Hello, Mr. Jacoby."

"Jonathan, I'm relieved you're awake from your surgery. Titus told me what happened. Awful, just awful."

Hearing Harvey Jacoby's voice, Jonathan felt his heart thudding. *Why does he need to talk to me? Has Scott taken a turn for the worse? Will he be in a coma indefinitely?* His chest tightened. He could hardly breathe.

"Jonathan, are you there?"

"Yes… yes, Mr. Jacoby, thank you. I'm relieved as well. How's Scott?" he managed to say calmly.

"I have great news. Scott came out of the coma this morning, but he's resting at the moment. He has some crucial information regarding the case, but he doesn't want to share it with you over the phone."

Jonathan exhaled a heavy sigh of relief. "Mr. Jacoby, that is great news. I'm thrilled that Scott is conscious. When can I come see him?"

"The doctors said his condition is stable, so there's no reason you can't see him after he awakens."

"That sounds great. I'll come by after I get the okay from my doctor to walk around. I'll check back in an hour or so."

"I'll let him know you're coming."

"Thank you, Mr. Jacoby."

"You're welcome, Jonathan. We'll see you then."

Jonathan hung up the phone. *Finally, a glimmer of hope.*

An hour later, the doctor cleared Jonathan to walk around inside the hospital. As he headed for the door in his hospital gown, escorted by Titus, his mind raced, thinking about the nature of the information Scott had. He had no clue what it was, but it could not have come at a better time.

"What do you think he wants to tell you?" Titus asked, holding his friend by the arm as they stepped into the elevator.

"I don't know. But I hope to God it's as significant as Scott thinks it is. Otherwise, we're dead in the water."

# Chapter 60

Jonathan prepared himself for a worst-case scenario. Even if the information was disappointing, he couldn't let Scott know it. He'd been through so much already, having been in an accident that could have killed him and then being in a coma.

Jonathan and Titus got off on the fourth floor and continued down the white-tiled corridor at a slow pace until they reached Scott's room. Jonathan eased the door open. Scott was propped against a couple of pillows, talking quietly with his father. The two of them looked toward the door. Scott beamed as Jonathan entered the room. Harvey Jacoby rose from the bedside chair and met Jonathan with a handshake.

"I'll come back to get you in about thirty minutes," Titus said, then left the room.

"Jonathan, thanks for coming," Harvey Jacoby said.

"Well, I didn't have far to go. Fortunately or unfortunately." Jonathan smiled. "I was already in the building."

Jonathan walked over to Scott and shook his hand, clasping it with both of his. "Hey, Scott. I'm so relieved you're okay."

"Nobody's more relieved than me." Scott managed a chuckle. "And I'm glad you're okay too."

An IV tube with clear liquid ran from Scott's arm to a machine positioned next to his bed. The left side of Scott's face sported a purple bruise, and a bandage covered his forehead where he'd sustained a gash from hitting the steering wheel. His right leg was wrapped in a cast up to his hip and elevated.

"How are you feeling?" Jonathan asked, releasing Scott's hand.

"Not bad, considering all that Dad and the doctors said I'd been through. I don't remember anything except being run off the road. The rest is a blank. I just remember waking up here."

"That must have been terrifying. But I'm glad you're safe and on the road to recovery. I feel terrible as it is, but I couldn't have forgiven myself if something more serious had happened to you."

"Jonathan, why don't you sit, please." Harvey Jacoby motioned to the chair where he'd previously sat. "Fortunately, Scott will make a full recovery now that the swelling in his brain has gone down." He walked across the room and stared pensively out of the window, with his fingers laced behind his back.

"Thank you, Mr. Jacoby." Taking the seat next to Scott's bed, Jonathan appraised his young assistant, feeling sick in the pit of his stomach.

"How's the trial going?" Scott asked.

Jonathan rubbed his chin, where a five-o'clock shadow had sprouted. "I'd be lying if I told you I wasn't concerned. We've had a few setbacks during the last week. Willie Earl Price was murdered two days ago."

Scott's face turned ashen. "Murdered? How?"

"A bullet to the back of the head."

"Oh my God!" Scott swallowed hard. "I'm so sorry to hear that."

Jonathan allowed Scott to process the information, then he continued. "Jim's business partner, Kade Wiley, who we thought might have a motive for killing Jim, has an ironclad alibi. So at this point, I could really use some good news."

Scott's face brightened, and his lips curved into a mischievous grin. "Jonathan, you are not going to believe what I found when I sneaked into Dr. Vincent's office on that Friday when I was supposed to meet with you and Titus in Greenville."

"You did what?" Jonathan leaned in, glancing in his father's direction. "You sneaked into Dr. Vincent's office?" he whispered.

"You can thank me later," Scott said. "But listen, everyone believed Jim Cunningham was killed by the severing of the carotid artery, right?"

"That's right. According to the medical examiner's report."

"That's not what killed Jim Cunningham."

Jonathan blinked and sat back in his chair. "What do you mean that's not what killed him?"

"I found the notes Dr. Vincent prepared for Mr. Cunningham, and it showed that he had documented the discoloration of Jim's fingernails."

"Discoloration of his fingernails." Jonathan thought back to a murder trial he'd litigated earlier in his career, in which the victim's nails had been discolored. "He was poisoned?"

"Yes, Jim Cunningham was poisoned."

"Do you have proof?"

"Yes. I photocopied the notes while I was in his office. The copy is in the glove box of my Beetle."

"Where's the Beetle?" Jonathan asked.

"The police impounded Scott's vehicle after the incident. I had it towed to the mechanic's the day after, and they finished repairing it yesterday. The vehicle is parked at our home."

"Why in God's name would the medical examiner withhold this crucial information?"

"Think about it, Jonathan." Harvey Jacoby turned from the window. "He had declared publicly that the murder was committed by severing of the carotid artery. They'd arrested the prime suspect, a Black woman—open-and-shut case. Can you imagine the backlash if he'd recanted his findings after Annie Connor had been arrested? He was probably afraid to reveal the truth. He might have feared losing his job after making this colossal blunder in such a high-profile case—or he might have feared losing his own life."

Jonathan nodded. "That makes sense. Although someone did in fact attempt to murder Jim by stabbing him multiple times, he was already dead from being poisoned."

"So my question to you, Jonathan, is how can we use this *unofficially obtained* evidence to free Mrs. Connor?" Scott's blue eyes sparkled.

"Simple," said Jonathan. "I'll call Dr. Vincent back to the stand."

# Chapter 61

Court resumed Tuesday afternoon in the second week of Momma's trial. I'd begged Jo to come to the courthouse with me so I wouldn't have to ride the bike all the way to downtown Lowell by myself. I remembered Daddy saying somebody white might try to kill me just because I am Black. Initially, Jo said no because of her fear that Daddy would find out. But eventually she gave in because she was as curious as I was about Momma's trial, and she knew Daddy didn't come home anymore until after dark, and when he did, he'd be drunker than Cooter Brown. Sometimes he'd even have lipstick on his shirt.

We sneaked into the courtroom and slid into the back row. Mr. Sutton walked to the prosecutor's table and sat with a look of satisfaction plastered across his face. Apparently, he was confident he'd presented a solid case and was assured of a win. He chatted quietly with his cocounsel, a young man about half his age with dishwater-blond hair. Mr. Streeter flipped through the pages of his legal pad. I supposed he was reviewing questions he'd prepared to ask the next witness. Momma sat to the left of Mr. Streeter with slumped shoulders. Walter and Aunt Bernadette sat in the row behind Momma. Mr. Titus sat to Aunt Bernie's right.

After the bailiff called the court to order, Judge Boone entered the courtroom, took his seat on the bench, then advised everyone to be seated. "Good morning, Counselors. Mr. Streeter, are you ready to call your first witness of the day?"

"Yes, Your Honor. The defense re-calls Dr. Karl E. Vincent to the stand."

Dr. Vincent walked warily to the witness stand, like a man who would have preferred to be anywhere else except the courtroom. The judge reminded him that he was still under oath and asked him to be seated. Dr. Vincent ran an unsteady hand through his neatly trimmed brown hair and, through his silver teardrop-framed eyeglasses, watched Mr. Streeter approach.

"Good morning, Dr. Vincent," Mr. Streeter said.

"Good morning."

"Dr. Vincent, when you testified earlier in the trial, you told the court that you were the medical examiner who examined Jim Cunningham's body at the crime scene. Is that correct?"

"Yes, that's correct."

"You also determined the cause of his death at the crime scene. Is that correct?" Mr. Streeter asked.

"Yes, that's also correct."

"Since time has elapsed since your earlier testimony, would you please state for the court the cause you determined for Mr. Cunningham's death."

"As I stated previously, Jim Cunningham's death was the result of multiple stab wounds to the face, neck, and chest area, with the fatal wound severing his carotid artery."

"Was that your preliminary finding at the crime scene?"

"Yes."

"Thank you, Doctor. Now, once you took the body to the morgue, did you do a more thorough examination?"

"Yes, I did."

"And did your final conclusion support your earlier cause of death as determined at the crime scene?" Mr. Streeter asked.

"Yes, it did."

"Dr. Vincent, when you examined the decedent's body at the morgue, did you examine his arms and hands?"

"I did a complete and thorough examination of the decedent's entire body."

"During your thorough examination, Dr. Vincent, did you find any defense wounds on the decedent's hands, which would indicate he tried to fight off his attacker?"

"There were no defense wounds on the decedent's hands."

"Did you find any defense wounds on the decedent's forearms, which would indicate he tried to shield himself from his attacker?"

"No, I did not."

"Dr. Vincent, was there any skin under Jim Cunningham's fingernails that would indicate he clawed his attacker?"

"No, there was not."

"Did you find it strange, Dr. Vincent, that a man whose very life was at stake did not defend himself or fight back at all during the attack?"

"No, sir. Since the decedent was in bed, I drew the conclusion that he had either taken a sedative or consumed a significant amount of alcohol. Either scenario would have rendered him incapable of fighting off an attacker."

"Are you saying, Doctor, that the decedent may have been semi-unconscious or in a deep sleep due to having taken some type of sedative or consumed a certain amount of alcohol?"

"Objection, Your Honor," Frank Sutton said. "Dr. Vincent has already established that the decedent's death was caused by a severed carotid artery. Do we really care if he was drunk or not?"

Laughter and mumbling rumbled through the courtroom.

Judge Boone banged his gavel. "Order in the court!"

Mr. Streeter walked toward the Judge's bench. "Your Honor, if the court would indulge the defense a few more minutes so we can cross-examine this witness, we will establish that the cause of Mr.

Cunningham's death was not the severing of his carotid artery, for which my client has been charged."

Chatter erupted in the courtroom. Frank Sutton pushed up from his seat. "Your Honor, I object vehemently to this baseless assertion that Jim Cunningham died from something other than what Dr. Vincent has already confirmed under oath."

"Objection overruled. The court is most interested in hearing this information. You may continue, Mr. Streeter."

"Do I need to repeat the question, Doctor?"

"No, you don't. The conclusion I'd drawn was that the decedent had taken sleep medication or was highly intoxicated."

"Thank you. Now, Dr. Vincent, you stated you examined the decedent's hands and his fingernails. Is that correct?"

"Yes, how many times do I need to answer that question?"

"And when you examined his fingernails, did you notice anything peculiar about them?"

Dr. Vincent shifted almost imperceptibly in his seat. Beads of perspiration sprouted around his temples. He looked toward the prosecution's table then at the judge.

"Answer the question, Dr. Vincent," Judge Boone said.

"Yes." The doctor's voice cracked.

"What was peculiar about his fingernails, Doctor?"

"They had a yellowish color to them," he mumbled.

"Louder, Doctor, so the jury can hear you."

"They had a yellowish color to them."

"And when you saw the yellowish color of the decedent's fingernails, based upon your medical training, what conclusion did you draw concerning the cause of this discoloration?"

He swallowed. "I surmised there might have been poison in his system."

"What poison, Dr. Vincent, would cause this type of discoloration?"

"Arsenic," he said, barely audible.

"Louder, Doctor."

"Arsenic. Arsenic."

"Let the record show that Dr. Vincent stated that when he observed the discoloration of his fingernails, he suspected Jim Cunningham might have ingested arsenic poison. Doctor, did you order a toxicology report to confirm your suspicion?"

"Yes." The doctor's shoulders slumped. He retrieved a handkerchief from his jacket pocket and mopped his face, which had become white and pasty with perspiration.

"What were the results of the toxicology report, Dr. Vincent?"

"The report showed Jim Cunningham had consumed small doses of arsenic poison over a duration of time, probably two to three months, which caused the discoloration of his fingernails."

The courtroom fell silent. Shock registered on Frank Sutton's face. He sprang from his seat to object but slowly sat back down.

"One final question. Dr. Vincent, in your medical opinion, was it arsenic poisoning or the severing of Jim Cunningham's carotid artery that killed him? And I remind you, Doctor, you are under oath."

"It was... it was the poison."

Pandemonium erupted in the courtroom—loud gasps, angry protests, wails, and shouts of profanity ripped through the air. Reporters raced out of the courtroom to file their stories.

Judge Boone banged his gavel. "Order! Order in the court! Order! I will have order, or I will clear this courtroom."

The noise gradually leveled off. The people took their seats, and the courtroom eventually became silent.

"Mr. Streeter, do you have any further questions for this witness?"

"No, Your Honor, I do not."

Frank Sutton stood, scratched the back of his head, then sat back down.

Judge Boone turned to the bailiff. "Take Dr. Vincent into custody pending formal charges for perjury and impeding the investigation of a felony."

The bailiff handcuffed Dr. Vincent and led him out of the courtroom amid shouts, hisses, and baleful glances from the people watching.

"Your Honor," Jonathan Streeter said, "the defense would like to call one final witness who can identify the person who actually killed Jim Cunningham."

"If the prosecution has no objections."

"Prosecution has no objections, Your Honor."

"Then call your witness, Mr. Streeter."

"The defense calls Caroline Cunningham to the stand."

# Chapter 62

I watched from the back row in the courthouse, practically holding my breath, as Ms. Caroline sauntered to the witness stand, fashionably attired in a cobalt-blue designer suit with shiny gold buttons on the jacket. With her shoulders back and her head lifted in a royal tilt, she perched herself on the chair, crossing one leg over the other. I could sense that even though this would be her third time taking the stand, Mr. Streeter had not rattled her in the least by having her reappear.

"Ms. Cunningham," Judge Boone said, peering down at her from his bench, "you were sworn in by the court previously. Therefore, this is to remind you that you're still under oath."

"Of course, Your Honor."

Mr. Streeter rose from the defense table. "Your Honor, defense once again requests to treat Ms. Cunningham as a hostile witness."

"Noted. You may proceed."

"Thank you, Your Honor." Mr. Streeter walked toward the witness and stopped several paces in front of her. "Ms. Cunningham, in your previous testimony, you told the court that you had a close relationship with your cousin, the deceased, Jim Cunningham. Is that correct?"

"We were like brother and sister."

"And you also testified that you visited your cousin about twice a month when you were keeping his books. Is that also correct?"

"Yes."

"Would you tell the court what period of time you kept Mr. Cunningham's records?"

"From January 1967 to April of this year."

"So you kept his books and records for almost two and a half years. Is that correct?"

"Yes."

"According to the statement you gave to my investigator, Titus Jones, Jim Cunningham asked you to stop keeping his books four months ago because he'd planned to hire a CPA to get everything in order before he and Ms. Bingham got married. Is that a correct statement?"

"Yes, it is."

"Ms. Cunningham, isn't it a fact that your cousin asked you to stop keeping his books four months ago because you confessed your love for him, and he rejected you and told you never to come to his home again?"

"No, that is absolutely not true, and I'm highly offended by the suggestion!"

"And is it also true, Ms. Cunningham, that when your parents found out how you felt about your own cousin during your sophomore year in college, they had you committed to a mental institution?"

"That is a lie!"

"And isn't it true that because your cousin rejected your advances, you poisoned him to death with arsenic poison?"

"No, no, no! I didn't kill Jim. I loved him like a brother."

"Ms. Cunningham where were you on July 11 between the hours of one and two o'clock a.m.?"

"I was in bed, asleep."

"Is there anyone who can corroborate that?" Mr. Streeter asked.

"The entire staff could."

"Does your staff perform a bed check, Ms. Cunningham?"

"Objection, Your Honor," Frank Sutton said. "Mr. Streeter is ridiculing the witness."

"I will restate the question, Your Honor," Mr. Streeter said. "Ms. Cunningham, can either of your staff members state unequivocally the time you came home on July 11 and also vouch for the fact that you never left your home again?"

"My maid certainly could."

"Thank you. Now, Ms. Cunningham, when was the last time you saw your cousin alive?"

"It had been almost two months since I'd seen Jim."

"Ms. Cunningham, we have witness statements from two neighbors of the deceased, indicating that they saw your red Mercedes Benz parked at Mr. Cunningham's home during the last two weeks before his death." Mr. Streeter walked to the defense table and took several sheets of paper from a folder. "I'd like to enter these notarized statements as Defense Exhibits C and D." Jonathan handed the papers to the judge. "The witnesses are here to testify to these statements if necessary. Why were you there, Ms. Cunningham?"

"He was my cousin. I didn't need a reason to visit him."

"You had a reason, Ms. Cunningham. You were there to administer the final doses of arsenic to kill him. You were poisoning your cousin with the home-cooked meals your maid prepared for him. Isn't that correct, Ms. Cunningham?"

"I did not! I didn't kill my cousin!"

"You were enraged with your cousin because you confessed your love for him, and he kicked you out of his house. He rejected you while he continued to sleep around with other women. And the final straw was when you heard he was having an affair with a Black woman. That's when you decided to kill him, Ms. Cunningham. You had the motive—jealousy. You had the means—arsenic poison. And you had the opportunity. You methodically planned, and you killed your own cousin!"

"Stop it! Stop it! Stop it!" Ms. Caroline banged on the witness stand in front of her with an open palm. "I didn't kill Jim! I tell you, I didn't! I did not kill him!"

"Order." The judge banged with his gavel. "The witness will calm herself."

Ms. Caroline glared at the judge then defiantly tossed her ginger tresses over her shoulders. Mr. Streeter walked to the defense table and pulled out the pink envelope that smelled of vanilla and rose from his folder.

"Your Honor, I'd like to enter this letter as Defense Exhibit E."

Ms. Caroline leaped to her feet. Her green eyes blazed with fury. "How did you get that letter? You have no right! You have no right! That letter is private! You hear me? Private! I'll have you thrown in jail for trespassing! I'll have you disbarred from ever practicing law again! You hear me, you Black son of—"

"Order. Order." The judge banged his gavel. "The witness will calm herself and take a seat or be held in contempt."

Ms. Caroline remained standing. She adjusted her suit jacket then slowly sat back down.

"I vehemently object, Your Honor," Mr. Sutton said, standing. "The prosecution has not been made aware of this piece of evidence, nor have we had the opportunity to examine it. And as such, we request to have it excluded as evidence."

"Your Honor, defense just recently became aware of this evidence. However, we believe it is crucial in establishing the motive for Mr. Cunningham's murder."

"In light of the strong reaction from the witness to the very presence of this piece of evidence, the court is inclined to believe its contents may prove significant to these proceedings. For this reason, I will allow it. Counselor, you may continue."

"Thank you, Your Honor. Now, Ms. Cunningham, do you recognize this envelope?"

Ms. Caroline's face turned a shade of primrose, and her green eyes shot daggers at Mr. Streeter. "Yes."

"Ms. Cunningham, do you know who wrote the letter contained inside this envelope?"

"Yes."

"Who wrote the letter, Ms. Cunningham?"

"I did."

"Ms. Cunningham, would you please read the letter, or shall I have the stenographer read it to the court?"

Ms. Caroline settled back in her chair, with her hands folded in her lap. She stared into space as though seeing events unfold in front of her. "When I confessed my love to Jim back in April, he became furious. When I reached for him... to calm him down... he recoiled from me like I was a diseased animal. He said I was sick... and that I needed help. He kicked me out of his house and told me not to come back until I'd gotten some help. How dare he judge me? Mr. high-and-mighty, look-so-good playboy, sleeping around with every cheap tramp in the Mississippi Delta and even that Black hussy. Yes, he was living in tall cotton, all right. Well, he got more than he bargained for. I really didn't want Jim to suffer—I just wanted him dead. So I killed him. Yes, I did it! I gave him the arsenic poison!"

The courtroom erupted in a frenzy. A chorus of voices began shouting. Reporters leaped to their feet and tripped over each other as they raced out of the courtroom.

Judged Boone pounded his gavel vigorously. "Order in the courtroom. Order! I will have order!"

# Chapter 63

Judge Boone banged louder and louder with his gavel. "I will clear this entire courtroom if you do not come to order!"

The noise leveled, becoming a chorus of mumbling, then a whisper.

"I said silence!" Judge Boone pounded with his gavel once more. When the courtroom was silent, the judge turned to the bailiff. "Officer Monroe, take Ms. Cunningham into custody pending formal charges against her for the first-degree premeditated murder of James Cunningham."

Ms. Caroline slowly rose from her seat, and the bailiff handcuffed her and led her out of the courtroom.

"Your Honor, the defense respectfully requests that the capital murder charges against my client, Mrs. Annie Lee Connor, be dismissed," Mr. Streeter said.

Momma dropped her head. She wiped the tears from her eyes.

"Does the prosecution have any objections?" the judge asked.

"No, Your Honor. However, the prosecution would like to advise the court that formal charges will be brought against Mrs. Connor for the attempted capital murder of James Cunningham."

"So noted. Mr. Streeter your client is free to go, pending any future charges."

"Thank you, Your Honor."

"I'd like to thank the jury for your service," Judge Boone said. "Court is dismissed."

My heart overflowed with joy. Jo and I had helped Mr. Streeter win Momma's case. Momma stood and hugged Mr. Streeter. Then she and Aunt Bernie hugged each other and cried what I thought were happy tears. Jo and I pushed through the crowd to make our way to Momma.

# Chapter 64

Momma's trial ended on August 10, and Mr. Streeter left town the following day. He said he had to get back to his law practice and the youth basketball team he'd been coaching. We realized we'd been blessed that he showed up in Greenville when he did. If it had not been for Mr. Streeter representing Momma, she would have been convicted of killing Mr. Jim and most likely would have died in the electric chair.

With Momma being home, things returned to normal and, for a short period of time, better than normal. Daddy wasn't drinking any alcohol, and on occasion, I'd even seen him sitting on their bed, attempting to read the Bible the Mennonite church folk had brought to my school. But as the days and weeks progressed, things started to change. Daddy started drinking again, and the arguments between him and Momma became more frequent and explosive. Most often, he'd accuse her of having an ongoing relationship with Mr. Streeter.

One Friday night in late September, just past midnight, Momma and Daddy had just returned home from what she called one of their favorite juke joints. We could hear their loud shouts and the spewing of profanity before they entered the house. Jo and I had been playing Old Maid on the living room floor, but before they opened the front door, we grabbed the cards and retreated to our bedroom. We didn't want to get caught in the middle of their tirade, which carried the force of a destructive tornado.

We heard the front door open and then slam shut. Laced with rage and fueled by alcohol, Daddy's rants became louder, angrier, and more intense. Then I felt my heart stop. I heard the name—Priscilla. The day of reckoning had finally come.

*Jesus, help us all.* My breathing became rapid, and I thought I would hyperventilate.

The shouting and cursing continued for what seemed like hours. I put my hands over my ears, but I could still hear them. I wanted to run outside and hide. But it was dark, and I was afraid. Daddy told Momma that Priscilla and Matthew had to go. Momma told him if Priscilla and Matthew left, she would leave too. That angered Daddy even more. I thought for certain he would strike Momma, but he never did. Finally, she told Daddy she was tired and she was going to bed. Daddy continued to shout and curse and stomp around. When Momma didn't respond, he called her name. Still, she didn't respond. Either she was pretending to be asleep, or she'd actually fallen asleep despite Daddy's rant.

Finally, Daddy stopped calling her name. There was complete silence. But I was afraid to go to sleep—afraid the arguing would start again and yank me out of a perfectly good dream and thrust me back into a world of turmoil and terror. So I stared at the ceiling in the darkness until my eyes began to burn. When I could hold them open no longer, I gave in and drifted off to sleep.

During the early hours of the morning, while it was still dark, with only the moonlight casting shadows in our room, I was awakened by voices.

"No! Stop! Let me go!" Priscilla said.

"Get up—you comin' with me!" Daddy snarled.

"No, leave me alone!" Priscilla insisted. "I don't want to go with you."

I lurched forward in the bed. "Daddy, what are you doing to Priscilla? Stop! Leave her alone."

"Shut up, boy, and go back to sleep. This ain't got nothin' to do with you! Now, get up, gal!"

"You're hurting my arm!" Priscilla said. "You're going to wake up Matthew!"

"Then get up now!"

Priscilla fought to free herself from Daddy's grasp, but being bigger and stronger, he dragged her out of bed and through the kitchen toward the back door. Her white nightgown disappeared into the darkness. I slid down the bunk bed ladder.

"Jo, Jo, wake up!" I shook her. "Daddy is taking Priscilla! Wake up!"

"What?" Jo said groggily. "Taking Priscilla where?"

"I don't know, out the back door... he's going to kill her." My heart pounded so hard I thought it would burst right through my chest.

Jo sprang upright in bed. "Where's Momma?"

"Asleep, I guess."

"Go get Momma!" Jo leaped out of bed and raced toward the kitchen, where Daddy had dragged Priscilla.

I raced into Momma's bedroom. "Momma! Momma! Wake up! Daddy's got Priscilla!" My tears tasted warm and salty. "Momma, Daddy is going to kill Priscilla!"

Momma rolled over and groaned. A rancid smell of alcohol and stale cigarettes escaped her lips.

I shook her violently. "Momma, please, please wake up! Daddy is going to kill Priscilla!"

Momma wouldn't wake up, so I left her and ran toward the back door. Priscilla struggled against Daddy's strong grip as he dragged her across the backyard and toward the cotton field.

"I'll leave. I'll never come back," Priscilla said through sniffles.

"It's too late for that now. You shouldna ever come back. Y'all fast-tail girls runnin' round with these boys... 'round here, gettin' pregnant. Now you gonna get what you deserve... what I shoulda gave you a long time ago."

I stopped in my tracks next to Jo. She was staring at the silver blade in Daddy's hand, glistening in the moonlight.

"Bailey, he's going to kill her. We've got to do something." Jo's voice trembled. Tears streamed down her face.

My legs felt like water. I could hear my heartbeat in my ears. Through my tears, I searched for a weapon and spotted the shovel. I grabbed it and raced toward Daddy. I swung wildly. Daddy snatched the shovel from my hands and tossed it behind him in the grass. I charged him and pounded him on his back. He turned and backhanded me. I landed hard on the dewy ground, tasting my blood.

"Y'all chillen' gon' on in the house. You hear me, Jo? You and Bailey. This ain't got nothin' to do with y'all."

Priscilla started crawling away, but Daddy grabbed her by her hair. She screamed out in pain.

"Daddy, you let her go! You're hurting my sister!" Ignoring the knife, I started to charge Daddy again, but then I heard a sound. My knees became wobbly.

*Click-click.*

Momma stood in the open doorway. The light in the kitchen framed her silhouette. She aimed the shotgun at Daddy. "What you doin' with my child, Otis?"

"What I shoulda done a long time ago before she came up pregnant! She shoulda been mine before she got spoiled." Daddy pressed the knife against Priscilla's throat.

"You're not gonna hurt my daughter." Momma's bare feet descended the wooden steps. "I will send you straight to hell before I let that happen."

"You won't shoot me, Annie. You ain't got it in you. Now, you need to put that gun down before somebody get hurt."

I eased into the darkness, crawled behind Daddy, and found the shovel. With all the strength I could muster, I whacked Daddy over the head with it. He staggered then lashed out wildly at me. I fell back on the ground.

"Priscilla, Bailey, run!" Momma screamed.

I grabbed Priscilla's hand, and we scrambled to our feet and raced into the cotton field, ducking among the stalks. We crouched down and peered between the stalks.

Daddy whirled around to face Momma. "You done messed up now, Annie!"

"No, Otis, you messed up when you tried to hurt my child."

Daddy started toward Momma. "Why, you ungrateful..."

*Boom!*

The pellets peppered Daddy's shoulder.

He screamed in pain. "I'll kill you!" Raising the knife, he charged.

*Click-click.*

*Boom!*

The second shotgun blast knocked Daddy back. He landed hard on the ground. In the moonlight, blood as dark as crude oil spewed from the hole in his chest, soaking his white T-shirt. He didn't move as Momma stood there, looking down at him.

After a moment, she tossed the shotgun aside and raced toward the field, calling out to us.

"Priscilla, Bailey, Jo!" Her voice trembled. "It's okay. Y'all can come out now."

# Chapter 65

Daylight had dawned when the police cars and the ambulance finally left our home. The ambulance took Daddy's body away, and the sheriff finished questioning Momma. He didn't arrest her because he said Momma killed Daddy in self-defense. He took Daddy's fishing knife as evidence. Once the strangers left, we all huddled together in the living room and cried. We cried tears of joy that Daddy hadn't killed Priscilla and tears of relief that the police hadn't taken Momma away for killing Daddy. We cried tears of gratitude that Priscilla and Matthew didn't have to leave. And above all, we cried because we were safe from Daddy's tyranny, and we had one another.

During the days that followed, we were quiet in our home but also sullen. We talked in soft tones, and there was no laughter. It seemed that since two tragedies had occurred, Daddy's and Uncle Earl's deaths, we didn't deserve to laugh—it would somehow be irreverent or disrespectful.

Momma and Priscilla talked quietly in the kitchen as they prepared our meals each day. Jo and I talked to each other about the recurring nightmares we had, knowing it would be a long time before we got over what happened, if we ever did. Tammy had slept through the entire ordeal, so she wasn't traumatized like Momma, my older siblings, and me.

The day after Daddy died, Mr. Eli went down to the police and told them about a conversation he and Daddy had while they were out drinking after one of their fishing trips. It had happened shortly after Momma's trial ended. Daddy had started drinking again, and he'd gotten extremely drunk. He bragged to Mr. Eli about how he'd stabbed Mr. Jim all those times with his favorite fish-gutting knife. Daddy said he pretended he'd gotten drunk that night and passed out in his car. He had been drinking, but he wasn't drunk enough to pass out. After he stabbed Mr. Jim, he drove out to Old Leland Road and poked a hole in his tire with an ice pick to make it go flat. Then he pushed a nail into the hole for the mechanics to find. He buried his bloody coveralls in a burlap sack underneath a tree behind the Mennonite church near the cemetery. According to Mr. Eli, Daddy had said he knew no one would go digging around in a graveyard, looking for evidence. The sheriff found Daddy's bloody clothes buried beneath the tree just as Daddy had told Mr. Eli. And according to the medical examiner, Daddy's knife matched Mr. Jim's stab wounds.

Daddy told Mr. Eli his only regret had been that Mr. Jim was already dead when he'd stabbed him, although he hadn't known it at the time. Mr. Eli had told Momma all of this, and he'd told her that Daddy said he felt bad about her being on trial but knew she wouldn't be convicted because she had an alibi. But after Willie Earl was murdered, Mr. Eli said Daddy was about to turn himself in. And then Ms. Caroline confessed. Because of all that, Mr. Eli told the police. We were relieved that the DA declined to charge Momma with attempted capital murder in Mr. Jim's death.

Even though the court didn't get to prove Daddy's guilt, God did, and he'd received the punishment he deserved for trying to kill Mr. Jim and Priscilla.

# Chapter 66
# Six Months Later

"Bailey, don't you hear Momma calling you? Why are you just sitting there, staring out of that window?"

"No, I didn't hear Momma. I was just sitting here thinking about all that happened last summer, and I guess I got lost in my thoughts."

"Are you reading about the trial again?"

I looked down at the newspaper clipping in my hand. The title of the article read, *DC Attorney Jonathan Streeter Wins Dismissal in Sensational Murder Trial Amid Shocking Revelations.*

"Yeah, I guess so."

"Well, you need to come on," Jo said. "Momma wants you to meet Priscilla's father."

"Do I have to?"

"Momma wants you to, so yes."

"But why, Jo? He's Priscilla's daddy, not mine. Besides, it's been pretty nice not having a daddy around here."

"There you go, only thinking about yourself again. Priscilla hasn't had a daddy her entire life, and now he may be visiting from time to time, so Momma wants us to get to know him too."

"I'm not selfish, and why did Momma wait all this time to find Priscilla's daddy, anyway?"

"You can ask Momma that question, but one reason is probably Daddy wouldn't have allowed another man to come around, especially Priscilla's daddy."

"I guess you're right about that. Have you met him?" I asked.

"Yeah, he's sitting in the living room."

"What do you think about him? Is he nice?"

"He's a man. You'll have to judge for yourself."

I sighed. "Thank you, Josephine, for all of your help."

"You're welcome. Now, come on."

I climbed from my perch in the windowsill, where I'd been admiring our lawn and our neighbors' lawn. Some had flowerbeds filled with a bounty of colorful spring flowers, and others just had green shrubbery. Momma had gotten a job at the Western Auto store in downtown Lowell, and we'd moved into a three-bedroom house in a new subdivision near her job. It was quiet and peaceful—with no cotton fields in sight.

I skulked down the hall, following Jo into the living room. Looking around for a stranger, I felt confused and disoriented. There, sitting on our new navy-blue leather sofa, was Jonathan Streeter, dressed in a casual light-blue pullover shirt and navy pants, cradling a glass of ice water. Priscilla sat to his right, bouncing Matthew on her knee, and Momma sat in the recliner opposite them.

"What... what's going on?" I asked. "Where is Priscilla's dad, and why are you here, Mr. Streeter?"

"Bailey, meet my father, Jonathan Streeter," Priscilla said.

"Wait... what? How can this be? Momma, you said you two were just kids in grade school when you met."

"We were. Then Jonathan moved from Indianola, where we'd gone to school together, and we lost contact. But we reconnected some years later. By that time, we were both teenagers."

"So, Mr. Streeter, why did you wait all these years to come and see your daughter?" I asked.

"Bailey, you can call me Jonathan. Up until a few months ago, I didn't know I had a daughter."

"When I found out I was having a baby," Momma said, "Jonathan had already left for college, and I didn't know how to contact him. After reconnecting during the trial, I knew I had to tell him about Priscilla. But I told Priscilla first and gave her time to process everything. Once she was ready to meet her dad, I contacted Jonathan."

"This is awesome!" I said. "Priscilla, how do you feel? Were you as shocked as I am to find out Mr. Streeter—I mean Jonathan—is your father?"

"Of course I was shocked. Momma never talked much about my father, especially with Otis being around. She'd call him JD for Jonathan David, and she'd say JD was a kind young man, good-looking, and smart. She said I looked a lot like him. And I guess I can see the resemblance." Priscilla smiled, and Jonathan patted her on the hand.

"Jonathan, can I ask you something about Momma's trial?"

"Sure, Bailey."

"What ever happened to that guy who was so disrespectful to you in court—the one who owned that fancy car dealership in Greenville?"

"He got sentenced to twenty years in a federal penitentiary for drug smuggling and money laundering."

"What happened to Ms. Caroline?"

"Oh, I suppose she's tucked away at a mental institution for a lot of years."

"Okay, Bailey, enough questions," Momma said. "Jonathan came to get acquainted with his daughter and grandchild."

"Well, can he get acquainted while we're eating?" I asked. "I smell something delicious coming from the kitchen, and I'm starved."

"That's a great idea," Momma said. "Jon, are you hungry?"

"Famished. Let's eat."

I raced to the dining room, jockeying for a seat beside Jonathan, knowing that Momma or Priscilla would sit on the other side of him.

# Acknowledgments

First, I must thank God for giving me not only the gift of writing but also the gift of storytelling. It's the passion that gets me out of bed each morning and fills me with anticipation for the day ahead.

Next, I want to express my gratitude to my publisher at Red Adept Publishing, Lynn McNamee, for recognizing something special in *Tall Cotton* and making my publishing dreams a reality. I also owe a heartfelt thanks to my content editor at Red Adept, Angie Lovell, whose gentle guidance and exceptional editing skills helped to make *Tall Cotton* the best it can be. Additionally, I'm deeply grateful to my line editor, Sarah Carleton, for her thoughtful approach and sharp attention to detail in editing my manuscript.

I would also like to thank my two Pitch Wars mentors, Alex Segura and Manju Soni. The contributions of these two incredible individuals were instrumental in improving the overall structure of *Tall Cotton,* shaping it into the best version of itself. I will be forever grateful for their expertise and encouragement.

A special thanks goes to LaRee Bryant, my first editor and a founding member of Dallas Mystery Writers, who taught me so much about the craft of writing. I'll never forget her initial advice: "Hold on, Catherine. Don't quit your day job just yet." (Lol!) I knew I had made significant progress when after reading the first five chapters of *Tall Cotton*, she said, "Catherine, I really think you've got something here." I am deeply saddened that LaRee didn't get to see *Tall Cotton* in print, but her influence remains with me. I'm also incredibly thankful to Sandy Steen from Dallas Mystery Writers, who was the most amazing plotting partner I could have asked for. Her insights and collaboration were a joy.

The Dallas Area Writers Group (DAWG) also played a vital role in my writing journey. Founders Patsy Summey and Alan Elliott created a warm and welcoming environment where I honed my writing skills through workshops and critique sessions featuring the expertise of exceptional authors Michelle Stimpson and James Gaskin. I must also thank my dear friend Lily Welborne, who accompanied me to every writer's group meeting I attended. Lily has been an unwavering source of encouragement and support.

Through the challenging journey to publication, I've been blessed with the steadfast support of two incredible prayer warriors, Downie Craig and Tamatha Dixon. These amazing women encouraged me through the most discouraging days, when rejection after rejection made the goal of publication appear unattainable. Their prayers and motivation kept me going.

Last but certainly not least, I have to thank my family: my sister, Mary Ann Griffin, after reminiscing with her about our childhood, the idea for *Tall Cotton* emerged; also sisters, Louise Henderson and Dorothy Levy Wofford; and nieces, Catelin Dunn, Erica Logan, and Roxanne Abushehab. These remarkable women have been not only my beta readers and critique partners but also my most loyal and enthusiastic supporters. I am eternally grateful for their love, support, and prayers.

# About the Author

Catherine grew up in the small town of Leland, Mississippi. For amusement, she read the dictionary from cover to cover. But she later discovered a better escape: fiction. As a teenager, she fell in love with all things mystery and never looked back. Catherine's imagination was nurtured by the Delta's vast cotton fields, soulful blues, and deep-rooted traditions, which influence her books.

When Catherine is not writing, you can find her reading a thriller or binge watching a mystery series. She also enjoys traveling, teaching Bible classes, devouring decadent chocolate, and savoring a steaming cup of coffee. Catherine currently resides in Houston, Texas.

Read more at https://www.catherinetuckerauthor.com/.

# About the Publisher

Dear Reader,

We hope you enjoyed this book. Please consider leaving a review on your favorite book site.

Visit our site to find more quality books!

Read more at https://RedAdeptPublishing.com.

Made in the USA
Middletown, DE
30 March 2025

73387441R10184